THE WIND
AND
THE RIVER

Kim Won-il

translated by
Choi Jin-young

Si-sa-yong-o-sa, Inc., Korea
Pace International Research, Inc., U.S.A.

Copyright © 1988 by Si-sa-yong-o-sa, Inc.

Published simultaneously in KOREA and the UNITED STATES

KOREA EDITION
First printing 1988
Si-sa-yong-o-sa, Inc.
55-1 Chongno 2-ga, Chongno-gu
Seoul 110-122, Korea

U.S. EDITION
First printing 1988
Pace International Research, Inc.
Tide Avenue, Falcon Cove
P.O. Box 51, Arch Cape
Oregon 97102, U.S.A.

ISBN : 0-87296-033-1

This book is a co-publication by Si-sa-yong-o-sa, Inc.
and The International Communication Foundation.

Preface

The title of this novel, *The Wind and the River*, best exemplifies the several themes and levels of symbolic meaning contained within the story of Yi In-t'ae. Specifically, it is the philosophical relationship between wind and water that composes the core of this tale. Mr. Choi, the geomancer, speaks of this relationship while describing the concept of "Ki" to his friend Yi. Ki is an invisible force of nature that both the living and the dead depend upon. It is carried by the wind and empowered by water, according to ancient philosophy, Mr. Choi explains.

This relationship between wind and water also sets forth more prosaic notions; it is a metaphor expressing principles of movement and stillness, change and permanence, yang and yin. It represents the lives of Yi and Mr. Choi, the wanderer and the stationary. Yi leaves home to escape the stifling lack of change he feels, yet is never fully free from a longing for permanence as he travels about. Mr. Choi never wanders and is bound to his home, yet he longs for a life of movement and change. This novel chronicles their contrasting existences in detail.

Male-female dynamics are also suggested in a scene in which Mr. Choi contemplates the relationship between his friend Yi and Yi's wife, Madam Wolp'o. Mr. Choi muses, "Flowing water may look the same, but if one observes it more closely, one will see changes caused by the wind, the temperature and the changing colors of nearby mountains reflecting on the water." Elements affect the water just as man affects woman. Yi and Madam Wolp'o are yang and yin, wind and water, as well.

The mountains and rivers of Ibam and its surrounding areas form an integral part of the story, lending import to Mr. Choi's role as a "reader" of land, as well as providing an appropriate background for the people who live and die in the village. It is through references to nature that much of the story's conventional wisdom is expressed.

The historical background is also critical to the fabric of the story. Yi left home at age eighteen in the year 1920; one year after the Samil Independence Movement, and a decade after the Japanese occupation of Korea. During the period of occupation, thousands of Koreans fled to Manchuria, living as expatriots. Yi was trained at a Korean military school for two years, and later fought in guerrilla attacks against the Japanese occupying forces. In 1922, he was captured by the Japanese and severely tortured.

Under torture, Yi finally broke down and betrayed his Korean compatriots. He was the sole survivor among those who were captured. Upon his subsequent release he limped to the small Korean village, where people had often fed and hid him, only to find that it had been decimated by the Japanese forces, who had used the information Yi had surrendered to them. Yi was assaulted by the few remaining Koreans in the village who had learned of his betrayal. They beat him mercilessly and severed both of his ears.

Half-deranged at his point, Yi wandered aimlessly throughout Manchuria, living like a dog. He had been heinously tortured by the Japanese, unforgivingly tortured by the betrayed Koreans, and he suffered the private torture of his own guilt.

Eventually he drifted into a group of travelling musicians from Korea, and it was from the troupe's sole female singer that Yi first encountered sexual love. For years, he begged and stole, only working occasionally, and fathered four children. He continued to wander around throughout Manchuria, China, and Japan.

It was not until 1945, when Japan surrendered and Korea was liberated, that Yi finally returned to his homeland. He was a middle-aged, ravaged and diseased bum, with years of pain and suffering burning inside him.

Bypassing his hometown, Yi settled in the town of Ibam where he promptly married a widowed tavern owner named Madam Wolp'o. Her tavern was Wolp'ook, and it was there that the simple village people speculated on the mysterious eccentric ways of Yi.

Yi succeeded in cultivating a deep friendship with only one man, Mr. Choi, the well-known geomancer. Mr. Choi was an honest, wise man and was Yi's sole confidant. It was only he who would slowly learn of Yi's life story, including the painful details of his betrayal and the loss of his ears by the hands of his countrymen.

In fact, Mr. Choi was also a victim of history. He had lost his eldest son to the frontlines of Southeast Asia during World War II, and his second son was an amputee from the Korean War.

Indeed, death, pain and suffering were facts of life for all Koreans during the thirty years from 1920 to 1953. Yi's life was symbolic of Korea's terrible struggle to survive the Japanese occupation, the two wars, and the precarious peace following the armistice. Life had exacted very heavy sacrifices from Yi and others of his generation.

Plagued by kidney disease in his later years, Yi sensed his life coming to an end. Facing impending death, he struggled desperately to find atonement for his sins, hoping to alleviate his feelings of guilt. He consulted a Christian preacher and a Buddhist monk, becoming obsessed with exonerating himself before death took him. He found no hope for forgiveness or salvation in either of the religions.

He found comfort only in Mr. Choi's land-divining theories. Mr. Choi told Yi that someone as guilt-ridden as he could only gain peace through the proper choice of a burial site. Mr. Choi promised Yi that he would divine a good resting place for him, on a site that would insure Yi of eternal peace.

Placing his trust in Mr. Choi's words and choice of a burial site, Yi died a peaceful death. Despite his suffering and sinful past, Yi discovered redemption in his struggle for forgiveness and salvation. "Aunt said his eyes were closed and there was a peaceful smile on his face," said Myŏng-ku, the errand boy and Yi's heir apparent.

Choi Jin-young

CONTENTS

CHAPTER I

It was the year the armistice was signed. Chŏng Myŏng-ku, now a tall good-looking young man, was an all-around errand boy at Wolp'ook. Wolp'ook was a tavern in the rural town of Ibam. Drinks and food were sold there, so it could be called a restaurant, but it also accommodated a few overnight customers on market days, thus making it an inn as well.

Wolp'ook was located at the head of the Ibam market place, right across from the town hall and the police station. A few paces down the road there was a bus stop where an old rickety bus stopped once a day. The bus ran between P'ohang, the port city, and a few other towns like Ch'ŏngsong and Andong.

Wolp'ook was a small mud-shack with one glass door which had taken the place of a mud-wall, long since gone. It wasn't a place worthy of a signboard or a restaurant title, but people around the town called it Wolp'ook after the woman owner who had originally come from Wolp'o. She was Madam Wolp'o, so to speak, and "ok" was a title given to small eateries.

On days when there was no market, the woman sold rice wine by the bowl to a few of her neighbors. There weren't enough people to do a regular business. However, on market days, her business was brisk. She served vegetable soup with rice, fried vegetables, and rice wine.

There were a few other such eateries scattered around the town, but people were attracted to Wolp'ook, perhaps because of its good location and Madam Wolp'o's "dirty mouth."

On market days her business was so good that she needed more space. She would put a canopy of coarse white cloth next to the glass door, and sell her food and drinks in this crude open-air cafe. For seating space she spread a few straw mats.

The husband of this woman of Wolp'ook, Yi In-t'ae, was a man in his mid-fifties. He was tall and big-framed, and his sallow face was always slightly swollen, making his face look like a blown-up bile-sac.

His long hair, covering both his ears, came down to his shoulders. If his forehead and the top of his head hadn't been bald, he would have looked somewhat like the image of Jesus Christ or a hermit philosopher.

His long face, big fleshy knob of a nose, and glazed hallucinatory eyes, were flanked on both sides by long hair. These features, while inspiring awe in some onlookers, made for a strange face indeed.

He was not a native of Ibam. He was passing through Ibam when the country was liberated. For one reason or another, he lingered on in the town and willy-nilly, settled down. He had been a bum, if the truth be known.

Yi became a kind of gigolo living off the woman's income. Despite his good name, and the nickname *T'angnip,* given to him after he settled down, people around the marketplace more often than not called him Yi Tae-mal, half jokingly and half affectionately.

"Tae-mal" was a shortened, round-about way of saying "big penis of a horse." "Tae-mal" was in fact a euphemism that the town people had adopted in deference to his age.

During the hot summer months while everyone took baths in the clean water of the Chayang River, Yi refused to even wash his back there. He was so lazy that he did not wash his face in the mornings, so few people had actually ever seen his famous male organ.

When men got together and there was a lull in conversation, they turned to the question of how big his organ might be. Some would have it that Yi's organ, when not erect, was no bigger than a long piece of rice cake, whereas others insisted that it was so big and long that it had to be bandaged against his thigh. All in all, they agreed that stories concerning his organ would not have started unless it was exceptional in some way.

"I've heard that if his organ happened to drop into a basin full of water, all the water would spill over," one wag of the town reported.

"Mr. T'angnip, how big is your organ really? Let us view it just once. We'll buy you all the wine and side dishes that you can eat," another ventured more directly.

Whenever he was asked such questions Yi would look at them with his small slitty eyes and with a hint of disdain, would say,

"It isn't worth betting anything on. Contrary to what you may think, it isn't that big of a deal."

But the men did not give up easily. One or two would say,

"Oh, come on, Mr. T'angnip. There must be a reason for all those stories about it. If I dare guess, it must be at least as big as my arm."

At such moments, Yi would smile an enigmatic smile and neither deny nor agree with the speculations.

There were other stories about him. One story would have it that his lady-killing techniques were so potent that once he seduced a woman, the woman would rather die than let him go.

However, since he had settled in Ibam, no one had ever seen him using his rumored techniques. Town people whispered that it was because the woman of Wolp'o had an equally potent organ herself. Her organ was so gooey and gripping that once Yi's organ was grasped, it was held and never let go. Thus people came to the conclusion that their Yin and Yang were so perfectly matched that they would never part.

The errand-boy Myŏng-ku's father was beaten to death by his

neighbors when the Republic of Korea Army recaptured his town of Ttakpatkol. Being a tenant farmer and somewhat bright, he had been elected by the Communist occupying forces to serve in the infamous internal security (police) station. That two and a half month collaboration with the enemy was enough to earn him the hatred of the whole town.

Myŏng-ku's mother, unable to endure the hate-filled eyes of her neighbors, decided to send Myŏng-ku, then 15, to the market place of Ibam. She also sent her 13-year-old daughter to a brewery in P'ohang to work as a babysitter, and her youngest boy to a distant relative of hers. Then she herself left the town.

The reason why she sent Myŏng-ku to Ibam was that Yi In-t'ae was from Ttakpatkol, where Myŏng-ku's family had lived for generations.

After she left town she sent only two letters to Myŏng-ku. The first one was sent from Yongch'on where she said she was working in an eatery. It was near the end of the year when Myŏng-ku received the letter. The second letter was sent from Taegu. She said she was working in the kitchen of a restaurant, and that she was planning to move to another place.

This letter read, "Tears blind me whenever I think of you three kids. But what can I do? Please be patient and carry on until good times come to us someday. When I do well enough to rent a room, I'll call all of you back. Then, we'll be together."

Since Myŏng-ku's mother could not read or write, somebody must have written it for her as she dictated. As soon as Myŏng-ku received this second letter he wrote to her. But his letter came back, stamped with "Addressee Unknown."

In the three years since she had left home she had never come near Ttakpatkol. After the two letters there was no more news from her.

Some old-timers from Ttakpatkol who had traveled afar, as well as strangers from other places on their way to Ttakpatkol, would tell Myŏng-ku that they had heard rumors that his mother had remarried. According to the rumors, she was either running a laundry in front of an American army base with her new husband, or she was a housemaid at the home of a sock-manufacturer. But no one had actually seen her.

Mrs. Yi, the owner of Wolp'ook, came from the fishing village of Wolp'o. Both her family and her husband's family were fishermen. One stormy day her husband drowned on a fishing trip. Leaving her two daughters with her husband's parents, she went around peddling whatever she could get her hands on. There were only a few villages and towns where she didn't go.

Toward the end of World War II, she finally settled in Ibam, buying her present house and starting her tavern.

Ibam was at that time a town of about two hundred homes. Nearly one hundred of them belonged to the powerful and prestigious Kwon family of Andong, who had to take refuge and settled here when the Japanese Army invaded Korea in the year of Imjin(1592). The remaining households were tenant farmers who worked the Kwon family land, and strangers who had wandered into town.

Ibam was located in a crater-like basin, surrounded by high mountains. The basin itself was more than 300 meters above sea-level. Ibam was strategically located as the *national* road that led to Ch'ŏngsong and Andong crossed through the town. Another road, though only a mud path for horse carriages, led to Kasa-ri, Koch'ŏn-ri and Sangok-ri, and crossed through Ibam as well.

When Japan lost the war, and Korea was liberated, more and more people began to arrive in Ibam. Although there were no inter-town buses then, since Ibam was the capital town of Chukchang county, the Wolp'o woman's business prospered. She bought two majigis (1 majigi equals 640m²) of rice paddies and leased them. She became quite comfortable, and was able to relax enough to recall all her days of hardship with a rueful smile.

It was about this time when Yi In-t'ae, looking for the whole world nothing better than a beggar and bum, happened to stay one night at Wolp'ook.

During that one night Yi must have wreaked his magic on the

Wolp'o woman, thus ending her long widowhood. Though they met in middle age, their union seemed to be made in heaven. It was as if an old shoe had found its right mate.

Before this union was formed, the Wolp'o woman had married off her older daughter to a family that didn't have to worry about where the next meal was coming from. Her 22-year-old second daughter was a gentle, lovable girl. She helped her mother with the housework and waited for a suitable husband.

The Wolp'o woman wanted to marry off her second daughter as soon as possible, but the majority of marriageable men had gone off to the war, and few respectable families would accept the daughter of the owner of a drinking place as a suitable bride.

CHAPTER II

Between market days Wolp'ook served as a kind of salon for the community. Here in a tiny room with only four straw mats covering the dirt floor, middle-aged idlers would gather to play *hwat'o*, a traditional card game. The winner had to treat others to drinks.

If there weren't enough men to make a card game interesting, people would look out the glass door and gossip about anybody and everybody happening to pass by.

On a late autumn day, while the rice stalks were heavily ripening, a few old-timers played cards, as they were wont to do almost every day. Tobacco smoke filled the room. Among the players was the Wolp'o woman whose game was particularly bad; it was in fact so bad that she didn't bother to collect money for drinks. Her dark-complexioned face was a fierce brown and her mouth was clamped tightly.

"Wow, the rice wine tastes especially good today. Free drinks make me pleasantly dizzy," said the salt-peddler Kim. The tip of his nose had pockmarks on it. He chewed on a piece of kimch'i while stealing a glance at the Wolp'o woman.

"Now don't make me angry. Just wait and see, I will make a bee-hive of your scarred nose," the woman sassed back at him.

The next game was not any better for her though.

"Woman, good cards don't stick to you today. At such times it's best to go and relieve yourself in the bathroom, because it gives you a break and puts a temporary halt on your opponent's lucky streak. Then you come back and start over," said Kwak in his nasal voice. He had been watching the game from behind the woman's back.

"If the cards decide not to come to you, there is nothing in the world you can do. Even if you take your underwear off and pull the hair from your crotch, they won't come to you. As far as hwat'o is concerned, I know much more than you do. So just shut up," she shot back to Kwak.

The Wolp'o woman was short and skinny, but her temper and sharp tongue were well-known among the men.

"Your playing is so bad that I said what I said out of sympathy," said Kwak, crestfallen. He had a cold, and a stuffed-up nose. In addition, he hadn't been able to pay for his food and lodging for several days.

Kwak was a lumberjack from a logging camp where he was one of the carriers who moved logs down mountains. He hurt his back one day and decided to stay at Wolp'ook until his back healed.

At this time the government was not strong enough to enforce environmental protection policies, so there was a crowd of loggers who had gotten, through bribery or other devious means, permits from government officials. Their position was that forests had to be cleared to stop Communist guerrillas from hiding in them. At any rate, the loggers cut down trees, some more than a century old, without scruples. The logs were then sent by freight trains to P'ohang and Taegu.

Yi In-t'ae sat a little apart from the card players and looked out the glass door. When he was young, he learned the Chinese game of *36* in Manchuria. Once he tried to cheat, only to be immediately discovered. He ended up being knifed by one of the players. Since then he had never touched cards.

The kind of game his neighbors played, with the winner

treating players to drinks afterwards, was too trifling to bother with, he thought. Free drinks aside, if someone continued to win much more often than another, more often they would end up being hated. So Yi decided long ago not to ever get involved in a game.

In fact, Yi was an expert card handler and could do many tricks. When a player stacked the cards, he could already guess what the top and the bottom cards were. When he picked up a card he pretended to pick the top one while actually picking up the bottom one. If there happened to be two decks of cards, he could do more wonderful tricks. He could hide a card in his sleeve, under his knee or even in the neck-opening of his shirt. And he could swap one of these cards with a card in his hand. His neighbors and casual onlookers found it almost magical. At night when on oil lamp was lit, he also performed shadow plays with his hands.

About eight years ago, when Yi first came to Wolp'ook, he joined in on an on-going card game. Within an hour, he had won every last penny of the betting money. From beginning to end, he never uttered a word or did anything suspicious.

As the other players stared hungrily at the pile of money in front of him, he said, "It is a very small man indeed, who would put away in his pocket the money he won at a gaming table," and he spent the entire amount on drinks for everyone. He did this in spite of his obvious poverty and beggar-like appearance. The woman of Wolp'o and the other men mumbled, "He is indeed a big man. A big man is different."

On January 15 by the lunar calendar of the same year, he showed his card tricks to all the people of the market place, but that was the end of his involvement. Since that day never he touched a card, except to play solitaire to find out his luck for the day.

Once a young man came to Yi and offered him a huge fee, equivalent to two kamanis(1 kamani equals 80 kilograms) of rice, and he asked Yi to teach him the card tricks. Yi refused because, he told the young man, "Gambling is the shortest way to ruin yourself and your family." Thus, Yi showed the town people an unusual and awe-inspiring side of his character.

Today Yi was sitting patiently, chewing on his dry lips. In fact, he was seething inside. He turned his sleepy bedroom eyes to the window and looked out without a word.

"I told him many times that you wanted to see him today. I don't know why he is not here yet.... unless he had to attend to something more urgent," said Myŏng-ku, as if the absence of Mr. Choi, the town geomancer, were his own fault.

Myŏng-ku had grown enough to do a man's work, so he was paid a monthly salary in addition to his keep. Last year the Wolp'o woman gave him 40,000 won a month, an amount so small that it was equivalent to the price of 20 packs of the cheapest cigarettes.

This year, however, there had been a currency change and the won was reduced to one one-hundredth of its original value. Still, the woman insisted that Myŏng-ku get only 400 won per month. Inflation was so rampant that prices went up as fast as a loan shark's interest rates.

By now Myŏng-ku was familiar with prices and market values, and was discontented with his ridiculous pay. To make matters worse, the Wolp'o woman forced him to gather and bring home firewood from the mountains three days in a row between market days.

On market days there were a hundred and one small errands to run, but at least he didn't have to walk miles to gather firewood. Market days thus became days of rest for Myŏng-ku.

Today was a market day and yesterday was his wood-gathering day.

People of Ibam had to walk at least 50 to 60 ris (1 ri equals 0.4km) toward the Talŭi Pass and the Kuam Mountain to scrape up bundles of pine branches and needles, so Myŏng-ku made up his mind to go with some other men in this direction.

But at breakfast yesterday morning Yi had told Myŏng-ku to go over instead to Mr. Choi, and invite him to come see him the next morning. The Kuam Mountain and Talŭi Pass in the north were not as steep as the Pohyŏn Mountain in the west, which was near Mr. Choi's and the Pohyŏn Mountain did not yield as much firewood as the other mountain, which meant more work for Myŏng-ku.

"If I go to Tuma-ri, it will take me all day to collect a mere bundle of kindling wood," Myŏng-ku complained. However, he was secretly glad that he had an excuse to go to Mr. Choi's house. All the same, he complained specifically to the woman of Wolp'o.

"Hey, who do you think you are? All you have to do is obey the orders of your elders. Your head has grown too big for this work, huh? What's the big idea? Complaining and grumbling!"

Yi blew his top. He could be infinitely patient when he wanted to, but when he was in a hurry, he could blow steam at the slightest provocation.

"Mr. Choi will come here on his own in only three days. Why are you in such a hurry to see him anyway?" the woman spoke up in defense of Myŏng-ku because she felt a little sorry about the low salary she was giving him.

"Now, you too, are going to abuse me when you've squeezed every last drop of sweet juice from me?" Yi's anger was directed not only at Myŏng-ku but also at his wife.

"Please, that is enough. I'll go to Mr. Choi and get some firewood around there," Myŏng-ku spoke to appease both of them.

Since Myŏng-ku had to take a detour, he put his lunch on his A-frame and started on the long journey.

In the Chayang River, icy cold water flowed over smooth flat rocks. Myŏng-ku crossed the river, went over the Kyeyang Pass and walked for miles along a narrow path. On the slopes of the mountains there were rice paddies, and further into the mountains there suddenly appeared a sun-drenched village of about a hundred thatched roof houses. This was Tuma-ri.

Tuma-ri was a tiny village composed of two families—the Wolsŏng branch of the Choi clan, and the Kyŏngju branch of the Kim clan. As both family groups were quite prestigious, the larger town of Ibam established a branch school in Tuma-ri.

Mr. Choi, the geomancer, was the head of the mainline Choi clan and the administrative head of the village. The Choi house was one of the few with a tile roof.

When Myŏng-ku stepped inside the straw gate, he saw the family busy thrashing beans. Mr. Choi was thrashing and Mrs. Choi was stacking up the bean stalks in front of an empty cow shed. Myŏng-ku told Mr. Choi that his uncle wanted to see him on some urgent business.

On the wooden floor of the central hall, Mr. Choi's old mother was peeling and cutting a pumpkin into long, spiral strips to dry. The crisp, warm autumn sun was shining upon the old lady's cotton-white hair. Beside her sat Mr. Choi's daughter, Kye-yŏn, leaning against the hall column. She held up her face toward the sun like a sunflower. Her complexion was dark and sickly. She looked at Myŏng-ku with utterly expressionless eyes. She showed no hint of interest in him.

She was completely indifferent to the clear warm fall air, the majestic Pohyŏn Mountain with its snow-covered top, and the autumn colors of its trees, as well as to Myŏng-ku, an old friend.

Her face was like a mask. She seemed as if she were rid of all human feelings. Neither the wonderful fall scene nor any other pleasure of life held her interest. Looking at her, Myŏng-ku recalled the face of his sister, who was about Kye-yŏn's age, and who was reported to be working in a brewery in P'ohang.

These days his heart beat wildly at sudden unexpected moments, and now gazing at Kye-yŏn's scrawny appearance, his heart began to beat as if it would burst open.

Kye-yŏn, on the other hand, looked at him with vacant eyes, then closed them as if even the sunlight were too heavy upon her eyelids.

"Then I'll tell Uncle that you'll be coming tomorrow," said Myŏng-ku, and he left. He felt desolate.

On every roof there were red peppers drying in the warm sun. Their bright red color seemed to stab his eyes. With the empty A-frame on his back, he crossed the river. Under the crystal clear water, he noticed one round white stone that reminded him of Kye-yŏn's face. The double image of her face and the stone remained long in his mind's eye.

"He did promise, didn't he?" Yi asked Myŏng-ku, upon his return.

"Yes, he did. He said he was going to come to Ibam anyway, because he had some business to do at Mr. Chang's place," Myŏng-ku answered. Chang was a Chinese herb doctor.

"I guess he is going to take his own time. Maybe he will have lunch and a long nap before he starts. Usually he is as quick as a squirrel, but today he isn't going to be like that," Yi said.

"You act like a little kid with his candy on fire, more restless and impatient than Mr. Choi ever was," Madam Wolp'o said.

Ignoring her remark, he rubbed down his swollen face with his huge hand. The swelling went down a little, but his slitty eyes were still deep in his face.

At that moment, Preacher Min was passing by Wolp'ook in his worn all-weather coat. He carried in his hand his usual big beat-up black bag, which looked like something out of a thrift shop. Preacher Min was a bachelor living alone in a small rented room behind the kitchen of the house next to Wolp'ook.

He had been an elementary school teacher in Angang when he got conscripted and sent to war. After being discharged from the army, he began to study theology through a correspondence school. He was a preacher at the Ibam Church. Wearing thick glasses, he walked with a serious face, always as if he were deep in thought.

"That man must be a real disciple of Jesus Christ. Day and night, he is at work," said Yi, eyeing the preacher who was hurrying away, his shoulders hunched, his face serious.

"Every night before he goes to bed, he prays for as long as an hour," said Myŏng-ku.

"How do you know that?"

"When I go around the pigsty in the back of the house, I can hear him. He always kneels to pray under the date tree beside the kitchen."

"I've heard that all in his squadron except for him died in a battle near Ch'ŏlwŏn. He said it was because of God that he alone survived. I don't know about that. But he said the night before, he had seen Jesus Christ in his dream as clearly as if He were standing there in front of him. Anyway, he doesn't seem like a madman, but he is very strange all the same," Yi concluded.

In the market place, every time the cool autumn wind blew, straw and bits of debris blew around. The sun was already sinking in the west and long shadows were stretching from the houses. Stray dogs were the only moving creatures on the deserted plaza.

Children had gone off to rice fields to chase away sparrows or to the mountains to gather chestnuts. Men had gone to the mountains, too, but to collect firewood. Women stayed home to do all the pickling of vegetables and the fluffing of cotton quilts in the sun in preparation for the long winter.

"Hey, Tal-gon, give me a bowl of rice wine. Why, my insides are on fire. I can't wait any longer," Yi called to Sohn, the owner of the bicycle shop.

"What? You know your days are numbered, and you are going to cut them short like a silkworm winding itself shut. Tae-mal, you have lost your power just like my card game," Madam Wolp'o sneered at her husband.

"Lost his power? That's not a normal thing to say. Madam Wolp'o, is something wrong?" Kang, the briqutte-seller, joined in.

"Hey, why are you so interested? You have a healthy wife. Even cucumbers and eggplants taste best when they are just plucked. Once plucked, they don't stay fresh," Madam Wolp'o said with a provocative, sly smile, and snatched up her cards. This time the cards were good.

"You over there, I told you I wanted a drink. I know you got bad cards. Don't try to guess others' cards," Yi shouted at Sohn, instead of at his wife.

"Why are you telling him to fold? He means to stay on. If you want to die, prepare to salt your own flesh," Madam Wolp'o's voice rang with vitality because her cards were good.

"You dirty old woman. Why don't you jam a big stick into your dirty mouth? You are as rotten as salted anchovies, damned woman," Yi cursed at his wife and picked up the empty bowl lying beside Sohn.

"To speak the truth, you are a damned bum," his wife shot back.

Yi didn't say anything because he actually had been a bum. Crestfallen, his hands shook when he held the wine bowl. His eyes were glaring at his wife.

"Are you really going to drink that? Think of your condition," Madam Wolp'o said in a gentler voice.

"What would you do if I did?"

"Is Mr. Choi going to bring you a bear's gall to make you stronger?"

"What if he brings instead a sea lion's testicles, huh, you damned woman?"

"Come, come, I thought you were a perfectly matched couple. Why are you at each other's throats tonight? Really, there must be something wrong with your bedroom business," Sohn threw down his cards and picked up the bowl.

"Okay, Mr. Yi. Just one bowl. I won't give you anymore. I don't know what kind of big deal Mr. "Stick" Choi and you are up to, and I don't understand why you are so petulant and impatient today," said Sohn as he poured rice wine into the bowl Yi held out.

They called Mr. Choi "Stick" Choi because he always carried a stick with him.

Yi downed the drink in one gulp. He was about to pick up a piece of kimch'i when he remembered that salty things were bad for his kidney trouble. So he just swallowed his own saliva instead.

He yanked a piece of straw from the ragged edge of a mat and picked his teeth with it. His knee joints hurt, so he stretched his legs. As he kneaded his knees, he recalled that Choi's daughter had a disease of the joints.

"There he comes," Myŏng-ku shouted, pointing at the market place.

Yi quickly turned and looked out the window. From behind the fabric shop, in the dusty wind whirling around, Mr. Choi was coming in his quick gait, swinging his juniper cane.

Short and skinny, Mr. Choi was wearing a black coat and a dark brown hat. A bundle in one hand, he was coming straight to Wolp'ook.

"He's here! He's here! Now, I'm going to my room," Yi said. His face smoothed, he stood up. Pounding the boy's back with his fist, he said to Myŏng-ku, "Make a big fire in the fuel hole of my room tonight. Make the floor scorching hot."

"Humph, he must be happy now. I wonder what big secret deal there is between them," Madam Wolp'o said to herself.

Yi opened the door and the smoke in the room was sucked into the cold air outside. No sooner had Yi stepped down into the yard than Mr. Choi came through the fence door.

"My dear man, my nose grew by several inches today, just waiting for you. If you were coming in today, why didn't you leave after breakfast? Was somebody going to snatch you away if you left early?" Yi said affectionately.

"You don't know what you are talking about. I had to take care of something," Mr. Choi said with a deep sigh.

Mr. Choi was about the same age as Yi, but because of his mustache and beard, he looked close to sixty. During the war when Red guerrillas were running wild in Tuma-ri and Sangok-ri around the Pohyŏn Mountain, he thought looking older was advantageous in order to survive, so he began to grow a mustache and a beard.

"Why, now that the war is over, there aren't any Red guerrillas sneaking down, are there?" Yi asked.

"No, no. Such things should never happen again. By the way, you know I always come here on market days. Why did you want to see me so urgently? You and your wife are not scheming to take away the lease of your rice paddies from me, are you?"

Mr. Choi grew rice in Madam Wolp'o's paddies on a 50/50 profit-sharing basis.

"How can you say such a thing? Aren't we the best of friends? Now I see you are a born worrier."

"It wasn't you I suspected. I thought your wife might have suddenly gotten a bright idea."

"She wouldn't do that, at least for the sake of Ch'an-kyŏng. She isn't a very generous person, but she has always liked you."

"I've had so much bad luck this year that even small things scare me."

"Let's go in and talk. It's cold out here." Yi let Mr. Choi go in first. The inner room was very small.

"I had to ask Mr. Chang to give me medicine on credit again. I'm ashamed," said Mr. Choi.

"Medicine again?" Yi had noticed the bundle Mr. Choi had in his hand.

"Yes, for my daughter."

"What is that long bundle under the other one?"

"Centipedes."

"Centipedes?"

"Mr. Chang says they are a last resort. I don't know how effective they will be. I'll have to wait and see."

"Let's go in first."

Mr. Choi stepped on the stepping-stone and propped his cane against a hall post. Above the door, there were three pictures on the wall. One was the picture of Madam Wolp'o's daughter's old-style wedding, the next one a picture of Yi, and the last a picture of the Madam.

Eight years ago when Yi came to Ibam and married Madam Wolp'o, they thought they were too old to have a regular wedding and a wedding picture, so they had individual pictures taken instead, as tokens of their pledge to love each other until their hair turned white.

Yi's face in the picture was austere and stern, like that of a ascetic hermit, while Madam Wolp'o's was sly and street-smart.

Following Mr. Choi, Yi was about to step into the room

when he changed his mind. He went over to the other room and coughed a couple of times. He had already seen a pair of light blue rubber shoes in front of the room.

"Are you in there, Suk-kyŏng?" he asked.

"Yes."

The door opened from inside. Suk-kyŏng was embroidering a big cross on a piece of white tablecloth.

"Suk-kyŏng, will you bring me a small table of drinks and some side dishes? Don't let your mother know of this. As you know, I must not drink, so bring just one bowl. Bring rice wine and seasoned snipe-fish. It was very tasty when I had it at breakfast. Will you do this for me? Now there's a good girl."

When Yi wanted to persuade a person he used his special, smooth talk in a purposely melodious voice. His wife's younger daughter looked like her mother with a narrow chin and thin lips, which, Yi thought, indicated that she would be sexually active and aggressive.

He thought of the older girl who had produced two children, a boy and a girl, and who was reported to have a very good marriage.

"All right," Suk-kyŏng said. Her stepfather's knowing glances sent a chill down her spine, so she avoided his eyes and answered curtly.

Yi thought to himself, "If only I had the sexual prowess I used to have, I could have that one, too." Then, he reminded himself that he should not sin any more. When he entered the inner chamber, Mr. Choi was sitting on the floor with his hat beside him and turning a worried glance at the medicine he had brought. Through the back window, hazy light was coming in, but the room was almost dark.

"Your daughter's condition has worsened, I gather?" Yi asked, lowering himself down on the floor.

"I wish she would just die in her sleep. She has given us so much pain and suffering. To have good and healthy children is one of five happinesses, they say, but this daughter of mine has been not a child but an enemy."

"My dear man, don't complain about your children in front of me. As you know, I have none."

"Why don't you hear me out? Last night, after a few hours of rather uneasy sleep, she couldn't sit up. No matter how she tried, she could not. When we asked her what the matter was, she said her legs didn't feel like her legs. True, her legs were as stiff as two sticks of wood. My wife and I were so scared that we gave her a hot massage all night. Still, her skinny legs merely twitched a little and had no strength in them. Toward the afternoon, she began to move her legs like a baby, leaning against a wall. I just don't understand what's wrong with her." Mr. Choi's lamentation was long.

"Hmmm. I don't understand it, either. On the last market day, she managed to come here, didn't she? Even though you carried her on your back half the way."

"She did." Mr. Choi looked again at the medicine. "Centipedes. They are quite potent. I don't know whether her frail body will be able to take them."

"Ah, it's such a pity that a young girl has to suffer so much. Maybe your ancestors chose the wrong grave site."

"Hold it right there. One doesn't criticize one's ancestors."

"Do you think the Choi family is equal to the Kwon family of Andong?"

"So, what do you think you are? You're nothing but a destitute country bumpkin."

These two were always exchanging such jokes. Mr. Choi took a tobacco pouch and a pipe from the inside pocket of his coat. Feeling the air over the brazier, he found there were embers in it.

"Here, why don't you smoke these?" Yi gave Mr. Choi a pack of Mugunghwa cigarettes.

"If it were a lung disease, it'd be just in the chest. But my girl coughs all the time and the germs have gone into her bones, too. Germs are not bullets; I don't know how they infiltrated her bones." Grumbling thus, Mr. Choi lit up a cigarette with an ember from the brazier.

"It is called tuberculosis in modern medical lingo. Tuberculosis is not confined to the lungs. You can have tuberculosis in bone marrow, in the joints, in the skin, and in the kidneys. Meningitis, pleuritis, peritonitis are all caused by tubercular germs. And your young daughter has bone marrow tuberculosis. Poor girl, it's just bad luck," Yi nodded and tut-tutted in sympathy.

Because he had travelled widely, he had learned a thing or two, and people sometimes called him Know-It-All Yi. He looked over at Mr. Choi's worry-ridden face. He was inhaling the cigarette smoke so avidly that his cheeks were sucked in.

"Have you heard from your son?" Yi asked.

"The last time I heard from him, he said his leg was going to be amputated. I haven't heard from him since then. You know, fall is such a busy season that I don't have time to go and see him. Besides, I have no money, unless I borrow from someone again. I feel like a person staring at a scorching sky in a summer drought."

Mr. Choi's son was at an army hospital in Taegu. Since he was drafted the year before last, he came through many battles, miraculously unscathed, until last April when he was shot in the thigh in the Kŭmhwa battle.

"We are back to the same divided situation anyway. I wonder why we fought. We sided with the Americans and the Russians, but the result was that we poor people got killed. They talk about democracy or communism, so we go along with this or that. In the meantime, we try our damnedest to preserve our necks. I'm sick of the whole thing. Rich and powerful guys never have their sons sent to the front. Those rich kids either get easy work in safe places or are sent to America to study. So, all the poor men's sons become bullet stoppers." Mr. Choi was vehement.

"They say that college students don't get drafted."

"Damn this world. Those guys in high positions telling everyone else what to do, they are the vile ones. I thought heaven would punish me if I did wrong, so I wandered around the world, all alone, frustrated and furious. I was the fool in the end," said Yi, getting excited, too. The veins in his neck rose in an angry red color.

"Damn it all. I'm sick of this fighting. What difference does it make whether this side wins or that side wins? It won't make the least bit of difference to people like us land-scratchers."

"Come on. You are the administrative head of your village. If the Communists win, they won't let you do ancestor worship. They won't let you keep your family geneology, either."

"Have I done anything bad because I am an administrative head? As for ancestor worship, you can always lock the door and put a bowl of cold water on the altar. It's your heart that matters. As for geneology, my family line never produced a prime minister nor a vice minister. So, what's the big deal? For generations, we never had enough rice to eat, and yet, we had to obey, obey, all the time. Who cares if I can't keep my geneology? You can take it for all I care."

"Wow. You are really pouring out a piece of your mind today. You can say all those things, but my case is different. Since I have wandered around the world and idled my time away, Communists will certainly make me a target of criticism. What use am I going to be? If we want a comparatively easy life, the Republic of Korea is better still."

"As fortune-tellers read palms, I read land, but I am sick and tired of this farming life," Mr. Choi said. He rubbed out the half-burnt cigarette and leaned the butt against the rim of the brazier.

"In war, the only survivors are people like me. We lie low, crawl around like dogs, and wag our tails at whoever rules over us. People like me have no courage when a gun is pointed at us. If the Red soldiers tell us to say hurrah, we will. If the Republic Army tells us to do the same, we will. Ah, this damned world. What good is ideology anyway? Useless dog bones," Yi shook his head, remembering the terror-filled days under the Communists.

Then, Yi suddenly turned very somber and began to speak seriously.

"The poor Korean people! They have persevered for generations like weeds, having no place to lean against for support. If they don't work, they don't eat. They say heaven is on the side of people, but does heaven hear their cries?"

"It's too late for my generation, but if my children want to leave Tuma-ri and live somewhere else, I will not object. Perhaps my ancestors will also understand and give their permission," said Mr. Choi as he wiped away tears from his eyes.

Even as recently as the previous spring, Tuma-ri, having been situated deep in the mountain side, would raise the *T'aegŭkki*, the Republic of Korea flag, during the day at the elementary school. At night the whole village trembled in fear because the retreating Red Army soldiers would often raid the village.

Young men of the village, therefore, either volunteered for the ROK Army or left the village for other places. Left behind were old people, women, and children.

The series of reversals between the Red soldiers and ROK soldiers began in 1948 before the Korean War broke out. The first national election to be held in South Korea, the May 10 Election, met with fierce opposition from the Southern Communist Party, whose followers began to flee into the mountains to plan a revolutionary war. For a time in 1948 and until the spring of 1950, Communist guerrillas considered the villages of this area their own territory. They came and went as they pleased.

In 1949, the Communist government in the north sent Kim Dal-sam and 300 armed guerrilla fighters to the south. They merged with the other fighters deep in the Pohyŏn Mountain area and formed what they called the third field infantry.

The ROK Field Army in turn set up its headquarters in Tuma-ri and evacuated everyone in the village to Ibam. They built small mud shacks and barely survived on the government-issued rice.

At the beginning of the war, wherever soldiers went, regardless of which side they were on, villages were ruined. Chukchang county, having been located near the famous Battle of the P'o-hang-Hyŏngsan Rivers, was devastated.

After the sea of fire swept through Tuma-ri, it took some time before people began to re-emerge. It was fall when relative peace began to reign. By then, the Red Army stragglers had been completely wiped out throughout the T'aebaek Mountain areas or had fled north through a path in the Odae Mountain range. Suk-kyŏng brought in a small table with a kettle of rice wine, an empty bowl, kimch'i, and snipe-fish. Though Yi didn't tell her so, she brought two pairs of chopsticks.

"How is my sister's family?" Suk-kyŏng asked Mr. Choi.

"Everyone is busy harvesting, as you know. Yesterday when I went to the field, I saw your sister with the baby on her back, shaking empty cans to chase away sparrows."

"I wonder if she can come and see us at Ch'usŏk."

"I'll tell her that you miss her."

"Thank you. I hope you have a pleasant time."

"Thank you."

Suk-kyŏng went out, holding the side of her skirt.

"When you are depressed and angry, drinking is the best cure. Now, drink this bowl of wine in one gulp." Yi poured wine into the bowl for Mr. Choi.

Mr. Choi, instead of drinking the wine, just stared down at the cigarette butt. In deference, Yi merely sat there and watched him.

"Mr. Choi, why don't you use your magical stick this time?" Yi didn't want to wait any longer.

Mr. Choi raised his head and looked at his friend blankly. He looked as if he had no idea what Yi was talking about.

"Use my magic stick? What does my stick have to do with curing my daughter?"

"I'm not talking about your daughter. I'm the one. I'm going to die soon."

"What are you talking about?"

"Will you find a good burial site for me? I know I won't live out this year." Pretending to be thick-skinned, Yi came right out and asked Mr. Choi.

"As you know I've led a worthless, idle life, so I have no regrets even if I died now. Frankly speaking, I'm ashamed that

I've lived this long. You know me well. Since the age of 22, I've lived like a weed, barely surviving when trodden, and using all kinds of lies and tricks. Three times I've felt death knocking on my door; the first time was when I was tortured by the Japanese military police, the second time when I was doing forced labor at a Hokkaido mine, and this time. When I think of ending my life here in Ibam, I don't feel sad, but the first thing that comes to my mind is that sheep-like face of yours. For the last time in my life, I wanted to ask a big favor of you. So I sent Myŏng-ku to you. I wanted to see you right away. You know how impatient I am."

"What a thunder out of the blue sky this is! This must be some sort of practical joke gone too far. You are too healthy to die. The way you talk, you're going to live a long time, till senility hits you."

Mr. Choi dismissed what he had just heard, snorted, and drank the bowlful of milky white wine. Then he picked up a piece of the fish and chewed it, bones and all.

"Hey, do you think I sit here and consume expensive rice wine to pull a joke on you?"

Yi picked up Mr. Choi's bowl and poured the wine for himself. "If I'm going to die, I'll drink and die."

"This isn't the first time you've asked me to find a grave site for you."

"That was different. Everyone dies sooner or later, so I just wanted you to hear it often and get used to it. But this time, it is urgent, very urgent."

"You sound like a person caught with diarrhea in a moving bus."

"Listen. This is not a time for jokes."

After making sure there was no one nearby, Yi began to talk in a low voice.

"You know how to read land and I know my sickness."

Sensing that Yi was not joking, Mr. Choi became serious.

"It was nine years ago in Hokkaido when I got this kidney ailment. During those years in the mines, there weren't women around, so I didn't get to use my famous tool. It kind of hung there, loose and useless. Still, I was virile enough to make one or two women taste a piece of heaven several times a night. Fortune-tellers say they can tell whether a woman was born to be poor or rich, but I can tell right away what her hole would be like just by looking at her face. It is just as you can find a truly good burial hole with that stick of yours."

Yi stopped, poured more wine into the bowl, and gave it to Mr. Choi.

Mr. Choi, momentarily forgetting his daughter's disease, sat there with a smile on his face. He smoothed down his beard.

Yi had not gone hungry all his life solely because of his legendary lady-killing techniques, Mr. Choi thought. In light of that fact, his lewd talk must not be idle talk but a tale of true experiences.

There was no man in the world who didn't like dirty talk, but Yi didn't tell such stories just to anybody. If he were to tell his whole life story, it would be endless. However, seduction techniques that made women cling to him as if to a magnet, were a precious secret he would not divulge easily. Consequently, he would simply clam up on the subject.

"Yi Tae-mal, my friend, stories of women need some spice. Before you came to Ibam, how many different women had you slept with? Did you ever sleep with a Russian woman with blue eyes?" If the oldest man among those gathered in the tavern, like Kwon from the upper village, asked such a question, Yi would simply grin and clam up.

"Yes, I did experience many different kinds of women, but all I can say is that Korean women are the best. The structure of their private parts differ according to the region they live in. Women in the tropical region have very stiff and coarse hair, so your skin can be scraped off. They have narrow openings, but inside they are damp and soft. The private parts of women in the cold region are weak and watery so that you feel no friction. Inside, they are loose, wide, and dry. Compared with those women, Korean women have just the right combination because we have four distinct seasons, and a small but interesting geography.

So, my advice to you all is that you cherish your own wives. From ancient times, Chinese aristocrats preferred women from Shilla or Paekche rather than blue-eyed Western women. My conclusion, therefore, is that Korean women's private parts are the best."

Yi would not go further than this, though the men became thirstier than ever for more details. But they had to be content with slight stirrings between their thighs. To them, Yi's story was like a few drops of rain on parched land.

Ever since Yi settled in Ibam eight years ago, he told what was really deep in his heart only to Mr. Choi. Of course, he didn't tell about every woman he had known, even to Mr. Choi, but he did describe in detail his escapades with a few women who stood out in his memory. Whenever he did this, he made Mr. Choi promise that he would not tell anyone else.

Since Mr. Choi had become friends with Yi, he had heard many stories about women, but being the head of his family branch and of a fastidious turn of mind, he didn't feel the need to repeat the stories to other people.

On the other hand, Mr. Choi noticed that his friend's stories had grains of truth about the Yin and Yang of man-woman relationships, that made people think. It was like finding truth in a rare book.

It seemed that the gossip and rumors about Yi's virility came more likely than not from Madam Wolp'o's mouth, and became greatly exaggerated.

"Did Madam Wolp'o suggest a divorce? If she and you were divorced you could just walk out since she is not your long-married first wife nor has she produced any children with you. Simply go off to some place. Stop this sudden talk of finding a grave site. Are you going to shut yourself up and die?"

Knowing that Mr. Choi had a habit of creating a joke from every story, Yi answered serenely.

"My dear friend, I'm telling you a secret that I haven't told anyone. Frankly speaking, my tool is not working anymore. Until now, no matter how drunk I might get, my tool always worked. If I decided not to have intercourse at all, that was another matter, but for the first time I wanted it, but couldn't perform. Even at this age, I do it once every day. Occasionally, on a market day, I skipped, but these past five days, I wasn't able to get an erection. Even when I get one, it is so soft and weak. From a long time ago, I knew that the day I couldn't do it would be the day I should prepare myself for a final resting at Puk-mang Mountain."

Yi heaved a long sigh. On his sallow swollen face there was resignation written all over.

"Come on, my man, at your age it is time the thing didn't work. Besides, you have used it so strenuously, so long that you have exhausted it," Mr. Choi said in earnest.

Truthfully speaking, Mr. Choi couldn't remember when he had last had sexual relations with his wife. When they were young, he and his wife had had a very good sex life, until World War II broke out. His eldest son was drafted and hadn't been heard from since, and his second son went to the Korean War and became an amputee. After losing his sons, he lost all interest in sex. On top of this, his daughter became seriously ill. "Come to think of it," he thought, "I've forgotten that my wife was a woman capable of sex."

It was a matter of stimulation. People used to eating meat always craved it more than those who ate less of it. So it was with sex. Those who had sex more often thought of their organs in a sexual way, while those who went without it thought of their organs as good for only urination.

"Husband, please don't touch even a drop of alcohol. To you, alcohol is poison. If I smell alcohol on your breath later, I'll tear you apart. Remember." Madam Wolp'o's sharp voice was heard from the yard. She was on her way to her room from the outdoor lavatory.

"I say this only for your sake, so listen and remember for your own good."

"I'm not drinking. I'm just treating Mr. Choi," Yi said, a little annoyed.

"Mr. Choi, please bring me some red peppers and sesame if you've finished harvesting them. I'll pay you market prices," Madam Wolp'o said to Mr. Choi.

"Why do you want to buy mine? Your in-laws have them, too," Mr. Choi opened the door and asked.

"I'll do something else to help them. If I pay them, they won't like it."

"You are right. This year my peppers are the best in my village, if I may say so."

Mr. Choi agreed and shut the door.

Yi chewed a fish piece while listening to the conversation. Finally, Madam Wolp'o's footsteps faded away.

"She is really lucky. In a busy season like this, she has time enough to play cards, unlike other people."

"You know, honestly, that woman really loves me. Only, her tongue is sharp and her mouth is dirty."

"As a rule, married couples are like that. Once they mix their bodies, they develop a deep bond."

"Married couple? Even children become strangers once they leave you. She and I may have a physical bond, but there is no bonding of minds between us. We weren't married first to each other. We just happened to run into each other, and that's different."

"Do you really think of Madam Wolp'o that way?"

"What difference would it make if I felt otherwise? Do you always think of your wife as a part of you? Have you ever gotten angry and wished her dead or for her to return to her family?"

"One should not talk like that."

"You talk like an ethics teacher, but that is a kind of hypocrisy."

"But there have to be morals and ethics in the human world."

"But if you take off the veneer, you'll see a base nature. Mind you, what I've said is true."

"No wonder why people call you Yi Tae-mal," Mr. Choi said

and laughed.

"You are probably right. If you just love someone and don't have physical relations, it is easy to part. But, once you have physical relations, feelings of love begin to develop. That's the mysterious nature of human relationships. That's why my wife does everything she can for my health. She worries about my kidney disease and brings me all kinds of special medicine. Why, she somehow even got the rare 'gobon' root and boiled it for me. Another time, she bought eels and steamed them with pumpkins. She said that these things were aphrodysiacs too. But what's the use of my woman's concern? I know my own body better than she. When I wake up in the morning, my legs are so heavy that I can hardly sit up. My hands and my face are swollen too. Look, look at my legs."

Yi untied the laces of his pants and pushed the material up over his knee to show a hairy, muscular leg. When he pushed down the fleshy part of his leg with his right thumb, the flesh went deep down but didn't spring back up.

"It is swollen quite badly."

"Now you know. Around noon, the swelling goes down a little bit, but then, the swelling starts again in the afternoon. My hands, too. My urine is thick and dark brown in color. It was long ago when I urinated with such force that a chamber pot nearly broke."

"Please, that's enough. I understand now."

"I, too, went to Mr. Chang yesterday and bought some medicine."

"Your sickness is quite advanced, too. Yes, your body is cracked, as you say."

Then Yi began to plead to Mr. Choi. "You see, my time has come. I can't eat anymore. At times like this, I want to go off and wander around, but this body of mine won't last long in this cold weather. So, please, before the fall is over, find me a good grave site. I hate even the thought of my hometown. I won't so much as urinate in that direction."

"I really don't understand this hatred of yours about your

own hometown."

"Standing alone in the whole wide world, well, that is me. I have no one above me, no one under me. The land-god of my hometown won't accept me, nor will I feel comfortable lying there. When I settled down in Ibam, I decided to clear it out of my mind completely. To tell you the truth, the best burial site I would want would be a place in the Yaji Village in Kando, Manchuria. But you can't go there, even if you are healthy and strong. So, find me the place you've often described as the best. On top, there is the head mountain, beneath which there is the main mountain. Under a tall mountain top spreading its wings, there is a cave. On the left, there lies a blue dragon and on the right, a white tiger. In front, there is a river. Across the river, there sits a red peacock kneeling humbly. Isn't this the right description of the best burial site? Please get me such a one." Yi repeated word for word what Mr. Choi had told him.

"But, my dear friend, it all depends on who the individual is. A chicken can't turn into a swan simply because it has a good burial site. A burial site should always fit the person. A hole in the middle of a vegetable field can be the best grave site in the world."

"Anyway, you know me well. Find me a site that suits me. If you find it for me, I'll go up there and get used to it even if I have to lean on a stick to do it. Now that I am sick and near death, my thoughts go out to all my children, scattered around God knows where. I have had a hard fate. A fate like mine ought to stop with me. No one should ever live like me again."

"What's the use of thinking of your children when you are in this condition?"

"You are wrong. Because of my condition, I think of them. Poor devils! What is the meaning of being born into this sea of suffering!!" said Yi as he raised a trembling hand and wiped his eyes.

Yi grabbed Mr. Choi's hand and carried on about his sickness, his wish for a good burial site, his hard life, and finally he wept over his children. He insisted that when he was comfortably buried near Ibam, his scattered children should stop wandering around as he had done, and settle down in one place to live like human beings.

A man who lived all his life solely by his wits, Yi performed well enough today to persuade Mr. Choi. Though Mr. Choi was himself troubled by his own problems, he was moved by Yi's sad story and reluctantly agreed with him.

Though Yi insisted that Mr. Choi have dinner with him, Mr. Choi decided to leave as he had to arrive home before sundown. He didn't have time to listen to and commiserate with his friend. He had to hurry home to boil his daughter's medicine.

When he got outside, the evening fog was dense and the wind blew hard. The noises of the forest, coming from the surrounding mountains, were deafening.

Yi came out with Mr. Choi to the market place where he bought a couple of salted fish for him, and asked him again to find a good burial place.

Then Yi turned back to his home, but passed by it instead and walked north along the Chayang River, cold wind was blowing. He arrived at the T'angnip Rock outside the village. Looking up at the rock rising high like a dragon's head, he prayed.

"Please, god of the dragon-head, do not punish this Yi In-t'ae anymore, and grant me an immediate death." Tears ran down his cheeks and his long, wind-blown hair fluttered like a shredded rag.

CHAPTER III

It was early autumn in 1945 just before *Ch'usŏk,* the Harvest Festival Day. Mr. Choi and his wife came to Ibam every two or three days, as well as on market days. They were desperate for news of their eldest son who had been sent to World War II.

Out of the six young men from Tuma-ri who had gone to war, three had returned two weeks ago and two had been killed, one in the spring, another in the fall. The Chois' son was the only one yet to be heard from, and their anxiety was overwhelming.

It was a market day. The sweltering summer had spent its fury, and a cool breeze began to blow early in the morning and again in the evening. Mr. Choi sat under Madam Wolp'o's makeshift canopy and had a bowl of soup with rice and a bowl of rice ale.

Mr. Kim the salt-seller happened to be seated next to Mr. Choi. He was having a good day because people had bought his salt and many other things for the Harvest Festival.

"Mr. Choi, they say that boys who were sent to the South Sea are regarded as war criminals and are put in American prisoners' camps."

"I hope that's true, because that means he will come home someday."

"Don't worry too much, Mr. Choi. Human fate is in the hands

of God in Heaven," Kim said, while eyeing Madam Wolp'o.

"Look at Madam Wolp'o over there. Watch her hand ladling the soup. It looks as alive as a moving fish."

At that moment, Madam Wolp'o was putting some soup into a bowl and chatting away with a customer. She was giggling too. Her neat shiny hair was parted in the middle and a round bun at the back of her head was tied with a red ribbon. A long jade hair pin was stuck in the bun.

"I've heard that she is buying some rice paddies. Must have made quite a bit of money. Everyone gets three chances to make money in his life, they say," Kim said. Mr. Choi nodded while he too, watched Madam Wolp'o.

Mr. Choi had thought on his part, that since the last market day, Madam Wolp'o had been too ready with her laughter and too full of energy. He had figured that because people were now coming back home in droves, her business was booming. So he didn't pay much attention to her sudden bursts of energy and her coquettish laughter.

According to rumor, even on ordinary days, she had so many overnight customers that she could not accomodate them all. The lucky ones would spend the night in her one small, foul-smelling room, bitten by fleas and lice. They paid not only for lodging but also for supper and breakfast, which was usually accompanied by a so-called "waking-up wine." No wonder she was making money.

"Mr. Choi, have you heard the rumor?" Kim asked. "What rumor?" Mr. Choi was hoping to hear some more stories about the boys sent to the South Sea.

"Good heavens, you are slow. The rumor has spread all over the market."

"What rumor are you talking about?" Mr. Choi stared at Kim who was winking and tut-tut-ing.

"A stranger came to Wolp'ook the other day and spent the night here. The next day he looked around the Ibam Academy and the T'angnip Rock, and didn't seem to be in a hurry to leave. The most incredible thing is that from the next night on, he began to sleep in Madam Wolpo's inner chamber instead of in the room for customers. It's already been five days. Madam Wolp'o cooks fresh rice three times a day, puts everything on a special lacquer tray-table, and serves him in her room. At each meal she even gives him a raw egg, which as you know, is as rare and precious as anything. Can you believe it? Can you? You know a lot about the Yin and Yang of man-woman relationships. Tell me what you think of this?"

"This is indeed top news," said Mr. Choi with a smile.

"If I may speak the truth, Madam Wolp'o is a woman in her prime, so once in a while if she needs a man, she should have a quiet affair with any man she fancies. But how could she invite a man into her inner chamber after knowing him only for two days? I can't believe it. As for Madam Wolp'o, she is no ordinary woman. She came from a fishing village, peddled, and raised two daughters alone. She wouldn't give you so much as a bowl of cold water unless she was sure she could get something in return," Kim finished and gulped down a bowl of rice ale. He looked as if he had had his best-laying hen stolen during the night.

"Maybe, he is a distant relative of hers or someone she knew long ago."

"No, no, no. If that were the case, no one would talk about it. He is an absolutely total stranger."

"No, he can't be."

"That stranger came here from Chayang and asked around for a place to sleep. He finally came to Wolp'ook. He was wearing a ragged army uniform and torn army shoes. His toes were sticking out of holes in his shoes. They say that he was originally from the Ttakpat village, about 30 ris from here. From Yŏngch'ŏn to Chayang, he rode on a truck, but from Chayang he walked 40 ris to Ibam. By the time he got to Ibam, his legs had given out. At first, he thought he would force himself to go as far as Kasa-ri, but he was so worn out that he decided to stay one night at Wolp'ook. He told people that he had come to Korea for the first time in 25 years."

"Touched Korean soil for the first time in 25 years?" Mr. Choi asked himself.

"That's what he said."

"How old is he?"

"About forty-four or five. About your age."

"That's very strange. A man who has come home after 25 years decides to settle here and become the gigolo of a tavern owner? And his hometown is only a little distance from here?"

"Well, gigolo or not, aren't you more interested in how this man took her heart away? What kind of fantastic techniques did he use, huh?"

"The relationship between a man and a woman is never fully understood. It is always an inscrutable thing."

"That's what they say. For example, look at Madam Banguri. She is an amazon and can carry a huge sack of rice without any difficulty. But she worships her skinny runt of a husband. He barely reaches her chin, but when he orders her around, she moves like a slave. They tell me the reason for this is that he makes her extremely happy in bed."

"I don't know about that, but that man from the Ttakpat village must have fantastic bedroom techniques. Otherwise how could he have conquered a widow and occupied her inner chamber? There is a grown daughter in the same house, at that."

"Mr. Choi, that is not all. His history is fantastic too. He has been to every place in the world. He speaks Chinese, Russian, and Japanese. You can't help being overwhelmed if you listen to him. He is also an expert card handler. These days Madam Wolp'o's place is jam-packed every night. People want to hear about his wanderings around the world."

Mr. Choi's ears seemed to open suddenly at Kim's story of this incredible man who had traveled around the world, crossing mountains, rivers, and fields. Mr. Choi had been drinking heavily and worrying about his missing son. Perhaps, this strange man might be just the right person to get to know.

"What is his family name?"

"It's said to be Yi."

"Can he drink?"

"Yes, he s gulped down bowlfuls."

"Really? By the way, are you going to spend this whole day gossiping? Have a good day of business."

Mr. Choi ordered a big kettle of rice wine and a side dish of seasoned raw fish.

"Mr. Choi, what's going on? Have you found a sack full of money or something? How are you going to drink all that by yourself?"

Madam Wolp'o cried, giving him a side glance. Her eyes had a cold vitality, as if winter icicles were melting in her eyes.

"Whether I drink it alone or with a friend is none of your business. Put it on my credit. I'll pay it off after the harvest is over."

"I'll give you all the wine you want for free. Just find me a good young man for my girl Ch'an-kyŏng. She is good and gentle. She is pretty. She is first-class bride material. Please find me a young man in Tuma-ri. I'll send a considerable dowery to him. And of course, I'll not be stingy in a gift to you, either."

"All right," Mr. Choi answered curtly. He picked up his four-legged tray, and went into the house. On the stepping-stone in front of the hall was a pair of torn army shoes.

"Is the master of the house in?" Mr. Choi coughed a couple of times and called. No one answered. Only Ch'an-kyŏng, the eldest daughter of Madam Wolp'o, came out with a few thin green-onion crepes on a platter. She had just made them in the kitchen.

"Mr. Choi, why are you holding a tray?"

"Is there a man named Mr. Yi here?"

"You mean the strange man? He is in the back," Ch'an-kyŏng answered and grinned.

Mr. Choi took the tray, turned around the kitchen, and went to the backyard. Red peppers were ripening in the vegetable garden. Beside it, under a paulownia tree, there lay a man on a wooden cot. Like a mythical figure in a dream garden, he lay on his side with one arm under his head and another lightly touching his back.

"Are you the master of the house, Mr. Yi?" Mr. Choi called to him very politely.

"My family name is Yi. But if you are looking for the master, go back to the store. The lady master is doing business there, don't you know?"

Yi answered in a clear voice without getting up. His eyes were turned to the pigs in the sty. He would not even look up.

"I've come here to speak with Mr. Yi."

Hearing this, Yi raised himself on one elbow. He squinted his eyes and looked up at Mr. Choi.

Yi saw a short man wearing a shabby cotton coat and a crushed, grimy hat. The man, holding a tray, looked like a sycophantic servant in front of his master.

"I don't know who you are. But if you want to see me, sit down here."

Yi didn't sound pleased at all as he sat up, with one knee erect. He pushed away the wooden pillow and patted his back again. His eyelids were swollen and his eyes were red, apparently because he hadn't slept well the night before.

Mr. Choi thought to himself, "That man must have used all his energy last night to show off to Madam Wolp'o. Look at him, he is just a husk today." Then he put the tray down on the cot and took off his shoes. They sat facing each other, introduced themselves and bowed deeply. Mr. Choi began to look over Yi carefully. He couldn't tell whether Yi himself had bought it or Madam Wolp'o paid for it, but Yi wore a brand new suit of light green, a traditional jacket and pants like a bride-groom. He also had on a deep-purple vested overjacket.

Mr. Choi wasn't impressed by the attire, but he knew right away that Yi was not an ordinary man. The long hair and his rather handsome horse-like face were impressive, but what struck Mr. Choi most were his deep dreamy eyes.

On one hand, his eyes had the profound, transcendental light of a hermit philosopher. On the other hand, they had the damp, lewd appeal of a man who had mastered all the sexual secrets of the world. Mr. Choi suddenly felt a shiver going down his spine, as if a worm had crawled down it. He poured rice wine into a bowl and offered it to Yi.

"I live in Tuma-ri, about 20 ris west of here. It's a small village deep in the Pohyŏn Mountain. I'm just a small farmer from an old farming family that has lived there for many generations. But I have studied the secrets of land by myself for some years, and I know a thing or two about it. I've heard that you have traveled to many countries in the Orient and I hoped that you would tell me of your experiences. I thought I could learn much from you. That is why I dared to show myself here."

Mr. Choi spoke like a disciple visiting a venerated teacher.

"A geomancer?" Yi put his knee down and sat properly. He rubbed his beardless chin and nodded slowly.

"Then you are a site-finder, too, aren't you? You say you've studied land alone. Then how much have you learned?"

Using the disrespectful form of address, Yi spoke to Mr. Choi as a seer would to an ignorant man. Yi's question implied that he didn't believe in the knowledge of Mr. Choi, a country bumpkin from a mountain village.

"I don't know whether you've heard this, but among geomancers, there are four classes from the ordinary all the way up to the divine. As for me, I can read the rise and fall of a land form, and the shape and direction of a mountain. I am an ordinary geomancer."

Mr. Choi, intuitively knowing that Yi was neither as learned nor as old as he, went on explaining himself, using big words here and there. He was not offended by Yi's disrespectful manner of speaking.

"Is that right?" Yi plucked a hair from his nostril and threw it over the cot. He nodded again.

"I am on the lowest rung, yet, but I am rather well-known around here. I've read the shapes and directions of quite a few houses and burial sites."

"A geomancer has always been regarded as middle class. Of

course, the Buddhist monk Muhak was raised to become a royal teacher," continued Yi. "You say you've studied land by yourself? How and when did you begin to learn?"

"When I was a child, I came from Tuma-ri to Ibam to learn Sohak (a Confucian book for school children)at a school here."

"Did the Kwon family accept a child from an ordinary farming family? Times have changed, but at that time the Kwon family was the most powerful one."

"My grandfather asked the teacher for special permission. He wanted me to learn, as I was the eldest son of the mainline Choi branch."

"Hmmmm. Today's world doesn't care about family power and prestige. The Chosŏn Dynasty was ruined by excessive adherence to those things, as you know. Still, as I wandered around the world, I found that children of a famous family were different. It's just like that. Even pigs take generations of selective breeding to produce outstanding studs."

Yi glanced at the pigsty and returned to the main subject.

"You read Sohak. Then did the teacher open your eyes to land divining? A confucianist would never do that."

"Of course not. When I became a young man, I began to get interested in it by accident. So I searched and got as many books as I could and read them. When I became familiar with reading mountains, I traveled on foot to famous mountains and rivers around here, during the months when farm work slackened a little. I'm still a small frog in a small pond."

Mr. Choi drank up the wine and returned the bowl to Yi. He wanted to see what Yi was really like. At that moment, he looked like a poor, hungry school dog.

"You have traveled millions of ris, so you must know a lot. From the Paektu Mountain down to the long tail of this Korean peninsula. What do you think of our land here in comparison to the big continent?"

"I have merely wandered around without paying attention to such things. The Korean peninsula is like a piece of rice paper crumpled up to be used in the bathroom. It is small in scale and has too many mountains and valleys. There are no wide plains nor any majestic mountains."

Yi drank the wine in front of him and handed the bowl over to Mr. Choi. Yi's hands shook as he poured. He committed the grave error of spilling the wine as his eyes roved around. From the first moment he met Mr. Choi, his eyes had wandered from the sky to the vegetable garden, to the pigsty, back to Mr. Choi. Yi's eyes were like those of an amnesia patient's, unsettled and wandering. Mr. Choi congratulated himself, "I'm right. That is the very way of a man whose fate was to wander forever."

"The old geomancers from China were deeply touched by the beauty and goodness of our mountains and rivers, which they called "Gold-Embroidered Land," the very best of land. Of course, I've only heard it said," said Mr. Choi.

"Since you are so good at reading land, will you find me a good burial site? A very good one. It's been said that one good grave site in three or four generations is enough. I really need one because I have had a hard life and too much bad luck."

"Now that you have said so, I'll be frank with you. Your face shows that you are the kind of person who needs a good burial site." Mr. Choi said this with the full knowledge that it would bring home the painful truth of Yi's life.

"Well, I don't know whether my burial site will be of any good to anyone as I am childless," Yi said pretending indifference, but he was secretly surprised at Mr. Choi's insight.

"As I have learned land, I've also learned a little about reading faces. If you go back to the origins of geomancy, they are the same."

"In that case, you must have read my face pretty well." Yi thrust his upper body toward Mr. Choi, while realizing that Mr. Choi was using the same technique he himself used when he approached a new woman.

"According to books, if your face shows a dragon flying off to heaven, your children scatter all over the world, always moving, but doing nothing that matters."

Mr. Choi stopped, piquing Yi's curiosity, and drank some

wine. He had already clearly seen Yi's constantly moving eyes and big-knuckled hands with their inappropriately long, thin fingers. These were signs that Yi was an incomparably lazy man, destined to wander around.

It went without saying that salt-seller Kim's remarks had given Choi a clue. Moreover, Mr. Choi found that despite the first impression he gave, Yi was diminishing right before his eyes as they went on talking. As familiarity bred contempt, this diminishing of Yi's stature meant that they were in fact becoming more friendly.

"Busy movements without actual gain! That's an excellent expression. Korean people, as you know, are born with a blue Mongolian mark on their buttocks. We have descended from the Mongolian nomads and there are millions of Korean people who wander around. I'm not the only one. Still, your perspicacious remark about my fate has an especially profound meaning for me."

Yi nodded and picked up the wine bowl. He was gradually absorbed by Mr. Choi's observations and they ended up changing their positions completely. Unlike the beginning of their encounter, Mr. Choi came to hold the upper hand.

"Mr. Yi, listen to me. The reason why I introduced myself to you was that when I heard about you, I was immediately fascinated."

Mr. Choi went on, "Ever since I was a young boy, I've always wanted to wander around this whole wide world, without a house or a family, like a puff of a cloud. I wanted to move around. So I left home twice. The first time, I wanted to become a monk; the second time, I just wanted to flee to Manchuria."

"To Manchuria?"

"Yes, to the wide plains of Manchuria! But wandering wasn't written in my fate. I failed in both of my attempts." Mr. Choi sighed. He didn't say it to please Yi. When he heard about Yi from the salt-seller, Mr. Choi felt a deep longing in his heart that had been dormant for many years. Yi sounded like the very man he had always wanted to be. That longing had pushed him toward Wolp'ook.

"It is true that unless your fate says so, you cannot go off. On the other hand, no matter how much you may want to settle down in one place, if your fate says otherwise, you have to move on."

"You are right. My fate must have said I could not leave here. When I was about twenty, I went to a Buddhist temple called Myogak, in the Kiryong Mountain. But before I had my head shaven, my mother came and brought me home quite forcibly. The second time I made it as far as Andong, but my father found me and dragged me home. Ever since then I have stayed in Tuma-ri, doing my duties as the eldest son of my family."

Mr. Choi's story was true. He wanted to be a monk, not just a stay-in-one-place meditating monk, but a wandering monk who would see the world and learn the meaning of life. The second time, he decided to go to Manchuria with the money he had gotten from selling three pigs at the Ibam market. He was again caught, this time at a tavern in Andong, by his father. His father borrowed a horse and chased after him all night.

The family elders had had a meeting and came to the conclusion that marriage was the only cure for his wanderlust. So he was married. Children followed, and then his father became ill with asthma and soon died. Mr. Choi finally gave up his ambitions. For three years he had had to perform the duties of a mourning eldest son. Supporting the family fell squarely on his shoulders.

Then, near the end of the year, at the market place of Ibam, he happened to find *The Predictions of Mr. Chŏng* and *The Condensed Book of Divining Theories* among other books such as *Ch'unhyangjŏn, The Sad Story of Chang Hwa Hong Ryŏn, Fortune Telling* and others. He bought the first two books, worn and thin, and brought them home to study.

As in other areas of life, even his intellectual curiosity was connected with the natural surroundings in which he lived. He began to visit scenic places near Tuma-ri and to study at night, despite the fatigue he felt from doing farm work during the day.

He read the books over and over again until he memorized which phrase was on what page. He realized that the wide world he had dreamed about was contained in those books.

With a beginner's enthusiasm, he would go to the market and ask book peddlers to get him such books as *the Principles of Reading Land, Finding the Right Home and Burial Sites,* and *Geography.* In these books, he found profound truth. During the months when the farm lay idle, he would pack up a bundle like the famous map-maker Kim Chŏng-ho, and travel to Ch'ŏng-song, Kunwi, Yŏngch'ŏn, Wŏlsŏng, and Yŏngdŏk. He explored their hills and rivers, studied their forms and directions, thus gaining first-hand knowledge of the land.

In every village he visited, he found a geomancer from whom he drew whatever knowledge he could. In the meantime, his reputation as a geomancer grew, and people began to ask him to judge a house to see if it was good or bad, or to find a burial place that would ensure prosperity for later generations.

After hearing Mr. Choi's history as a geomancer Yi began to laugh uproariously.

"Ha, ha, ha. I've met a true friend in you. You have found the truth by self-study, and as for me, I traveled to Russia, to southern China, and to Japan. I did not study as you did, but I saw much. Now we are true friends of the mind. Let's drink to our friendship."

Yi raised the bowl contentedly. Though he didn't know how long he was going to live in Ibam, he knew he needed some close friends to make life more bearable. He would rather have someone from the mighty Kwon family, but Mr. Choi seemed as good a neighbor as he might get.

"Pardon me, Mr. Yi, but how old.... What zodiac year were you born in?" Mr. Choi asked after emptying the wine bowl.

"October in the Year of Imin."

"Then you are one year younger than I. I was born in May of the Shinch'uk year."

"Why don't you call me Brother Yi instead of Mr. Yi?"

"Brother Yi? That is too informal. Only young ones use such

words. Don't you have a good nickname?"

"A nickname? I will choose one right now. How is T'ang-nip?"

"T'angnip is the name of the dragon-head god in the Ibam area."

"That's why I chose it."

"T'angnip, that sounds rather good."

Mr. Choi thought with a smile that the pronunciation of the word T'angnip was becoming to Yi. Now that he had a nickname even his character seemed to get better. Anyway, what is a title, Mr. Choi thought.

"By the way, T'angnip, with your hometown not far from here, do you still want to live here the rest of your life?"

"Well, a road is made as people tread on it, and when people go on the road, it usually leads to a house. If there is a house, one lives in it. And I live in this house here."

Yi raised his slitty eyes and looked at Mr. Choi as if he were trying to see through him.

"Are you asking the question because my face tells you that I will move on again?"

"No, not specifically...."

Mr. Choi felt the same chill down his spine and saw a peculiar light in Yi's eyes.

"I've wandered around so much that I cannot promise that I'll settle here for good—but...."

"That means you have no intention of returning to your hometown?"

"I know I'll have to visit it sooner or later, but I'm not too eager to do that. To be honest with you, I do not want to live there. According to my calculation, it will have been twenty-five years since I left it. If I go there now, a middle-aged pauper, will anyone give me a house, a family or rice paddies? Of course, when I came here, I thought about going home, but my heart was not in it. I walked along the Chayang River wondering how I could go there in this condition. There were moments when I wanted to turn around and go back to Yŏngch'ŏn. I put one heavy foot in front of another and asked myself why I was going in the direction of my hometown, against the stream like a salmon. My heart was as dark as the night. I could not understand it myself. I didn't have any money... then..." Yi squinted his eyes and grinned.

"You found Madam Wolp'o to your taste?" Mr. Choi asked immediately.

"Hmmm. You aren't jealous, are you?"

Instead of answering Mr. Choi's question about Madam Wolp'o, Yi changed the subject.

"You know how life is. I go wherever my fancy leads me, like the wind and like a wisp. If I feel like it, I stay for a while. If I get bored, I leave. Then, I'll die someday. Isn't that life? A man's life is as short as a wink. While roaming around the world, I felt one thing deeply in my heart, and that was that people on the bottom rung of life are nameless blades of grass. They are mere wild flowers in the field. In the summer when the sun is hot, they turn green, and when fall comes, they wither away, leaving behind their seeds. That's how they live their short lives. Life is a ball of sorrow, here now but gone the next minute."

Yi's eyes were filled with a pathetic smile as he looked at Mr. Choi in the most touching manner.

Mr. Choi on the other hand, thought that that particular smile of his must have captivated Madam Wolp'o's heart. If not, it certainly must have had some strange sexual appeal. Yi's remarks showed a profound philosophy he had formed about life. He linked his own sorrow with the sufferings of all living beings, thus arriving at a universal truth. So his remarks kindled a warm little flame in Mr. Choi's heart that had been desolate because of his eldest son.

"People at the bottom are mere nameless blades of grass and wild flowers in the field," Mr. Choi repeated and nodded. Those are beautiful words. You know divining is like that. A human being is no better than a blade of grass, so he has to live in accordance with natural laws, and when he dies, he melts back into nature. It is just like the grass and flowers that grow and die. Westerners find joy in conquering and destroying nature but Orientals always wish for complete harmony with nature whether they are living or dead. Even when you decide on the architectural form of your house or the location of your grave, you have to consider the geography, soil quality, water flow, and weather, because all these elements must be welded in harmony. If a wild flower blooms mistakenly in someone's yard, it will be plucked. If the flower is beautiful and attracts human desire, it is no longer a wild flower. The same principle applies to other things. One doesn't build a house facing a northwesterly direction, nor does one dig a grave near a stream or on top of a mountain. All things have their proper places in nature, thus geomancy means finding the right place in nature.

"What you've just said is true. But, let me ask you this. If one is forced by circumstances to build a house near a stream that is often flooded, what should one do?"

"A likely question. If there is a geographical shortcoming, people can improve upon it. That is another principle. The reason we build artificial supports is to use them as bulwarks when the river-side plain is flooded. We plant trees to stop the wind and build dams at the bottoms of steep hills to make a reservoir. If a hill is too steep, we smooth it ; if a place is too damp, we air it. In other words, divining land means harmonizing nature and men for the good of both. In political terms, a government based upon this principle is the best. In terms of geomancy, the ideal is to realize the principles of harmony."

Mr. Choi relished this opportunity to explain what he knew. He had not done this in a long time.

Yi, who had been listening to Mr. Choi, occasionally cocking his head or nodding, gazed at Mr. Choi with obvious worry in his eyes. His expression was almost child-like.

"If I understand you correctly, I have roamed around the world all these years because I failed to find a place that was in harmony with me, am I right?"

"T'angnip, do you mean that you are going to settle down here, even though you may go off again some day?"

"If you put it that way, well, I guess, that is what I mean. I feel I should settle somewhere on account of my age and...."

"Do you like Ibam?"

"When I lived in Ttakpatkol as a little boy, I used to follow my parents to the Ibam market and wished that I could someday live in a busy place like this. Ibam is known in this area for its beautiful scenery. After the war with Japan in 1592, a famous Confucian scholar, Yŏhyŏn, wrote a poem about Ibam's natural beauty. Though I am not a diviner, I know this is as good a place as any for men to live. During the Japanese occupation, there was an entertainment house full of girls, so shipowners from P'ohang and other idle rich men came here for boating and feasts. I know Ibam is a good place for me. I am not a geomancer, but I know what to look for in a place, what is good for people."

The day after Yi had arrived in Ibam, he woke up very early and went up to the T'angnip Rock that gave this place its name. The Rock rose nearly 30 meters high beside the icy clear waters of the Chayang River, about 200 meters toward Sangok-ri from Ibam.

Yi's hometown was located nearly 30 ris north of the Rock, which, was a familiar sight to him. The Chayang River flowed into the Kŭmho River. The Kŭmho River then found its way to the Naktong River, which went down all the way to the South Sea.

The Rock, stood where it had always stood, majestic and erect. Its erect form looked a little like the male organ, with which Yi felt a strange sense of identification. On that very day he decided to call himself T'angnip, should he ever have a nickname.

Behind the Rock, a little way off, there was an arbour called the *Manhwaldang,* reportedly built during the reign of King Hyojong. Its sharp, curved roof lines were clear against the blue sky. It was a gathering place for scholars and poets. They composed poems and had parties there. If one followed the river upstream, one came to a beautiful lake under a high cliff.

Legend had it that angels came down from heaven to bathe in the lake. Across the lake, on the smooth flat top of a knoll, stood an old-style schoolhouse planted among ancient pine trees and elms.

During the reign of Taewongun, old-style schools in the entire nation were closed. Even so, the school building stood majestically, reminding everyone of the mighty power of the Kwons of Andong and the high reputation of the school as a center of learning and teaching for scholars and students.

From his walk that morning around Ibam, looking at its natural beauty, its pure air and its old and clean aura, Yi returned with a quiet determination that he would take it easy and put in order all his past history. Though he had not a penny to his name, he had found a means to survive in Ibam.

Yi found the wine kettle empty. "This time I'll buy," Yi said and went off with the empty kettle. "I bought this pair today at the market," he said sliding his feet into new shoes. Yi went to the outer court where Ch'an-kyŏng, Madam Wolp'o's older girl, was busily going about her mother's business. He went over to her and asked for another kettle of wine and a plate of scallion cakes.

"Are you paying, Mr. Yi?" Ch'an-kyŏng asked sharply.

"You just wait. You'll know who I am soon enough. Don't worry about the bill."

Yi stared back at her and tried to smooth over the awkward encounter.

"She has already found out what's going on. That sly one. Just let her wait. I know what she thinks. I'll show her what's what," Yi thought.

"Are you really going to live here?" Ch'an-kyŏng shot at him angrily.

"I'll tell you the truth, whether you like it or not. I'm going to be your stepfather, for a while at least. I'll also help out your mother in her business," Yi thrust his face so close to hers that he could almost feel her smooth bosom under her shirt front.

"God, you are shameless. You must have cowhide or dog's

hide over your face instead of human skin," Ch'an-kyŏng stepped back while covering her shirt front with both hands.
"Okay, you are right. I'm a male dog. A virile male dog," Yi
hissed.
Ch'an-kyŏng blushed deeply and ran away.
"Hey, girl," he called after her. The whole time, he leered at
her round buttocks hidden in her purple skirt.
"Are you calling me?" Ch'an-kyŏng stopped and turned
around. The deep blush wasn't gone completely, and her expression was anything but friendly.
"Yes, but for no particular reason. Your back looks so much
like that of my old sister-in-law. When you get married and bear
a big healthy son, you'll have no difficulty," Yi said, grinning
like a fool.
Mr. Choi and Yi became good friends within an hour of their
first meeting. They began to drink again the wine Ch'an-kyŏng's
younger sister had brought. As the day waned, a cool breeze
began to blow and early autumn leaves whirled down to the cot.
The two men went on talking like old childhood friends who
had met again after a long separation. While drinking and
conversing, they agreed that they should address each other
informally, without using their titles.
"Well, Mr. Yi, let me hear your already famous life history,"
Mr. Choi said. It was about sundown and the market was
closing up.
"Now, don't call me mister. I am neither a philosopher nor a
beggar. Just call me T'angnip," Yi said and looked far away into
the reddening sky in the west.
"If I write down my history, it will run to several volumes. If
I tell my story every day in installments, it may take more than
a year to finish it."
"Yes, I can see that. You are not like someone who is born
and dies in Tuma-ri."
"I was born in the little village of Ttakpat to a poverty-
stricken family without even a vegetable bed to its name. To top
it off, I was the second son. It was the year when I turned

eighteen...." Yi thus began telling his history.

It was written in Yi's fate that he should be footloose and restless. As soon as he reached adolescence, he quit his private laborer's job for a rich family and left his home.

Chukchang town in Yŏngil County was famous for its Korean paper, and his hometown, Ttakpat produced an abundance of Ttak trees that were the source material for paper. The name of the tree gave his town its name.

But the reason why Yi wanted to leave Ttakpat was not because of what was written in his fate, or the boredom and despair over his job, or the typical restlessness of a young man. The real reason was that he was deeply moved by the speeches and lectures given by college students who came to his town during vacations as a part of what was called the rural enlightenment movement.

The time was immediately after the March 1 Independence Uprising in 1919 and the new Japanese viceroy was changing the oppressive military rule to so-called cultural policies. The three college students from Seoul stayed in Ttakpat for only one week. Each day, when it was dusk, they gathered all the illiterate village people and taught them to read, lectured them on Korean history, and emphasized the necessity of a new life. Then, at night, they divided people into smaller groups and instilled in them the idea and the method of emancipation from Japan. The students were captivated by the radical leftist anarchism. One night, one of the students called all the young men of the village and told them the following story.

After the March 1 Movement of the last year, many Koreans had left for a new world. They wanted to be free, away from the Japanese oppression. There were more than half a million Koreans in Manchuria and Russia, and three hundred thousand Koreans in the Kando area north of the Hamkyŏng Province.

Manchuria was originally a part of Korea, but Japan turned it over to China in return for the railway construction rights in Manchuria. Though Manchuria belonged to China, Koreans there didn't have to live like the slaves in Japanese chains. There were limitless arable plains where Korean people raised rice and lived freely. The land was the old territory of Koguryŏ. Every Korean there dreamed of Korea's independence, and there actually was an army under the leadership of Hong Pŏm-do, an independence fighter. The well-armed Korean soldiers raided several Japanese guard posts not long ago. They were victorious. Additionally, in T'onghwa and Yuha, there was a military school to train Korean independence fighters.

Yi began to nurse a dream in his heart. Instead of being tied to 20 sacks of rice a year, a slave-level wage, he yearned to go to Manchuria to the military school, to learn to ride in the wide plains and fight the Japanese.

It was a vague dream, though, for a poor, illiterate farmer in a mountain village. But daring to have such a dream was an indication that he was destined to lead a different life than other young men of the village.

In order to realize his dream, he learned to read and write. On market days, he would walk two and a half hours to Ibam to buy books. He read every night. Then in the fall of that year, one of the poorest families in Ttakpat decided to leave for Manchuria to develop the land there, as they were going to starve anyway in their own village. Yi told them that he would meet them in Ch'ŏngsong, and he left home one night. He had managed to save a handful of pennies. It was the late fall of the year after the March 1 Independence Uprising in 1919.

"It was late fall in Korea, but it was the middle of winter in Manchuria. When we crossed the Amnok River, it was beastly. There were some twenty people with me. All they wanted was to grow enough rice to eat. The temperatures were near minus 40 degrees Celsius. Across the river, there was a sea of trees. I saw an entire family starve to death. Mr. Choi, try to imagine the scene! Women in tattered rags were carrying babies on their backs in that cold. They tried to warm each other with their body heat. But a baby's foot would protrude through a tear and freeze. The little toes were frozen stuck. Those who went through such agony had to work like slaves for years for Chinese land owners before they could get a patch of land of their own. It was a time of blood, sweat, and tears. If famine hit them, children would die first, then the whole family...."

In the meantime, Yi had gone straight to the military school in Yuha and finished the lowest level through sheer hard work and determination. Then he was sent to another military school in T'onghwa. The school was to educate noncommisioned officer candidates.

The second military school he attended had been built for Koreans by the family of Yi Hoe Ryŏng who had taken 60 members of his extended family across the Amnok River in 1910. They named the school Shin Hŭng Academy but when it became a military school they renamed it and moved to another place. It had to be relocated deeper in the mountains because the school became bigger and the first location was teeming with many people.

After the 1919 Samil March 1 Movement, hundreds of young men fled Korea to Manchuria. The school had to expand to accommodate them. They built new buildings and changed the name to Shin Hŭng Military School.

Yi finished the N.C.O. course in three months and was assigned to a guard post as an ordinary soldier. Later, he was re-assigned to the Independence Army and fought in the famous battle of the Hŭk River. He fought for two years in battle after battle. His life was often more painful than his old one, but he felt proud. His life had a purpose, a worth-while purpose.

Yi continued, "It was June, 1921. The Hŭk River battle was fierce. The year before in the Ch'ŏngsan-ri battles, the Japanese Army lost more than 2,000 men. They were raging with feelings of revenge. In order to counter the concerted "search strategy" of the Japanese Army, every branch of the Korean Independence Army converged in the Hŭkryong River region near the Russian border. At that time, a Russian called Lenin had succeeded in a Communist revolution and declared his support for all the nations seeking freedom and independence. So we thought he was on our side. But do you know what he did? He met with a

Japanese delegation in Beijing and agreed to a fishing treaty
with Japan. In return for the treaty, he promised Japan that he
would disarm all Korean soldiers within the Russian territory.
Things like justice and freedom could be sacrificed for actual
profits, as you know, and in international politics, yesterday's
friend can become today's enemy. In fact, for quite some time,
Korean and Russian armies had won battles against the
Japanese.

Russia was a vast country stretching from Europe to Asia.
This Russia, our friend, suddenly demanded that the Korean
Army lay down all the weapons it had. But do you think we
would obey? We were hardened fighters who had left home with
one purpose, to die for our country. We couldn't fight without
arms. The only solution left for us was to fight against the
Russians. That was the famous Hŭk River battle. Though we
fought with all we had, we were no match for the Russians
armed with artillery and machine guns. More than 300 Korean
soldiers died, about 1,000 were taken prisoners, and several
hundred were missing. General Chi Ch'ŏng-ch'ŏn was caught
and taken to a Russian camp where many Koreans were execut-
ed. Many were sent to Siberian labor camps to work with old
Russian Czarist soldiers and aristocrats. They weren't given
definite sentences, so they were there for life. You know, people
without a country are easy prey for any fierce predator no matter
where they may go."

Yi was quite aroused when he related these long-ago battles.
He stopped and heaved a deep sigh. He took a box of cigarettes
from his vest pocket and lit one. Exhaling a stream of blue
smoke, he gazed at the pigsty. It was evening meal time and the
pigs were frantically fighting over the trough.

Yi's eyes, steadily turned to the sty, took on a look of sadness.
The date tree was shedding yellowed leaves in the evening wind.
Ripe, red dates were clustered on the branches.

"T'angnip, let's move into the house. The breeze is quite
chilly, I'm afraid," said Mr. Choi. On any other market day, he
would have left long ago, but as he was absorbed in Yi's story,

so he stayed. For a while he couldn't even breathe, so intently was he listening to his new friend.

"Yes, let's move into my room." The two men picked up the wine kettle and the tray. The room was dark except for one small window that retained a little bit of sunset in its frame.

"So how did you survive that Hŭk River battle?" Mr. Choi asked as soon as they sat down.

"It was toward the end of June, so the river was swollen. I plunged into it and swam with all the strength and skill I had. Bullets were hitting the surface like a hailstorm. I don't know how I crossed the river. Anyway, I re-entered Manchuria. More than thirty people drowned, but I was one of several hundred who made it across the river. Among those survivors, some went all the way to Shanghai to join the Korean government in exile and others scattered in every direction. I joined a group of about thirty people and went to Kando and we sporadically continued the fight.

Our clothes were made of coarse thin cotton and our shoes were made of straw. In the winter, everyone suffered frostbite. One man standing on guard froze to death. Northern winds blew mercilessly, our clothes were thin and ragged, and the roof over our heads was the wide cruel sky. I can't even describe the suffering we endured.

But the Korean people in Kando regarded us as heroes and treated us royally. They would gladly give their own meager food as if we were their own lost sons. When we got together, we comforted each other with tears and warm words. When we parted, we reminded each other of our unwavering determination to destroy our enemy, Japan.

The Koreans fed us while we ambushed any small Japanese squad, and then ran and hid. Once in a while, we would stage a sneak-attack against a small Japanese military police detachment. Anyway, we were using the same strategies that Mao Tse-tung had used. Come to think of it, war and life are the same. They both use lies and tricks.

Pretend to be weak when you are not; use tricks while

pretending that you don't; draw the enemy out as if you would offer him some advantages, then confuse him and take advantage of him. If he is well prepared, step back and be cautious; if he is strong, avoid him, or confuse him by infuriating him. If he is comfortable, attack him; if he wants compromise, slander him; if he is not on guard, attack him mercilessly."

Yi was truly eloquent. Then he stopped suddenly, tense.

"Then it was around the middle of June of the following year. Sparrows were back from the south, fields and mountains were green. Flowers bloomed. It was beautiful. There was a hamlet of about 20 houses called Yaji, west of the town of Yŏngjŏng. It was a Korean village, and about a hundred ris from this hamlet we ran into a Japanese search party. The result was that several of the group were killed then and there, three were captured, and the rest escaped, helter-skelter. It was an utter rout."

"Sounds like the ROK Army that pushed North Korean stragglers into a corner like so many mice." Mr. Choi was thinking of what happened last winter at a temple in Mt. Po-hyŏn.

Communist soldiers were reported to be spotted there, and the Army and police from the Chayang Police Station found them and shot them all. The Red soldiers were apparently trying to find a path in the T'aebaek Mountain, back to the north. Mr. Choi and several young men buried them on a sunny slope. They were young men reduced to skin and bones who would have died in a few days if they had been left alone. Among the seven dead soldiers there was a young girl who was clutching a first-nurse's aid kit.

"My friend, don't compare my story to such an incident of fratricide because we never killed our own people. We also had leftists and rightists among us, but we were firmly united in the great goal of our nation's liberation. From this point of view, Kim in the north and Rhee in the south were fools. They were simply puppets of Russia and America. For the long-term future of the nation, they should not have done it. They were blinded by their own personal ambitions. They were no different from animals." Yi talked as if he were some great patriotic savant. Mr. Choi didn't dare open his mouth. He was overwhelmed by his friend's eloquence. Yi ejected a long stream of smoke, all the while staring into Mr. Choi's eyes. His eyes were deadly and there appeared a few drops of sweat on the tip of his doughy nose. Mr. Choi felt a chill running down his back and cast his eyes down.

If Yi stared, as he did now, into the eyes of a woman in the deep of night, no woman would dare refuse to do whatever he demanded.

"Mr. Choi, have you ever been tortured?"

"No, I haven't...."

"Shall I tell you how I was tortured by the Japanese?"

From this moment on, Yi's voice took on a harsh tone. It was as if a column of spiralling water was pushing up from a quiet surface of a lake. His voice sounded more like a scream.

"I was dragged to Hoeryŏng to a Japanese military police station where they tortured me mercilessly. They beat me, poured water into me, hung me upside down, stood me up under bright lights for three days without letting me rest or sleep... they even gave me electric torture."

He was almost breathless. "For a month and a half, I was tortured by every means imaginable. I never thought that humans could be so cruel to other humans. At that time I thought that burning in hell would be better than what I was going through. My flesh was torn, my bones were crushed, and so were my intestines."

"You really are a rare person," Mr. Choi said looking at Yi with awe and admiration. But Yi ignored him and went on with his story.

"Do you know how they pour water into you? They take you to a bathroom where they tie you down on a long chair. My hands were tied to the chair legs, my belly and legs to the chair seat. My head was hung down. Then they poured water into my mouth. Every time I tried to breathe, water would come back up and flow into my lungs. I could not breathe. I passed out.

Several times they did that to me and demanded that I confess where our headquarters were. As for keeping you awake for days on end, it was unbearable. If you don't sleep that long, every nerve in your body becomes a needle and bores into every part of your body. Sooner or later, you go mad. And the airplane torture—they tie your arms behind your back, tie your hands together and fasten them around your waist. Then they stick a gun through your arms and hang you up. Then the pressure of the gun makes it very hard to breathe and your chest aches unbearably. As time passes, because your body weight weighs you down, the pain is so great that you pass out again. Most people pass out within ten to fifteen minutes. Sometimes, they turn you round and round in the air. You get dizzy, nauseated, and pass out. The electric torture was the limit. They stripped me naked, pasted wire tips on my fingers and toes, and later under my tongue and on the tip of my penis. Then they sent electricity to those spots on my body. Every hair on you stands on end and you feel as if bits of flesh and bone are being torn off by a pair of pincers. You defecate and you faint. All your guts burst open... it was pain beyond any possible description. I think that during those days of torture, my penis lost its nerves and became numb. That was why I could do it to a woman as long as an hour or even two hours."

Yi had to stop himself because he was almost breathless. As if he were back in the old days, Yi swallowed hard and covered his crotch with both hands. He poured wine for himself and gulped it down. His hands were shaking violently. Mr. Choi himself got so excited that his lips were dry and his palms wet.

"I wished that they would simply cut my head off and get it over with, but no, they wouldn't do that. Finally, one guy died in torture, another lost his mind and was sent back to Seoul to his family. I heard later that the mad guy refused to eat and died mad in a university hospital. No man is a hero once he tastes torture. Let me tell you, no one in the world who has not experienced torture will ever understand what it's like. Never!" Yi banged his fist on the floor and screamed.

"My dear friend, pull yourself together. Calm down. I think I understand. Please lower your voice, lest people think we're arguing." Mr. Choi held his friend's hands and tried to calm him down, but it was in vain as he was too aroused to calm down.

"Loyalty, faithfulness, patriotism? Good words, sure, but let anyone who utters those words be naked and beaten for two days, and see what happens! Torture him till he throws up bile and his eyes pop out! Those pen-scratchers who write about patriotism and those politicians who shout patriotism, let them taste electric torture! I dare them to call anyone betrayer or traitor! I dare them!" Yi's face was flushed and sweat was pouring down his face. Mr. Choi could not get a word in edgewise because Yi was too excited.

"Mr. Choi, look at my ears. Look at these ears of mine!" Yi pushed back his long hair. There were no ears as if someone had cut them off cleanly with a knife. Few people pay attention to other people's ears because they take it for granted that everyone has ears. Mr. Choi, seeing for the first time an earless man, found it almost unbearably horrible. Mr. Choi thought a one-eyed man or a harelipped man looked better.

"Did you lose your ears then?" Mr. Choi asked with astonishment.

"During the Japanese invasion in the Imjin year, they cut off 50,000 noses and ears of Koreans, salted them, and buried them in a mound. When I went to Kyoto, there was an ear-tomb in front of a Buddhist temple. It brought back those horrible memories, so I sat in front of the tomb and cried...."

Yi's voice trailed off. He covered his eyes with his enormous hands and began to sob. His shoulders shook. He was crying hard. Mr. Choi too, felt a lump in his throat and fell silent.

"From that day on I grew my hair to cover the hideous scars. I was half-insane, too."

"Insane?"

Yi didn't answer that question. His sobbing stopped after a while. It was completely dark in the room. The wind shook the paper doors. Calming down considerably, Yi started again.

"After a month and a half, I was released. It was early August. I went around, mumbling to myself, because I was out of my mind. I was alive but I was not a whole person. I was no longer an independence fighter. I couldn't be because I was insane. I was no more than a wisp in the wind, being blown here and there. I begged for food around the Yongjŏng area. I was a wandering beggar. There were many Koreans who took pity on me and gave me food. Sometimes I stole potatoes or sweet potatoes from Chinese farms, sometimes I went hungry for days. Other times, I would eat dirt, field mice, whatever I could get my hands on. It was still summer, so I had no shirt, but only a scrap of cloth to cover my private parts. You can imagine what I looked like. No one recognized me. What I didn't understand was why I didn't die. The life force in me was mysteriously tenacious."

"So why didn't you come home at that time?"

"Come home in that condition? I wanted to kill myself, but I wasn't gutsy enough to do that. Suicide is not for everyone. Suicide was not in my fate apparently. Only special people can do it, but I am one of the common people who live on, like weeds and dogs. To speak the truth, I was in no mental condition to be able to distinguish between life and death."

Yi's wrinkly throat was soaked in sweat.

"You really did have awful experiences," Mr. Choi commiserated.

"Then autumn came around. I was in Yongjŏng. There was a huge 60th birthday celebration of one of the richest men there. His house was 12 kan (a unit of measurement, one kan is equivalent to one room), which meant it was a big house. Ordinary houses were 4 or 6 kan. A four kan house consisted of a kitchen, a small room next to the kitchen, an "upper" room with another smaller room attached to it. Six kan houses had two additional rooms, a stable and a mill next to it. Therefore, a 12 kan house was a huge one with a couple of servants. Hoping for a hot meal, I went in. There, lo and behold, were a band of singers who had come from Korea. It was true that people from any country would carry on their own cultures no matter where they went and settled. It's true of the Chinese, the Russians, and the Japanese. They live the way their ancestors used to live. Koreans in Kando made kimch'i, wore Korean clothes, and had kept up the Tano(spring festival in May) and Ch'usŏk(fall festival in August) festivities. On Tano Day, even the poor had new dresses made. The rich, of course, had many new clothes made. Ch'usŏk in Kando was already cold. Frost and snow covered everything. People were very busy harvesting. They made rice cakes and other goodies. The singers had been invited to provide entertainment. One of the singers was a woman in her mid-thirties. And the drummer was a gray old man. When they sang, everyone sang along. I was a beggar in rags, but I went in anyway and sat in the front row of the spectators. The singer was singing the farewell song of Ch'un-hyang. It was such a sad song that everyone shed tears. Tears poured down my face, and I ended up crying loudly. All farewell songs are sad, but Ch'un-hyang's song for her lover and Shim-ch'ŏng's song for her father are the tops." Yi's voice restored its normal tone.

"T'angnip, as you know, there are short songs and *t'aryŏng* (a kind of lamenting chant) in the Kyŏngsang provinces, but there is no *p'ansori* to speak of. Real p'ansori (a song that tells a story) exists only in the Chŏlla provinces, in such towns as Sunch'ang, Naju, and Posŏng."

"You are right. Arts and food are the best in Chŏlla provinces. Because they were mistreated by the Court, they must have directed their energy to music and arts. Anyway, a band's reputation is dependent on its drummer, and that old drummer was outstanding. The singer saw me crying uncontrollably and sang with her eyes turned to me. She was obviously feeling sorry for this poor beggar. After a little while, the spectators complained that my loud crying was drowning out her songs. Even the master of the house frowned, so his servants dragged me out of the house. I sat outside the door and cried my heart out.

Then, like a flash, an idea hit me. If I followed the band

around, at least I wouldn't starve. So I followed them everywhere they went, whether they liked me or not, I didn't care. I got to know women for the first time because of that singer. Those people in the band didn't care whether I was a common man or a noble man. They seemed to think that human fate was a strange thing, subject to mysterious changes, so why should they care whether anyone was rich or poor? They were not particularly respectful to people in high positions, but they were very warm to poor people. Later, I did become a member of the band and traveled around southern Manchuria. Several months passed and the singer got a letter that her mother was critically ill. By that time, my mental health was restored. I was twenty-one or two. My wandering life started in earnest."

It was the best time for wanderers as there was unrest in every northeastern region. While wandering here and there, Yi sired four children, three sons and a daughter. Each of them had a different mother. Yi himself left them in infancy, so he didn't remember any of them. When he was working at a lumber yard near Chongsŏng, he had an affair with a widow who bore him a son. But he left them before the boy was a year old. The next time he seduced a Korean farmer's daughter and had a son again. He was a servant in a rich Chinese house at that time. Soon he was bored with a servant's life and became a peddler. One day he was robbed by a gang of bandits and fled to Siberia.

Around 1860 there were many Koreans in Chita and Irkutsk. They had left their homes in Hamkyŏngdo and built Korean towns in those Russian cities. In Chita, under the supervision of the Commintern Orient, a Korean Communist party had been formed. Yi became a messenger for the party and was sent to the party's underground headquarters in Beijing to carry secret documents and operation funds.

He acted half-mad, so the Japanese police didn't suspect him, which made his errand easier to carry out. With some money he received, he goofed around in Beijing. Then the Japanese police got wind of what he was doing and began to tail him. Past torture scenes flashed back to him, and immediately he fled to

Shanghai.

Near the Hwangp'otan pier in Shanghai, he lived with an old Chinese madam. Again, he had an affair with a Chinese street vendor of hot cakes. This time, they had a daughter. After the woman died of post-natal complications, he abandoned the baby girl at the doorstep of a rich house and left Shanghai. The last child, a boy, was born in Pokchu in southern China. He was barely surviving by selling himself to homosexual men. He met a Chinese beggar-woman with a daughter. They lived together in a cave and had a son. They had lived together for a year and a half when the woman became seriously ill. He couldn't take it, so he sailed for Okinawa, where he worked in the sugarcane fields for two years.

By this time, he was nearing forty. While Japan was engaged in her foolish wars, Yi wandered around Japan, working here, begging there. As a matter of fact, he earned his food and lodging by fulfilling the sexual needs of Japanese women whose husbands were away at the war.

Yi's life story was so astounding that Mr. Choi didn't know which part was real and which was fabricated. However, he couldn't help himself being curious about certain details in the story. The biggest question was how did an independence fighter who had laid his life down for his country become such an animal, even if he were unspeakably tortured and without half his mind? How could he become a male prostitute for Japanese women? Mr. Choi could not believe this.

"T'angnip, after you joined the band, you washed your hands of the Independence Army, didn't you? Since you were tortured so horribly by the Japanese, your hostility toward them must have doubled. So how in the world could you sell yourself to Japanese women? Can you tell me that?"

"As I told you, after I was released from the torture chamber, I lived like an animal, a dog or a pig. My soul was gone, and only my body continued to live, until I hoped, it too, would be gone. Of course, once I got to know women, I enjoyed that part of life. When I make love to a woman, I don't do it like an ordinary man. I tell myself: 'You, dirty dog without ears, you are not a human. You are a dog and you are only fit for this. Do it as inhumanly as you can. Pour yourself into it!' So, the woman ends up having several orgasmic fits until she is utterly exhausted. I really kill them!" Yi went on heatedly, grinding his teeth and grinning like an animal. His sweaty face was the very image of a male animal in heat.

"It's an incredible story. How could you feel satisfied with killing women that way?"

"Let me tell you that a man like yourself who has never had another woman except his wife will never understand that. A faithful wife and a whore have different sexual relations. A man who decides to devote himself to it could do it easily. I was one."

"What happened to the documents you carried from Chita to Beijing?"

"When I ran that errand, it wasn't out of patriotism that I did it, but rather for the large amount of money they promised. Later, I found out that they sent another man to shadow me all the way."

"Your explanation sounds plausible, but I still don't understand." Mr. Choi felt sure that something important had happened around the time when Yi left the Independence Army. But as long as he refused to tell, there was no way to find this out.

"When I regained my sanity while traveling around with the band, I thought I didn't deserve manhood, so I tried to cut off my penis. Alas, I was too weak. Subsequently, I became a sexually voracious male animal. You know, it is very hard for a human being to elevate himself to a higher level. On the other hand, it is very easy to slide down to corruption. I was a weak, corrupt person in every sense of the word."

Yi's voice subsided to a low whisper. There was a rice-grain size discharge in the corner of his eye.

"According to your words, your days in Japan were the most animal-like days. You were killing various Japanese women then," said Mr. Choi, laughing a curiously empty laugh, like air seeping out of a rubber ball.

"But bad luck was lurking around me again. I think it was in Nikko. Nikko is something like our Kŭmgang Mountains. There were a great waterfall and a lake. A very famous tourist spot. Anyway, I seduced a Japanese widow. We were having a wonderful time when a Japanese detective burst in. Usually I escaped such police interrogations by acting stupid and insane, but this police detective was persistent. I was arrested again. I was born to be harrassed and tormented by the Japanese police. I wish I had been born fifty years earlier than I was...."

Yi was sent to a mine in Hokkaido. For two years he did forced labor. He was nearly killed several times when the mines caved in. His body was tired down to his bone marrow, and he was suffering from kidney infections. He had seen the world and he thought he was going to die like a mole in a dark cave.

Everyday dead miners were carried out on straw sacks. The miners were Koreans who were forced to work under the worst of work conditions. They died of malnutrition and disease.

One summer day, three hundred meters below the ground, he heard the most unreal news that Korea was liberated. Instantly, his past days came crowding upon him. He felt ashamed of himself while at the same time he felt elated at the prospect of living a normal life. Instead of throwing away his precious semen, he was going to enjoy giving it happily.

He remembered a poem in which the poet described the very feelings he felt at this moment. The poet said that when he was looking for his own burial site, as he sensed his end coming, he suddenly saw in his mind's eye the vision of his home. Yi joined other Koreans, thousands of them, on their trip back home. Their ship crossed the channel. Finally he stepped on his home soil for the first time since he had left, at the age of eighteen. It was his country, it was his land. As Yi himself said, he seemed to have a special fate as far as relations with women were concerned. On his way home, he came to Ibam, met Madam Wolp'o, and lingered on.

CHAPTER IV

As the summer was nearing its end, the Ibam market began to regain its vitality. Even as late as the previous July when the armistice was signed, few people bothered to come on market days, though the battle front was 1,000 ris far north of the town.

What little was available at the market left only some food items and a few basic necessities. Any other merchandise didn't attract anyone.

When the fighting ceased along the demilitarized zone, people who had gone off to safer refuges started to come back to their empty houses. They repaired roofs and built up new dirt fences. All farmers, they ploughed the land and sowed seeds as if nothing had happened. Human beings were unreliable, but the land always honestly rewarded them for their efforts.

The land reform that had been put into effect three years prior had been interrupted during the war. Now the government enforced its reform policies by giving 5 to 6 majigis to each farmer. Though the size of the allocated land was only about half of what the government had initially promised, people were nevertheless grateful. Everyone was happy to till his own land, and everyone worked hard. The result of this year was manifest in a better than average harvest.

Autumn was a busy season. People had to weed the rice paddies and raise fall vegetables to be pickled for the winter. On market days everyone came, not because anyone had anything to buy or sell, but because they missed their friends and acquaintances. They yearned for human contact.

Whenever they got together, they talked about the hardships of war, who was killed and who was wounded, and who lost his family in a bombing raid. They would shed tears over their common experiences, and for those who died.

Chǒng Myǒng-ku was having another busy day. He had to fetch some wine at the shop, make a fire to cook the usual soup with rice, and bring water from the well. Amid this continuous work, he would glance toward the southwestern corner of the market. Mr. Choi did not show himself till about noon. Myǒng-ku hoped that Mr.Choi would not miss this market day. He might bring his daughter Kye-yǒn with him to have Mr. Chang perform acupuncture on her. So he had sneaked off to a rice-cake shop this morning and bought some cakes sprinkled with mashed chestnuts to give her.

Yi also watched everyone who went by. When Mr. Choi didn't show up, he turned around and went inside. "Myǒng-ku, as soon as you see Mr. Choi, let me know," he said.

The day was a flawless autumn day, with a cloudless azure sky and cool fresh breeze. Over across the market place, one could see yellow and red autumn leaves in bright contrast to the green pine trees. Up in the sky, a hawk was flying around leisurely. Sparrows were flitting here and there like little children at play.

As the market was crowded, so was Madam Wolp'o's place.

If someone happened to say, 'I've been to Taegu...,' Myǒng-ku's ears pricked up. News of his mother's whereabouts was always uppermost in his mind. To find her and to reunite with his mother and sister was his preoccupation.

If only he knew where in Taegu his mother could be found, he would ask for a leave and go and get her. He was going to beg her to live with him, his sister and brother, as a family should, but he knew it wasn't going to be easy. Above all, he wanted to get out of this small mountain village. If he found his mother, he would find a job in a factory, a store, or a tavern. He was determined to work day and night to provide for her. When he saved enough to support a family, he would get his brother and sister, too. His mother had had to give away her children in order for them to survive, wherever it might be. But he was going to get them together first. His mother would come back from whatever difficult situation she might be in, he thought.

The sun was hanging low over the Pohyŏn Mountain, but Mr. Choi was still nowhere to be seen. He missed the last market day, so Myŏng-ku was sure he would come today. Perhaps Kye-yŏn's condition had worsened or he had too much work to do. Myŏng-ku's heart sank as he had been hoping to see Kye-yŏn to give her the delicious rice-cakes he had hidden behind the pile of firewood.

Yi too, was disappointed. He was looking forward to seeing his friend. He became so impatient that he walked out to the market place again. He walked like a duck. His pale face was so swollen that he looked like a person that had been submerged under water for some time. His big nose was sunk in the swelling.

After looking around the market, he looked into his wife's store. Myŏng-ku was putting dry branches and leaves into the furnace.

"Myŏng-ku, come over here," Yi said. Myŏng-ku shook off the dried pine needles from his palms and went to him.

"Mr. Choi hasn't shown up today, has he?"

"I've been watching the market all day. No, he didn't come. Maybe he came and went back right away," Myŏng-ku answered.

"Why don't you run over to Mr. Chang's? Maybe he is there. You could have missed him if he had gone directly to Mr. Chang," Yi said. "Damn him, so intent on saving a daughter whose bones are already rotten that he turns a deaf ear to my pleading."

"Why are you worried that you won't be properly buried when you die? Put your worries to rest. I'll personally dig the pigsty and bury you there," said Madam Wolp'o, who must have heard Yi.

"You bitch, why don't you shut up? This is not a matter you should stick your nose into. You don't know anything, so zip up your sassy lips, you she-devil," Yi screamed.

"I'll go and see if he is with Mr. Chang," Myŏng-ku interjected just to get away from their bickering.

Myŏng-ku quickly ran toward the Chang's pharmacy, which was located at the mouth of the road to Snake Valley. It wasn't really a proper pharmacy, but rather a room in Mr. Chang's house where he prescribed herb medicines for a variety of ailments.

Past the town hall, along a stream, Myŏng-ku went on. On the slope of a hill across the stream, there were a church and several rows of big tiled-roof houses.

The owners of the houses were members of the famous Kwon family. The area was called the upper village.

Mr. Chang Che-mun belonged to the Chang branch of Yang-dong, but he moved to Ibam where his in-laws lived, and opened the medicine shop. The upper village was known for its abundance of persimmon trees, whose branches of ripe red fruit hung over the mossy tiles of the dark roofs.

Myŏng-ku quickened his steps along the narrow path between some mulberry trees and went in the tall gate. There in front of him, sat Mr. Choi, on the edge of the central hall, gazing at a persimmon tree. He wore a quilted vest and had a scarf around his neck. Red persimmons on bare branches were bright against the blue sky.

"How are you, sir?" Myŏng-ku greeted and bowed to him.

"What in the world brings you here?"

"Good heavens, sir, Uncle has been waiting for you all day long."

Myŏng-ku looked around to see if he had come with his daughter. There were only a few chickens pecking at the dirt in the yard. No one else seemed to be there. It was eerily quiet. Behind Mr. Choi, in the hall, dried herbs were piled up against the wall. On the stepping-stone, there were a pair of men's and women's rubber shoes.

"I was going to drop in, but I haven't finished what I came here for," Mr. Choi answered in a subdued gloomy voice.

"Then you haven't had lunch yet?"

"Lunch is not important. Even at home, we only eat a few boiled potatoes for lunch anyway."

"Didn't you bring Kye-yǒn with you?" Myǒng-ku asked, blushing.

"She's getting an acupuncture treatment in that room. She has a needle stuck in every joint...," Mr. Choi glanced at the medicine room. Myǒng-ku followed his eyes to the same direction. The door was closed and not a sound was coming out of it.

Myǒng-ku could only imagine the pale and thin Kye-yǒn, lying on the floor with only her chest and stomach covered. Her limbs would be weakly spread on the floor, with needles sticking up from every part of her arms and legs. Her breath would be shallow. Imagining all this made Myǒng-ku sigh a heavy sigh. He could smell the bitter-sweet smell of the herb medicines being boiled.

"Now, now, there's a good girl. Don't move. If you do, you'll hurt," Mr. Chang's calm voice was heard through the paper door.

Myǒng-ku pricked up his ears. Mr. Chang's voice stopped, but he could hear Kye-yǒn's weak low moaning. It was like the moaning sound of a sick lamb. Every time she moaned under her labored breathing, all the thin needles on her body would tremble.

Myǒng-ku suddenly saw in his mind's eye a skinned frog. He shuddered. What a terrible disease she had. No longer able to stand it, he stood up.

"Please drop in before you go home, sir. I'll tell Uncle that you will."

"All right. Madam Wolp'o asked me to bring red peppers and sesame seeds to sell. So I brought them."

Walking heavily through the mulberry bushes, Myŏng-ku looked up to the sky. To his eyes the blue sky flowed like waves upon waves of blue water. Riding on the waves were two faces, the wan little face of Kye-yŏn and the face of his sister. His eyes filled with hot tears. Soon he heard the noise of the market place.

The afternoon was waning fast as the sun was slowly sinking behind the mountain. The market was closing up. The sky took on an opaque faded color and the cold evening wind began to sweep over the market. The crude canopies in front of the stores fluttered in the wind, their snapping sounds echoing in the air.

"Big discount! The last to go! Almost free!" cried the last of the vendors, but people from outside the town had already left and only a few stragglers were strolling around. Dogs were converging at the fish shop for scraps.

At Wolp'ook, the lunch hour at noon was its peak time. There was a long lull before the drinking and dinner hour for the peddlers, vendors, and the store owners, who came there for drinking and dining on their way home. They would bring their day's earnings in their money pouches to have a good time.

About dinnertime Mr. Choi finally appeared, carrying two huge sacks on his A-frame. Kye-yŏn was not with him, and his face had a deep, worried look. Madam Wolp'o was ladling the rice soup into a bowl when she saw him.

"Are you on your way to a widow for a rendevous or for a chat with your friends?" she joked. Too worried and tired to mind the woman's bad manners, Mr. Choi walked into her yard.

"Sir, may I have a word with you?"

"Don't bother me. I'm too worried and anxious. Just pay me for these peppers and seeds at today's prices. I have to pay off my debt to Mr. Chang."

"You do look worried. Your daughter's illness, isn't it? By the way, when are you going to cut the rice in our field? If I send my husband out, he might end up drinking somewhere, so I am going to take some time out and have a look."

"Ah, those measely rice paddies! No one will take them away. You must stay awake nights worrying over the rice," Mr. Choi retorted unkindly because he thought she dwelled too much on the fact that he was leasing her paddies.

Mr. Choi's retort wasn't particularly offensive because he usually talked like that to her. But she knew that he was scrupulously honest about reporting the amount of rice he raised. His life motto was one of honesty and integrity, and he observed all rules and promises to the last letter.

Everyone around the area was well aware of his honesty and clean reputation. Besides, he held a special place in Madam Wolp'o's heart because he had been the matchmaker for her older daughter.

"I was going to go to Tuma-ri to look in on my daughter. But today your brusqueness brings out that famous Choi streak. You act like a hungry beggar-monk who got stung by a bee. Ah, I think I should sprinkle some salt at my door."

Ignoring her chattering, he went into the yard. Myŏng-ku was cleaning grime off several oil lamps in front of the water pump. He looked at Mr. Choi stepping in without Kye-yŏn. He must have left her with Mr. Chang, he thought. He wanted to ask Mr. Choi about Kye-yŏn, but he kept his mouth shut since showing excessive interest in the girl was unseemly on his part.

No sooner had Myŏng-ku stood up to tell Uncle that Mr. Choi was there than Yi himself opened the door and shouted happily.

"Is that you? Damn the devil! What have you been up to? Why didn't you go home with your sick daughter on your back?"

"Did you wait for me to repeat that old story of yours? Huh? About your burial place?" Mr. Choi answered while slowly lowering his A-frame.

"Why didn't you come last market day? Were you looking for my burial site?"

"You are not going to die soon, I can tell from your loud

voice. In fact I'm the one who should get a grave ready. Both my body and mind are exhausted. I wonder what life is...."

"Come on in. You don't have to worry about your burial site since you have an ancestral family plot. Anyway, let's make a firm deal tonight about my burial. By the way, how is your daughter?"

"I'm afraid I have to impose on you tonight. Dinner and overnight lodging. Mr. Chang is going to do mugwort steaming on her all night. So I'll have to wait till tomorrow morning to take her home."

"That's good news to me. We will talk about your divining ways all night."

Yi told Myŏng-ku to bring some ale and side dishes. Mr. Choi leaned his A-frame against a hall post and stepped into the inner chamber. A little while later Myŏng-ku brought, on a lacquer table-tray, a wine kettle and two bowls of soup. The soup was a vegetable-meat soup and was eaten with the ale. The two men sat facing each other and talked late into the night. Their topic was of the various aspects and problems of land divining.

It was Mr. Choi who expounded while Yi either agreed, asked questions, or added what opinion he might have.

"You see, the history is really long. In the book *Samgukyusa* (the history of the three kingdoms), there is a story. The fourth king of Shilla, King Talhae had gone up a hill where he saw a house on a most auspicious site. He thought up a scheme to get the house for himself. At that time, he held only a high court position, Hogong, but later, after he became the owner of the house, he became king."

"Ha! An auspicious site gave him the throne. Of course, he was of the royal family, so he was different. That kind of luck is called a dragon dream, isn't it? He must have had a dragon dream the night before he found the house."

"I'll lend you a book I have. I borrowed it from an old monk at the Ch'ŏngok Temple in Ŭich'ang. I copied it and returned it to him. It's called *Ch'ŏngokyŏng* written by a famous diviner, Ch'ŏng O-ja, in the age of the later Han Dynasty. If anyone wants to become a diviner, he must read it. According to the book, when a man dies, he goes back to his real entity, his essence. While he is alive, he merely borrows from heaven and earth, that is, spirit from heaven and flesh and bones from earth. So, when he dies, his spirit goes back to the spiritual world in the universe and his flesh and bones return to the earth. The spirit and the body in their original spheres are called the real entity. If the flesh and bones happen to be buried in the right cave, his posterity will prosper; if not, his posterity will wither away. This can be translated into something like 'a favorable omen brings prosperity to one's offspring.'"

"That sounds very much like Buddhist teaching. It certainly is a profound philosophy," said Yi, nodding with a serious expression on his face.

"From what I have seen of your hometown, I can tell you it has a few good sites in it. The southern slope of the Talŭi Pass is one example. Six or seven years ago, I explored that region thoroughly. The water of the Sŏkkye River is very good. It flows from west to south, therefore, the area near the mouth of the river is without doubt one of the best sites. However, that pass belongs to the Chŏng clan of Kyŏngju, and they already have many graves there."

"Instead of the direction toward Sangok, how about the direction toward the Susŏk Mountain?"

"Why do you want to move away from your birth place? Don't you know the beginning part of the Ch'unhyang story? I haven't heard it sung by singers, but what I read was that a great beauty is born with the spirit of the place in her. Likewise, it is most appropriate to be buried in the same place where you were born. The spirit is still there. By the way, are you going to visit your hometown on Ch'usŏk Day?"

"How can I walk to and from there? It is nearly 80 ris. You saw how swollen my legs were. If I want to go there so badly that I would lay down my life for it, then I might go, but I don't want to. My hometown left my heart long ago. I am not fit to be buried at home. I'm no great beauty nor a great man born with the home spirit. No, I gave up on the idea of visiting it this year," Yi retorted and rubbed his eyes.

It was the year after Korea's liberation from Japan. Yi came home 25 years after he had left it at eighteen. The year's harvest was over. He was staying at Wolp'ook at that time. He kept saying every day that he was going to go to his hometown tomorrow. After nearly two weeks of hesitation, he decided to go.

No one in Ttakpat village recognized this strange-looking man with long hair, wearing a long black coat. His brother, who was still a tenant farmer, did not recognize him, either, at least not at first.

"Someone told me that there was a man from the Ttakpat village. How in the world could I know it was you the man was talking about? Oh, why were you so indifferent? If you were alive, why didn't you send us a line at least? I am almost fifty, and I didn't memorialize you in our ancestor worship rites. I thought you weren't in this world," Yi's brother put his arms around him and wept.

"I thought I would come home when I became successful. Not that I am now," Yi said. He had so much to say but he couldn't. Whether his brother understood him or not, he wanted to say to him, "Look, brother, though I didn't gain wealth or fame, I would have written you if I had lived like a decent human being. But I haven't." What good would it do if he said this to his brother now?

Yi had no intention of settling down in Ttakpatkol even if his brother insisted they share whatever he had and live like two loving brothers. Ttakpat was where he grew up, but it was not a place for a middle-aged destitute man to live. His past life was so shameful that he didn't dare face it. Yes, it was better for him to settle in Ibam.

"Big brother, unless you have much shopping to do, I know you won't come to Ibam. But if you do, please come and see me. Two weeks ago when I arrived from Japan, I met a woman there. If you come right down to it, Ibam is almost like home, don't you think? If I come here to live, it only means that you have an additional mouth to feed. So why don't we stay where we are and visit each other often?"

Yi consoled his weeping brother. Then he went up a hill to his parents' graves. They were bare mounds, smoothed down over the years. He stood in front of them, and cried with no restraint. He gave his brother some money to put grass over the graves. He spent one night with his brother and left the next morning.

Before he left, he told his brother and the villagers that he could be found at a tavern called Wolp'ook. At that time, one of the villagers listening and remembering what Yi said was Myŏng-ku's mother.

From that year on, at every Hanshik Day(the day families visit ancestral burial sites) in the spring, and on Ch'usŏk Day in the fall, Yi would get a bottle of rice wine and a hunk of beef and he would go to visit his brother and his parents' graves. His brother in turn visited him once every two months or so. But, perhaps because of the long separation, their relationship failed to become any closer.

"Are you looking for a resting place, too? Why are you standing there?" Yi said sharply to Myŏng-ku.

"Er, no, I...."

Myŏng-ku did have an errand but he was too scared to remember. Then he remembered why he had come there.

"Aunt says you shouldn't drink. If you do, she said you'll be in big trouble."

"Okay, tell her I won't. The bitch! If she feels so desolate in bed, why doesn't she get herself a gigolo? I'm not a man to get jealous at that sort of thing," Yi was swearing at the back of the retreating Myŏng-ku.

"So, your famous superman virility at night is coming to an end, eh?" Mr. Choi teased.

"Yes, it is gone. My organ is like a salted and fermented red pepper. It's shrivelled to nothing. That's why she sighs and thrashes all night. She has had it too good, and can't do without it."

As Myŏng-ku heard this, he found himself trembling with a sudden burst of desire. All the sexually charged intimate conversations between Yi and the Madam that he had secretly overheard flashed back to him. While eavesdropping on their pillow talk, he imagined the two of them, naked and engaged in sexual acts. His face began to flush furiously as if he were sitting in front of an open fire.

The first time Myŏng-ku began to enjoy eavesdropping and later peeking through a hole in their paper door was two months after he had first come to live at Wolp'ook three years ago. He began to pay attention to the rumors among the market people about Yi's "night work", and he himself became interested in sexual relations. But he wasn't interested in Yi's supposedly tremendous organ or his techniques.

He was only fifteen and rather slow, so he didn't know much about sex. One night he went into the backyard and crouched under the window of the Madam's inner room. Despite the freezing cold, his body was strangely infused with a kind of fever.

While waiting for them to put out the oil lamp, he formed in is mind such questions as, "Is it true that grownups make babies by doing the act? Then, why do they do it so often, apart from making babies? Is it so fantastically pleasurable?" Myŏng-ku wanted to look into this mystery by at least hearing what they said.

"What is the greatest pleasure of life? They say that among animals man is the only creature to have a soul. God selected a few men to work in soulful celibacy, but to most of us common people, He allowed for us to have sexual pleasure. For millions of people, life is empty without this pleasure. Fame, power, and children are nothing once you leave this world. Come, my woman, how many times shall I take you to an orgasmic climax tonight?" Yi's voice was clear and full of emotion.

"Your organ must be made of iron. It never loses its power, no matter how long you do it. Where in the world did you learn all those incredible tricks? You make me see stars and hear the earth explode, so many times a night, I can't even count," answered the Madam, her voice already nasal with desire.

Myŏng-ku heard them undress, the lamp still on in the room where their sweet talk went on. Their talk gradually became more graphic, as they spoke of each part of their bodies. Myŏng-ku was too excited to realize that their talk was lewd and dirty.

Their conversation evoked in him a clear image of their naked bodies stuck together in heated motion. He felt his own breath coming out in gasps. He could hardly restrain himself from poking a hole in the paper window in order to see them. He wasn't gutsy enough though. He sat there and twisted his legs while a strange heat ran through his body. He felt his own organ rising. For the first time in his life, he knew he had in him a healthy live thing that was going to be powerful and explosive.

He thought to himself, "Ah, this is what it's like to become an adult." From that day on, every night when it was time for the Yis to start their "night work", Myŏng-ku would find himself loitering around their window. He had already made a small nail-head size hole in the paper. It was a hole that could be covered by a tiny flap of paper. While he enjoyed this keyhole view of the couple's erotic and violent sexual acts, he did feel pangs of conscience that later bothered him oppressively.

But when it was dark and quiet, with only a distant dog barking at the moon, Myŏng-ku's mind slowly turned to that strange and exciting image of the Yis locked together as one body. Myŏng-ku's luck ran out one day the next spring when he got caught red-handed by Ch'an-kyŏng, who was by then engaged to be married.

There was the possibility that Ch'an-kyŏng herself had come to the spot to look in secretly, but Myŏng-ku could not say so. He only remembered later the blue eerie light in her eyes, which at the time reminded him of the eyes of a wild cat. After that night of the awkward encounter, Myŏng-ku lost the desire to continue his nightly peeping. Once in a while, his legs would carry him to the same spot, but the number of his visits slowly decreased. Instead, the newly-found pleasure of masturbation occupied him more and more. While he was engaged in this self-actualizing sexual pleasure, he always envisioned the scene in the Yis' room.

During the day Yi and the Madam looked just like any ordinary couple in town, and Myŏng-ku felt more ashamed of himself. Mr. Choi's occasional remark that "man and woman relationships are indeed very mysterious things" began to make sense to him.

Night shadows slowly descended upon everything, and the sad cry of crickets stirred Myŏng-ku's imagination. From the town's storage house came the wailing song of a popular singer. A movie was being shown there.

There was no sign of Mr. Choi when Myŏng-ku had dinner with three overnight lodgers. No sooner was dinner over than Kwak began to scratch himself all over. Finally he took his shirt off and began to hunt for lice in it. An old man from Chayang and a peddler were leisurely chatting.

As the evening advanced, neighborhood men, sated with dinner, began to appear one by one at Wolp'ook. As soon as there were four men in the store, they started a 'hwato' game. Salt-seller Kim brought some fresh cold radishes which everyone noisily chewed on. To them, a radish was a good dessert.

Having little to do at night, Myŏng-ku would sit behind the players and collect a kind of tip from them, which later went into the Madam's pocket. Myŏng-ku was in charge of serving ale and side dishes for night caps.

He also secretly read books since he had made up his mind to leave Ibam. The books were titled *General Knowledge* and *How to Succeed Without Help*, both of which contained stories of men who had made something of themselves.

Because a fire was kept going all day to cook the soup, the room was hot and stuffy. Everyone took off his outer shirt. Every face was shining with sweat and grease. Cigarette smoke, foot odors, and radish-digesting burps filled the room when the door burst open.

"Good heavens! Are you trying to smoke out a badger from

a cave? It feels like a hot-spring bath. Oh, the salt-seller is here, too, eh? Then, no one has to worry about making soy sauce for the year, I presume."

It was Madam Wolp'o who wanted to join in the game after she had counted up and put away the day's earnings. Two latecomers came in. Games and drinking went on in the crowded room. Some were playing or watching the games while others chatted quietly.

After dinner, Mr. Choi and Yi talked for a while about the theories of divining land configurations. Later, Mr. Choi went up to Mr. Chang's. He wanted to sit beside his daughter while she was being treated.

The game slowly came to an end around ten o'clock. One or two onlookers had already fallen asleep. The neighborhood men left one by one. Yawning loudly, Madam Wolp'o also went in, having won back the money she had lost at the beginning of the game.

Myŏng-ku picked up empty wine bowls and dishes, and swept the floor. There were some covers for the lodgers, but no one needed them. An old man and the peddler of needles, thread and buttons were already snoring.

Kwak, who had gone into the mountains in order to dodge the draft, was writing his umpteenth letter home asking for money. He had hurt his back at the lumberyard and had been staying at Wolp'ook. At first his company paid for his food and lodging, but it had stopped the payments ten days ago. His back was nearly healed, but he was in no condition to do heavy work. Madam Wolp'o had confiscated his ID card and other possessions as security.

Myŏng-ku went to the backyard to retrieve the rice cakes he had hidden behind the firewood when he heard someone sneaking in quietly. He thought it was Mr. Choi, but it turned out to be Suk-kyŏng, holding a Bible to her bosom.

"Are you coming from church?"

"Oh, my goodness, you startled me! Why didn't you cough at least?"

"Why was the worship service so long? It's past ten o'clock." Myŏng-ku knew there was a service on Wednesday nights, but he suspected that Suk-kyŏng was seeing someone on the sly. He guessed it was Preacher Min. Because of him, the next door neighbor woman and Suk-kyŏng had started going to church a year ago. Suk-kyŏng had been baptized, too.

"There was choir practice," Suk-kyŏng smiled, showing her even white teeth.

"Why don't you go to church with me, Myŏng-ku? The Bible has such worthwhile things in it."

"How can I? I have to collect firewood on Sundays, as you know."

"That's right," she said and passed by him. He could smell the scent of her face powder.

For a moment, his desire to grab her was almost overwhelming. His crotch swelled up. But he couldn't raise a finger, let alone grab her. Downcast, he went back to the room and opened a book, but all he could see was Suk-kyŏng's round bosom. He closed the book and waited for Mr. Choi.

Moments before he fell asleep, he always thought of his parents, brother, and sister. Before the war, they had sat around and had had such happy meals. Now that his father was dead, such happy days would never come again. Myŏng-ku was dozing and sleeping fitfully when the door was opened by Mr. Choi.

"It is quite late, sir."

"Oh, are you still up?" Mr. Choi said and took off his hat and quilted vest. "It's almost like summer in this room," he said.

"Is Kye-yŏn any better?"

"No, I can't say that she is. Thank you for being so concerned about her," Mr. Choi said, smiling at Myŏng-ku.

"She reminds me of my sister in P'ohang, sir," Myŏng-ku stammered embarrassedly. It was true.

"In the past three years, Kye-yŏn and I have been good friends. I'm truly sorry that she is so sick."

"I know. So you can guess how I must feel. She is the only daughter I have."

Mr. Choi sat down and untied the ankle laces of his pants legs. He took off his socks that were thick with layers of patches.

"Other girls seem to grow up so well except for my own girl. I don't think there's much hope for her. I don't think she'll ever have a normal life."

"What time are you going back to Tuma-ri, sir?"

"Very early in the morning. I have to cut and gather millet, prepare the feed for the cows, weed the vegetable fields, and sow the wheat and barley seeds.... There's so much to do. I cannot sit here and waste time."

"May I come with you? I have to collect firewood tomorrow. Why don't we leave right after breakfast?"

Myŏng-ku had been thinking about accompanying him all evening. "To carry Kye-yŏn on your A-frame would be too much for you. It's such a long way. I'd like to help you carry her," he wanted to say, but didn't dare.

"Why not? That's a good idea. To walk together would be nice," Mr. Choi agreed and put some tobacco in his pipe.

The next morning at early dawn, Mr. Choi went up to Mr. Chang's and brought Kye-yŏn to Wolp'ook. The night-long treatment must have been severe because Kye-yŏn looked half-dead. When Mr. Choi lowered her onto the floor, she collapsed. Her shallow breath came out in small gasps and her eye-lids trembled minutely. Her thin and veiny neck showed signs of advanced tuberculosis.

Myŏng-ku swept the frost-covered yard with a bamboo broom. He didn't know what else to do. Kye-yŏn looked like a straw doll in a girl's dress. Myŏng-ku watched her with aching compassion.

"Why don't we take her into my room? She shouldn't stay out here. I'll pray for you with all my heart," Suk-kyŏng offered.

"Shut up. If praying can cure sick people, who would be sick in this world? That fool of a girl is under some Jesus spell," shouted Madam Wolp'o from inside her room.

"We are leaving in a minute. Myŏng-ku, if you are coming with me, get ready," Mr. Choi said.

"Listen, you can't leave without having some breakfast. Your daughter must be starving. If you go now, she may collapse from hunger. The early morning cold is very bad for her. She may not make it back home," Yi carried on like an old woman.

At that moment, Kye-yŏn began to cough a wheezing cough, from deep within her chest. Every time she coughed, blue veins stood out on her thin neck.

"But now is the best time for us to leave. If we wait until everyone has had breakfast, and come out, we will be presenting a pretty unsightly sight."

"Are you out of your mind? Is this a time to think about her future or your appearances? You are going to lead her to death if you insist on saving face. Haven't you heard that one step outside your door may be death?"

Yi looked at Mr. Choi and Suk-kyŏng alternately and said, "What are you standing there for? Carry her inside and lay her on the warm floor."

Kye-yŏn managed to stop coughing and opened her eyes.

"Father, let us go home now," she whispered. Her voice was full of sadness and her thin lips trembled. A stream of tears flowed down her cheeks.

"Oh, my poor girl. I myself raised two girls. I know what it's like," Madam Wolp'o said and held up Kye-yŏn's upper body. Suk-kyŏng stepped into the hall and held her feet. Together they carried her into Suk-kyŏng's room. Kye-yŏn moaned as if all her bones were breaking apart.

Mr. Choi hardly ate anything. With his daughter on his back, he stepped down to the yard.

"Please don't forget to find me a good site," Yi called to Mr. Choi when they walked out to the market plaza.

Myŏng-ku followed them, carrying Mr. Choi's A-frame on top of his. Kye-yŏn could swallow only a few spoonfuls of watery rice gruel. On her father's back, she looked like a corpse.

There were groups of school children on their way to school. From the church on the slope behind the town hall came the ding-dong sound of the bell.

Past the storage barn of the town hall, further down, there were stepping-stones across the Chayang River. The water level at this time of year was very low.

Since it was the dry fall season, the river bottom was shallow enough for people to cross by using the stones. Upstream, a few children were already at play trying to catch fish. The wind blew hard from the top of the valley. Mr. Choi and Myŏng-ku stepped on the smooth stones placed conveniently across the river.

Mr. Choi wobbled a couple of times but he made it safely to the other side. Once they went up the bank, there were no houses and only a narrow path between dense bushes.

As they walked on to the point where the path led to the Sŏwun Temple, Kye-yŏn lay her head sideways on her father's back. Her narrow back convulsed once in a while. Mr. Choi mumbled something to himself along the way, but Myŏng-ku could not make out what it was.

The rising sun warmed their backs. Frost on the leaves was shining like tiny gems. Squirrels darted away at the sound of their footsteps. Oak trees and black alders, heavily wet with frost, were shedding yellowed leaves in the morning breeze.

Frost from the grass and fallen leaves dampened the men's pants up to their knees. It was a 30-degree, steep uphill walk from the Chayang River to the top of the hill

Mr. Choi carried his daughter all the way up. Myŏng-ku thought that it would be easier for Mr. Choi to carry Kye-yŏn on his A-frame rather than on his back, but he kept silent. The path was like the winding peel of a pumpkin. Mr. Choi walked on, mumbling or quietly chanting, without once slipping or slowing down.

Myŏng-ku's eyes caught sight of Kye-yŏn's buttocks in the locked hands of her father. Her behind was that of an ordinary 17-year-old girl's, but under her black cotton skirt there was little flesh.

Myŏng-ku had gotten sexually aroused at the sight of Suk-kyŏng's high bosom and ripe bottom, but he didn't feel that way about Kye-yŏn.

Someday when Kye-yŏn married, she might also do what the Madam did, he thought. However, this seemed impossible to him, not because she was sick nor because she reminded him of his sister but because Kye-yŏn had always been such an object of sweet love and yearning to Myŏng-ku. He thought her to be unlike the Madam.

Three winters ago, when Myŏng-ku had come to Ibam, Kye-yŏn used to come with her parents on market days. She had a tanned, vivacious face then. Her sickness began to get hold of her only this last year around the early fall. He thought back on his encounters with her.

One day Myŏng-ku bought sesame seed-covered rice candy and gave it to her. She blushed furiously and refused to accept it. Embarrassed, Myŏng-ku said, "It's really sweet," and bit on the candy stick himself. Another day, she sat in front of a vendor's cart and looked at a small mirror. She held it, rubbed it, and looked at herself in it, and finally, she put it back. It was obvious that she didn't have money. As she walked away, she looked back at it again.

Myŏng-ku went over and bought it for 3,000 won. When he came home, Kye-yŏn was sitting on the edge of the hall.

"Kye-yŏn, will you have this?" asked Myŏng-ku as he tried to put it in her hands.

"We have a mirror at home," Kye-yŏn said coldly, and she shook her head till her two red-ribboned pigtails danced.

"But you don't have your own mirror, do you?" Kye-yŏn shook her head and hid both her hands behind her back. Myŏng-ku put the mirror beside her and went away.

After a long time Myŏng-ku glanced in her direction. She was sitting as primly as before, but the mirror was gone. From then on, whenever she ran into him, she would blush and give him a shy smile.

It was a market day in early spring of last year. Mr. Choi brought an A-frameful of cut wood to Ibam with Kye-yŏn, who also carried on her head a huge bundle of dried pine needles. Mr. Choi had to sell the wood and the pine needles to make enough money to buy various items for his grandmother's memorial rites.

Because of the war, everyone's life had become harder than before. Moreover, from the later part of the winter until the late spring, farmers everywhere had had to go through what was called "the spring hunger", a period of survival on wild roots and pine bark-and-flour cakes. Though Mr. Choi was the head of the Choi clan, he had no money either. Bored with waiting for a buyer at the wood shop, Kye-yŏn had strolled down to Wolp'ook.

Myŏng-ku saw her sitting in the hall.

"Kye-yŏn, you have come to Ibam many times but you haven't been to the old academy, have you? I want to show you around," he said.

Kye-yŏn looked down at her hands and said nothing.

"I have a sister about your age. She is in P'ohang," he said, to the speechless girl. Her coarse black cotton skirt had patches on it. Her thin legs under the skirt showed whitish dried skin and scratch marks that she had apparently gotten while gathering pine needles and branches.

Guessing that Kye-yŏn didn't want to come along, Myŏng-ku turned toward the door.

"I've heard from Father that the academy is very big," Kye-yŏn said to his back in a very small voice.

"I know you are too shy to come with me. I'll go up there by myself, then you can follow me a little later. The academy, the T'angnip Rock, and the Pise Arbor are worth seeing," he said and left. He didn't want to be seen by the Madam, so he quickly merged himself into the crowd at the market.

He tried to comfort himself with the fact that even if Kye-yŏn did not follow him, he had nothing to lose. But deep in his heart, he was burning with violent emotions. Passing by the grain shop, he glanced back but didn't see her. Myŏng-ku slowed down and sauntered down a narrow pebbled road.

By the time he reached the town boundary and turned on to the wide main road toward Sang-gok, he surmised that Kye-yŏn might be seen behind him. When he looked back however, there were only a few peddlers on the road. There was no sign of Kye-yŏn.

He felt as if a carefully-built edifice were suddenly crumbling in his heart. He also felt ashamed of the bold suggestion he had made. Suddenly his eyes began to cloud. He thought of going back, but decided he would walk around the stone walls of the academy first. He went to see the T'angnip Rock and crossed the narrow wooden bridge over the Chayang River. The wind from the valley roared down like a waterfall among the dense trees. Though the wind was cold, it had a tinge of spring in it.

Myŏng-ku flopped himself down under the pine tree in front of the academy's great gates. Then he watched the road. For a long while he sat there and regretted that he had ever made such a suggestion to her. The cold wind didn't help his desolation. He regretted also that he hadn't asked her to go and see the performances of the song-and-dance troupe in the yard of the town hall.

It was too late to retract what he had said. When he stood up to dust off his pants seat, he saw a black figure emerging on the road. Myŏng-ku hid behind a pine tree and watched the tiny figure. By the time the figure reached a tavern beside the road, he could see it was Kye-yŏn.

She walked lightly while patting one palm with a small branch held in the other. He knew she was pretending to be nonchalant.

Afraid that she might turn around and go back, Myŏng-ku walked back along the stone wall. "What am I going to say to her?" His heart was pounding uncontrollably. When he peeked around the next time, Kye-yŏn was trying the gate. Finding the gate locked, she peered inside through a crack.

Myŏng-ku thought about putting his hand over her eyes from behind, but he didn't have the courage to do that. Kye-yŏn craned her neck looking here and there, then started toward the river bank. Myŏng-ku decided to follow her quietly. She stopped on a sunny slope and exclaimed, "Wow, there are so many shepherd's purses here. I wonder why no one has taken them yet." She sounded as if the remark was meant for someone else to hear. Kye-yŏn picked a handful of shepherd's purses and put them in the front of her skirt. Myŏng-ku finally found something he could say to her.

"Let me get some for you, too." Kye-yŏn was not surprised. She seemed as if she had known all along that he was behind her.

"Yes, let's pick as many as we can. We eat shepherd's purse gruel for dinner everyday."

They continued the work for a long time. Myŏng-ku gave whatever he got to Kye-yŏn. Her skirt was full of the wild vegetable.

"What are we going to do with all this?" Kye-yŏn asked. She was near tears. If she stood up and held the edge of her skirt, her bare knees would show. On the other hand, she could not walk, squatting as she was.

"Kye-yŏn sat there, utterly helpless. Myŏng-ku thought that at the moment she was the cutest thing in the world.

"I'll go and bring you a basket. Wait just a few minutes," he said.

Myŏng-ku took off his jacket and spread it on the ground beside her.

"Put it all on this."

Kye-yŏn turned her eyes away from the unwashed undershirt Myŏng-ku was wearing.

"You'll be cold and...."

"No, I won't. Put the whole pile here. I'll wrap it and carry it for you. Quick. Won't you come with me to see the troupe? I have enough money."

Kye-yŏn threw the mound of shepherd's purses on his spread jacket. Standing near her, Myŏng-ku could smell a faint mysterious odor like that of fresh grass when he buried his face in it. It was like the smell of big trees when he stepped outside in the middle of the night. It was Kye-yŏn's breath. It was a sweet scent in the air like when grapes ripened. It was fresh, sweet, and warm.

Later in the night, while Myŏng-ku had tossed and turned in
his loneliness and longing, he remembered that mysterious odor
of Kye-yŏn's. Perhaps it was too faint even to be called a smell,
but it stirred him powerfully, far more than the powder smell on
the faces of the Madam and Suk-kyŏng. It was better than the
scent of a flower in full bloom.

Kye-yŏn's scent evoked a far stronger fascination and sorrow
in his heart. It didn't arouse him sexually, but made him more
lonely. He was caught up in his recollections until Mr. Choi's
voice brought him back to the present.

"Let's rest here awhile," Mr. Choi said when they reached the
top of the Kyeyang Pass. He gently put Kye-yŏn down on the
grass.

"Are you all right, dear?" Mr. Choi asked and wiped his face
with a towel that he had wound around his neck. He took off his
hat.

"Yes," Kye-yŏn answered weakly and re-tied the loosened
strings of her jacket.

Myŏng-ku put down his A-frame, too. The cool wind dried
the sweat on his face. The sun had risen a little higher and shone
on everything. Mr. Choi stuffed his pipe with tobacco. Insects
and birds were chirping.

The Young Pass was nearly 500 meters above sea level. The
area around it was flat and even. On the sunny southern side
where there was no wind, waist-high mountain bamboos were
growing in clumps. Brushy bushes grew, scattered here and there.
Other stringy vines were growing where there were no trees. The
red autumn leaves among the bushes were brilliant against the
other faded leaves.

"Look at this grave. I wonder whose grave it is. As time passes
by, it is forgotten and forsaken by everyone." The grave was so
eroded and bare that it no longer looked like a grave.

"Sir, come spring, I'm going to leave Ibam and go to Taegu,"
Myŏng-ku said as he tore apart some of the dry leaves he had
picked up.

"Leave here? Just like that?"

Mr. Choi looked over at him through the tobacco smoke. Kye-yŏn, who was resting her cheek on her raised knees, suddenly looked up and gazed at him but said nothing. Her lips trembled a little. She put her head on her knees again and closed her eyes.

She looked like someone resigned to whatever was being offered.

"Ibam is not my hometown. I've become tired of it. If you were going to live in a strange place, Taegu is as good a place as any. Besides, a big city like Taegu must have more job openings. It must be better than here," Myŏng-ku said.

"Your family was ruined by the war. The south and north both say they fought to unify the country, but both were spurred by vengeance, I'm afraid."

"It seems so. Though my father was a member of the Communist Internal Security Office, he never killed anyone. He didn't join because he wanted to, either. He wasn't educated enough to know the leftists from the rightists anyway. I don't know for sure, but that was why he didn't run away when the Republic Army recaptured our town. He thought he hadn't done anything bad."

Myŏng-ku could recall the scene clearly. Several young men of the village dragged his father to a field and beat him to a pulp with clubs and rocks. His skull was crushed, and his stomach torn open, as he pleaded for mercy. "Please don't kill me. What did I do?" But the bloodcrazed young men never stopped the beating until Myŏng-ku's mother and sister, screaming, covered his bloody, mangled body. They carried him home where he vomitted a bucketful of blood, and died before the day was over.

The next day the village head came. He told the family that the body would be cremated and the ashes strewn over the river. People wrapped the body with a straw sack and took it up to the caves where briquettes were made. Thus there was no funeral and no grave which the family could visit.

"We Koreans have been repressed for so long that we can be explosively cruel. We have been hungry and cold, that's why there have been so many instances of hostility and rebellion. On top of that, we are so ignorant and bad-tempered that we often fall into bloody fights."

"As for my mother, she could have stayed on in Ttakpatkol, but people were so cruel to her that she couldn't take it any more. The children wouldn't have anything to do with us. They called us 'red brats' and taunted us mercilessly."

"As the old saying goes, those who want a man to fall, will have their own feet smashed. They killed your father, and they couldn't stand seeing your mother because of the guilt they felt. That is the reason why they chased her out of the village."

"But I don't hate them. They were also victims of the terrible war. Besides, what good would it do if I nursed hatred toward them?"

"Yes, you are a good boy to think like that. If I hate someone, someone will hate me. Even if the world has gone awry, time will bring back the truth. It is wrong to live with hatred in your heart," Mr. Choi nodded his head and suddenly asked, "How old are you, Myŏng-ku?"

"Eighteen, sir."

"You are old enough to have 'the ole wander itch.' I had the same idea when I was your age. It was so strong that I could not stand daily farm work."

Mr. Choi gazed far away in the direction of his hometown. There, under the brilliant sun, Mt. Pohyŏn stood in all its magnificence. Its top, covered with frosty bushes, glistened like a white crown.

"So to ease my mind, I used to go up to the top of Mt. Pohyŏn, look around, and yaho at the top of my lungs. Those were the days of my warm-blooded youth. When young, everyone wants to run away and see the world. However, youth is short. As the day quickly wanes into evening, life flies by like an arrow."

"But sir, I don't want to just wander around. I want to find a way to make a living, to succeed."

"Success is not easy, but I like your ambition. A man with

courage and determination should go to a bigger pond to catch bigger fish. That is true."

Mr. Choi's eyes were still on the mountain top. "Have you ever been to the top?"

"No, sir. It may be safe now, but the Red guerrillas were living in the caves up there, so no one dared climb there. When father was living, we used to go to the Kuam Mountain, to gather firewood."

"No, you couldn't have been to Mt. Pohyŏn. That mountain holds all the tragedies of the war in its bosom. But it has been and will always be silent. It has the blood, bones, and flesh of all the dead people in its soil, but it will forever seal its lips. If you go up to the top, there are three enormous rocks which we call the 'three brothers'. Every mountain around here has lots of viney bushes, but Mt. Pohyŏn has giant-size bushes all over its surface. They are taller than I. Before the war broke out, Red guerrillas, dozens of them, would penetrate into the bushes, and unless they moved around, no one could find them. In order to catch them, you would need thousands of searchers. After the liberation from Japan, Red guerrillas began a massive operation there, so the Republic Army had to burn down the whole mountain. That's when millions of trees, pine trees, oak trees, and ash trees were burnt to ashes."

In 1949, Mr. Choi was forced to work as a porter for the guerrillas. He had to carry on his A-frame sacks of rice and barley, usually in the night, to the guerrilla caves on the mountain. At that time, he didn't know how much time he had to live before he would be shot to death. About a month before, he had overheard the wife of the head of the Andong Kwon family. She said, "Maybe he went up north with them. The armistice was signed, but there has been no word from him. I don't think I'll ever see my son again, unless the country is unified, which seems impossible."

Her son was one of the very few college graduates of Ibam. He had joined the guerrilla forces in 1948 and had gone into the Pohyŏn Mountain. While the Communists ruled during the war, he briefly appeared in Ibam in a North Korean Army uniform, riding a Russian-made jeep. Then he was gone again.

"I'm afraid I'm wasting time waiting for news from my mother. I'm now grown enough to support myself wherever I may go. It's been two years since I last heard from her. Maybe I'll hear something from her before the winter is over. Even if I don't, I'm going to leave, "Myŏng-ku said and looked at Kye-yŏn.

"Please don't tell Uncle and Aunt."

"I won't. But...." Mr. Choi thought that a healthy, strong and thoughtful young man like Myŏng-ku would be a perfect son-in-law. "If Kye-yŏn weren't so sick, but.... well," thought Mr. Choi.

"You will be drafted in about three years. You can see the world then. You'll learn many things in the Army, and then you can decide whether or not to come back to Ibam."

"Father, shall we go now?" Kye-yŏn asked. She had been looking down at a purple daisy in her hands. Her voice was full of sorrow.

"All right, dear. Let's go."

Mr. Choi stood up after shaking out the ashes from his pipe.

"Let me borrow your scythe, Myŏng-ku."

Myŏng-ku untied his scythe from his A-frame. Still tied to his A-frame were his lunch pail and a small bundle of rice cakes he had bought yesterday for Kye-yŏn.

"Sir, would you like to have some of these?" Myŏng-ku unwrapped the cakes.

"What is it?"

"Rice cakes. I bought them yesterday to bring along today."

"Did you?" Mr. Choi picked up two of them.

"Will you have one, Kye-yŏn?" he asked.

"No, thank you." Kye-yŏn shook her head and let go of the daisy. It floated down to the ground.

"Oh, they are delicious," Mr. Choi said with relish.

"Why don't you try one? If you chew it slowly and long, it will be all right," he urged his daughter, to no avail.

Myŏng-ku looked at her too, while chewing on his share. He saw on her thin fingers and orange-red finger nails. She must have dyed them with balsam petals as country girls did. He wished she would accept just one cake, but she said, "No, Father, I don't want any." She hung her head down and buried her face between her knees.

"Tut, tut. She's observing a girl's proper manners," Mr. Choi said, looking at his daughter's pathetic figure. Minute ripples moved across her back as she silently wept.

Mr. Choi and Myŏng-ku finished up three cakes each. Mr. Choi obviously enjoyed them, but Myŏng-ku found them utterly tasteless. They were tough and hard to swallow.

With Myŏng-ku's scythe in hand, Mr. Choi walked up the slope where there was tall grass. A startled pheasant flew up. He began to cut the grass by the handful. He brought down an armful and spread it on the seat of his A-frame. On top of the grass he spread two empty sacks in which he had brought red peppers and sesame seeds. He was making a soft cushion for his daughter to sit on.

"Will you hold the A-frame for me?" he asked.

While Myŏng-ku held it, Mr. Choi scooped up Kye-yŏn in his arms and put her on the seat. She was so ashamed to be carried this way that she buried her face against the back of the A-frame. Her eye-lids were red and swollen.

"Sir, don't get me wrong, please, but may I carry this A-frame? It may be too hard for you to...." Myŏng-ku said, blushing.

"No, no, Father," Kye-yŏn spoke up sharply against Myŏng-ku's suggestion.

"All right, dear, I'll carry it," Mr. Choi said, and smiled at Myŏng-ku.

"Thank you, Myŏng-ku, for offering, but I have to carry my own load. It is what my fate has given me to carry. As long as I breathe, I'll have to carry it. Why don't you just follow me?"

The two men walked on. Myŏng-ku, with an empty A-frame on his back, was ahead. Except for the swishing sounds of the grass and the occasional cooing of wild doves, there was silence. No one spoke. They came out of the mountain path on to a road that ran along the river.

Myŏng-ku wished that he had been allowed to carry Kye-yŏn, who was light as a straw doll. On the other hand, he was quite happy, no, in fact, elated, to be going to Tuma-ri with her. His steps were light.

"For a girl to be so sick when she should be blooming like a magnolia," he thought.

He felt deep sorrow and compassion. He was happy and sad at the same time. He also remembered the mysterious scent he had smelled last spring when they were together near the academy. He held onto it like a precious dream.

Mr. Choi began to chant a song. Its beat was slow and Myŏng-ku caught the lyrics:

When you are a child, ay, ay, ay,
You don't know your parents' love, ay, ay, ay,
When you are grown up, ay, ay, ay,
You can't repay their love, ay, ay, ay,
All is in vain, all is in vain,
Ay, ay, ay.

The song was called *Talgujil*. It was sung as the lead song in a funeral march when people carried the coffin and the bier of the deceased to the burial place. It was mournful.

Climbing a steep slope, Mr. Choi was nearly breathless, but he continued the chant as chanting seemed to help him push on. Myŏng-ku couldn't decide whether the song was meant for himself, for Kye-yŏn, or was being sung just out of habit. He didn't dare ask.

When we get old, ay, ay, ay,
We'll never be young again, ay, ay, ay,
Though we lived a hundred years, ay, ay, ay,
Sleeping days, sick days, ay, ay, ay,
Sorrows and worries, ay, ay, ay,
Take away many a life, ay, ay, ay.

Myŏng-ku found himself gradually drawn into Mr. Choi's song, his feet leaden as if walking in oozy mud. As he walked on among the fallen leaves, his A-frame straps dug into his shoulders as if he were carrying a heavy sack. He wished Kye-yŏn were sitting on his A-frame, light and dozing like a child. "I'll never forget the day when we were together. I'll always cherish her fresh sweet odor. Kye-yŏn, I could carry you all the way to Yŏngch'ŏn, even to Taegu, and I wouldn't feel a thing," Myŏng-ku thought to himself. He felt light and strong.

Mr. Choi's song went on and on....

Though you beg of everyone, ay, ay, ay,
Who will listen to you, ay, ay, ay,
Alas, what shall I do, ay, ay, ay,
Life's end is so searing, ay, ay, ay.
Flowers on Myŏngsashimni beach, ay, ay, ay,
Don't cry when you wither, ay, ay, ay,
You will bloom again, ay, ay, ay,
But our life never comes back, ay, ay, ay,
It will never come back, ay, ay, ay,
It is a farewell forever and ever,
Ay, ay, ay.

CHAPTER V

Yi's kidney disease worsened as quickly as the winter days became shorter. His tongue was covered with a white film because of the uraemia. Having no appetite, he skipped meals and became so weak that he was bedridden all day.

Insomnia kept him awake at night. In earlier days when he had had an active sexual life, Madam Wolp'o used to sleep holding his organ in her hand. Now that he had lost such desires, he found her hand a mere nuisance.

After she fell asleep, he would gently pull himself away and sneak over to the wine jugs. He sat and drank in the dark. Though he knew well that alcohol was poison to a kidney patient, he couldn't help it. Without alcohol, he would stay awake all night.

His insomnia was different from that of others, because he was also tormented by remorse and guilt about all the things he had done in his life. One night to him was like a month. Only under alcoholic influence could he hope for a few winks of sleep.

Just as a tubercular patient should not refuse meat, or a diabetic should not eat sweets, Yi should not have had alcohol. He knew the harm alcohol did to his kidneys, which were already badly damaged. At this point he could clearly see the awful black figure of a messenger from another world, and he lay in bed tossing and turning. Yi thus felt it more urgent than ever to find a suitable burial site. He begged and badgered Mr. Choi.

Myŏng-ku had been to Mr. Choi's home many times to convey Yi's urgent message.

"Myŏng-ku, you saw for yourself, the coffin I had Old Man Pang make for me. When you see Mr. Choi, tell him Old Man Pang has already painted, lacquered, and varnished it three times. Don't forget to tell him that," Yi said to Myŏng-ku who was leaving with an empty A-frame on his back for yet another errand of wood gathering.

After Ch'usŏk, days went by faster. Temperatures went down quickly and frost covered the fields and paddies. In the deep valleys, a thin film of ice formed. High up in the sky, rows of birds were flying south day and night. Small birds like Chinese mountain hedge-sparrows and big ones like ducks, geese, and cranes were flying in a straight lines or in Vs.

Before Ch'usŏk, Mr. Choi had gone hunting for snakes as Mr. Chang had told him to stew them and feed the soup to Kye-yŏn. During the summer, there were snakes everywhere in the fields and rice paddies, but they were nowhere to be seen now that the weather was cold. Mr. Choi was armed with a bamboo thong and a sack. Failing to catch any, he spread the word that he would pay for snakes. One day Myŏng-ku caught a big snake and gave it to him.

After Mr. Choi boiled the snakes, he told Kye-yŏn that it was chicken soup. Kye-yŏn was forced by her parents to eat the soup, but she never failed to have diarrhea afterwards.

One day soon after the harvesting was done, and the trees had lost all their leaves, Yi and Mr. Choi ventured on a site exploration. The only winter preparation left was to make kimch'i and to gather as much firewood as possible. For the farmers of the area, winter had begun.

Mr. Choi had two spots in mind for Yi's resting place. One was not a site that Mr. Choi had purposely chosen for Yi, but the other was. If one went from Ibam to Ch'ŏngsong about 10 ris on the national road, there was a village called Hap'yŏng. It was much smaller than Ibam. To the southwestern side of Hap'yŏng, there was the town of Yangji-ri. The Tal Mountain was a sharply pointed mountain facing Yangji-ri. There was a site on this mountain that Mr. Choi had been eyeing since before the war.

Another site was located between Ibam and Tuma-ri. It was midway up the slope of a hill. This site was nestled among the rather steep T'aebaek Mountains. It was nearly 600 meters above the sea level.

The day Mr. Choi and Yi decided to visit the Yangji-ri site was a cold, windy, overcast day. Mr. Choi left home at dawn and arrived in Ibam in time for breakfast. Since their appointment had been made on the last market day, Yi was waiting to have breakfast with Mr. Choi. Myŏng-ku had already left to gather wood.

At the breakfast table, Mr. Choi realized how dead serious Yi was. His hair had been washed and combed. He wore a neat light blue suit with a green vest. He dawdled over his food. The swelling in his face looked different from other days. His tense and melancholy face looked like that of a strong-willed scholar about to drink poison from a King sent for punishment. Mr. Choi decided to assume an appropriately serious mien.

"Master Choi, why in the world is he going on this trip when he is in such bad shape today? I can't understand. Even if a burial site were urgently needed, you'd take care of that, wouldn't you? He acts as if he had a set date to go. He had a coffin made already. Who does he think he is anyway? Can he see into the future like a high priest or something?" Madam Wolp'o carried on amid repeated sighs.

"You have a point there. Korean people have always believed in the continuity of life, so they believe your spirit will live on forever after you die. However, he isn't even sixty yet. There aren't many people who are in such a hurry to go...," Mr. Choi replied.

"When I was in T'onggu, Manchuria, I had the opportunity to see the old tombs of the Koguryŏ Dynasty," Yi began, "and inside a tomb, there were rectangular stone rooms. The rooms were *Changgunch'ong, Kakchŏch'ong, Sashinch'ong*, and *Kwigapch'ong*, each with its own characteristics. What all of them had in common was a clear indication that all Korean ancestors absolutely believed in the spiritual after-world. The murals depicted the ecstasy of the dead person ascending to heaven and angelic people in the after-world riding on cranes surrounded by cherubic friends. Truly, the other world is a paradise with no hatred or torture."

"Do you mean that you'll hurry up there ahead of me to find a new wife and live a good life?" Madam Wolp'o attacked angrily.

"No, but I would very much like to be born a different person and live a different life."

"You greedy devil! You're more likely to fall into hell, surrounded by all those women you violated," Madam Wolp'o continued her sharp attack. Yi didn't say anything to her, but his face was dark.

When breakfast was almost over, a horse-cart driver came in to tell them to hurry up. The one bus that went to Ch'ŏngsong and Andong via Ibam came at 1 o'clock in the afternoon. Yi had negotiated a ride on a horse-cart going to Ch'ŏngsong. Yi put on an overcoat and picked up a cane. To protect his head from the wind, he wore a hat. The long hair under his hat looked rather incongruous with his general appearance.

"I'm afraid he's going to die on the road. A death-messenger must have already attached himself to him, otherwise why would he insist so on going?" Madam Wolp'o wouldn't let up.

"He is so weird. I don't understand how you have lived with him all this time," Suk-kyŏng said to her mother.

"Perhaps because it was written in our fates. God forbid you meet such a man as he," Madam Wolp'o said sadly. She sniffed.

"I'm never going to marry a man unless he is a Christian. My husband has to be a believer in Jesus Christ," Suk-kyŏng said decidedly.

"Still, he is your stepfather. Don't be too hard on him. He is a good man deep inside," the Madam defended him.

Yi and Mr. Choi sat behind sacks of rice on the cart. The sacks protected them from the wind. When they crossed a stream and rode around the Talbawi Mountain, they could see only a few grade school students on their way home. There were few people on the road beside them.

The cart clattered as it moved on. The wind became cold.

"Why is the weather so gloomy, like the frown on the face of a hungry mother-in-law? It doesn't look like rain or snow. When you go to the after-world with a death-messenger, there is a long, long road that is gloomy like this, I bet. Then, you are pushed down into a pitch dark sea like a lump of dung. Finally you arrive at the gate," Yi mumbled while looking at the dark overcast sky.

As if to reinforce Yi's premonition, several crows flew across the road toward the river. Caw, caw, their metallic cawing ominously spread far and wide, making the village seem all the more desolate. Yi followed them with his deep-set eyes.

"I have in my life found many burial sites for people, but I've never met a man like you who wanted to check over his own grave site in person. Will you tell me the reason why? You know we have a lot of time to kill," Mr. Choi said.

"Frankly speaking, I do not deserve to have a grave site. But I guess I have the same human weaknesses as other people. Since my life in this world has been worthless, like that of a pig, I pin that much stronger hope on my after-life. People who have never been treated like human beings hang onto their last hopes, those being to have good after-lives. It is the last hope a man can hang on to," Yi said with a sad smile.

"You call yourself a pig or a swine, but a pig is an animal. Animals don't have graves for their posterity. Butchers erect a tower or a grave for cows, but those are not only for the cows, but more importantly for the butchers themselves. They want atonement for all the killing, they did and appeasement for their own repressed anger against any cruel treatment they might have had to endure in society," said Mr. Choi.

"Your words express my feelings exactly," Yi replied, but his eyes were fixed on the deserted road they were traveling on. Bare branches of trees were whipped by the wind and dust rose like clouds. Old willow trees stood like ghosts in the dusty air. Beyond them, the village of Ibam was hidden by a mountain.

"In that case, do you really know the day you will leave this world? Is that why you're in such a hurry to find your resting place?"

"I've seen so many deaths of all kinds in my life that I can guess when a person will receive his death messenger. You know, there are people who are under the spell of the death messengers. I'll tell you a story of a man named Kim Ch'ul. He and I were so close that I still remember his name. After the Hŭk River battle, he and I went back to Kando, as I told you before. Our Independence Army was stationed in Yajigol about 300 ris from Yongjŏng. It was my first summer there.

Yajigol was a small Korean hamlet of about twenty houses. There was a mill run by a Korean. In the Kando area, no matter which town you went to, there were more Koreans than Chinese.

I belonged to a squad of about 30 men. While staying in Yajigol, we were treated royally by the Korean residents. What I mean by royal treatment is that they would go hungry in order to feed us. After that, we moved on to South Wanrugu which was another big town with more than 200 homes. Yajigol, Wanrugu, both south and north, and Orangch'on were under the administration of Yidogu. Right here in Yidogu, two years earlier, several thousand members of the Korean Independence Army had a great victory. They killed more than a thousand Japanese.

Our squad walked through a path in the woods everyday. Then one day, this guy, I mean Kim Ch'ul, did something he hadn't done before. He washed his face in a stream and cleaned his old gun really thoroughly. We were nomads, and we rarely washed ourselves let alone our guns. Clean or not, guns were guns as long as they shot out bullets. Anyway, I felt strange about Ch'ul's behavior. So I told him to be particularly careful that day. I don't know why, I just felt that he was behaving differently, and that was a bad omen.

Ch'ul answered that there weren't many battles worth speaking of and once we got involved in a battle, being careful didn't do much good. When he said this, his face looked so sad.

Anyway we walked on about 30 ris when our reconnaissance mission found a company-size Japanese army. We divided ourselves into three groups and attacked them from three sides. Ch'ul fought valiantly. He shot well. Even when his jaws were broken and he was bleeding heavily, he fought on. The damnedest thing was that his newly cleaned gun got stuck again and again. Suddenly, Ch'ul stood up and rushed straight toward the Japanese.

He threw a grenade at them and then fell with bullets in every part of his body. In that battle, we killed eleven enemy soldiers," Yi stopped. Because of either the remembrances of his old friend or the chilly weather, his teeth clattered. Then he sighed deeply. Tears were welling up in his eyes.

"Ch'ul was from Hamp'yŏng, the Chŏlla Province. He was a quiet, shy man. He died like that in Yajigol." Yi wiped his eyes with trembling hands. Tears continued to stream down his face.

"Does this mean that you are under a spell, too?"

"Heaven gives a sign to everyone at least once. It tells one to be especially careful. Anyway, my friend Ch'ul died, and I was captured. Too involved in fighting, we didn't know a new reserve company of Japanese had arrived from behind us. So nine of us were taken as prisoners. The rest of the story I have told you already. We were sent to the Military Police and tortured till we were no better than dead."

"Yes, you did. But I got the feeling that you were hiding something there," Mr. Choi said, determined to find out the full truth this time.

"Wait a minute. Are you implying that I broke down and confessed?" Yi's deep slitty eyes were burning. They were bloody as those of a bobcat ready to pounce on a field mouse.

"No, not exactly. Don't get me wrong," Mr. Choi wilted because he was by nature a gentle man. Quickly he turned his eyes away. If he continued to stare back at Yi's eyes, he thought his own eyes would burn and become blind. Yi's eyes were that cruel. Mr. Choi felt a cold shiver going down his back.

"When I started raving and acted insane, they let me go free. They said I was more tenacious than a cat. As you know, a cat doesn't die easily from severe beatings as a dog or a cow might."

"Apparently you were born with more than nine lives. Otherwise, you couldn't have survived such torture," Mr. Choi said, even though his doubts about the circumstances in which Yi was released were as strong as ever. Whatever the truth might be, the fact of Yi's survival was real. He could not have cut off his own ears.

"When I was released, the first thought that came to me was that it was time for me to die. Heaven was telling me that. But then at that very moment, I felt a sudden renewed desire to live...."

"At that moment you made up your mind to live like an animal?"

"Right. My mind was in confusion, but my survival instincts led me to begging, stealing, eating whatever could be found in the trash....It is true that one's life is in the hands of someone up there in heaven."

"Do you mean that heaven has given you some sort of chilling sign this time, too?"

"I am already a tree without a root, a well without water. I don't know anything else, but I do know myself." Yi coughed a dry cough and looked up to heaven.

"I've heard that some people wake up in their coffins when the lids are about to be nailed shut."

"All human beings become weak before death. From an emperor to an animal to an insect, every creature is scared of death. But whatever lives on earth must die. Every living thing thinks that it may get lucky and live on. That is the biggest lie it believes. If I quit smoking and drinking, take care of myself with proper medicine and a prudent diet, I might live a few more years."

"Why don't you do that, then? You can't live twice. Your body, once dead, will simply rot away."

"For some reason, I don't have such a desire. I don't want to hang onto life anymore. That too, must be in my fate."

"But you know you can make your own fate. For a man who has seen so much, such a remark seems beneath you. Why do you think man is called the supreme being on earth?"

"Even the fate that one makes or controls was originally given by heaven. So man cannot ultimately extend his given life span or change his nature. If you feed tonic medicine and nutritious meals to a sickly rich boy, he still might end up having indigestion and diarrhea. He might not stand the smell of meat from animals or fish, and might end up only eating salted baby shrimps."

"There are times when you can't do anything, so you leave everything to fate. I admit that the habit of leaving everything to fate is not right. Only when you accomplish something on your own, do you feel a sense of fulfilment. In a certain way, heaven helps those who help themselves. Heaven stands on the side of those who try to do their best."

"You think I don't know all those wise words? Don't try to preach to me like a monk or a preacher."

Yi put both of his hands between his knees and gave Mr. Choi a mischievous grin.

"Listen, I'll tell you an interesting story. Once upon a time, the only son of a rich man lived in a huge house. This son was so weak and sickly that he could be blown away like a dandelion. His anxious parents forced down his throat all kinds of expensive tonic medicines like ginseng and deer antler brews. But no sooner did he swallow these than he lost them all in diarrhea anyway.

The rich man happened to have a servant whose son was a moron. He followed the rich boy around and slurped up the medicinal discharges from the rich boy. The rich boy died before he was fifteen, but the moron, having become strong from the dead boy's tonic medicines, lived a long life and had many children. I wonder how many people ended up hating the aged moron."

"Do you mean to say that human life is a mystery?"

"I guess so. Who doesn't know that gambling and womanizing are the shortest routes to ruin, but so many people still can't control themselves. Once I was a heroin addict, but I had to quit because I had no money to buy heroin. Maybe I was allowed to live on because my fate was to meet Madam Wolp'o.

Most people in the market can recite at least a few words from wise men. But how many can put them into practice? Man's life is the same. A strong man who can easily carry a heavy sack of rice doesn't necessarily live long, while a weakling may live to be eighty because he knows how to take care of himself. I'm sorry to say this to you, but your eldest son was born under an unfavorable star, that's why he died ahead of his parents. As for your second son, what happened to him in the war?"

Mr. Choi didn't know what to say. He merely stared at his friend.

"All of us were taught that we should follow truth and justice, never in your life should you follow injustice, and look at gold as if it were mere stone. Good and wise words! Teachers teach us these things. But perhaps, only one in a hundred really practices them. Of course, teachers know that too, and yet they keep on teaching them.

They call it education, therefore, education is mere words, pictures of rice cakes that we can't eat. All we can get from them is the fun of memorizing them."

Yi's face under his long hair was the image of a profound sage. Noticing the strange mist in his eyes, Mr. Choi thought that his friend was indeed an inexplicable, unfathomable person. He was full of contradictions. On the one hand, he was shallow and frivolous, while at the same time he was deep and taciturn. He was calculating and greedy, but he was also above materialistic pursuit. His behavior was often so low and tawdry that you wouldn't want to sit with him, while at other times, he was almost like a philosopher full of awe-inspiring integrity. Though Mr. Choi had never traveled extensively, or met a wide range of people, he had learned on his own a standard of measuring people. He however, threw up his hands on Yi. Yi was definitely a big question mark. Though Yi insisted that he didn't know anything about divining land, Mr. Choi often sensed that Yi might know much more than he himself did.

It took them about an hour to get to Hap'yŏng where they had to get off the cart. They bade farewell to the cart owner and stepped on to a path between many rice paddies. From Hap'yŏng to Yangji-ri it was around one kilometer. They could see the village beyond a long row of trees. The Tal Mountain was further off from the village which was located over a hill and on the slope of the mountain.

At first Yi's gait was strong and regular, but as they began to climb, his steps gradually shortened as did his breath.

"Why are you suddenly so breathless? Is walking too much for you?" Mr. Choi extended a hand to help support his friend.

"See? Now you know how sick I am. I knew it, but I am glad I've tested myself. When I was an independence fighter, I had to climb so many mountains that I felt it odd to walk on flat land. Alas, fifty years of human life seems as short as a wink. I am back to my infancy, walking as I do, like an infant."

Yi was almost doubled over like an old man. He barely managed a few steps, then had to flop down on the ground with his legs and breath gone weak.

While sitting on a rock and on the grass, gasping for breath, he still didn't forget to look over the land carefully.

Under the dark overcast sky, the road that they had traveled lay like a long winding rope. The pebbly shores of the Chayang River spread out in front of Yangji-ri. Mr. Choi wondered what the flitting little specks were. He later found that they were sparrows flying off the tree branches.

Yangji-ri was only about 400 meters from the sea, and the Tal

Mountain was only 100 meters high. When they were halfway up, Yi began to complain.

"This is enough. I've seen enough. Let's go back to Ibam," he said.

"Listen, we have been meaning to do this for a long time. So stop whining. We're almost there anyway."

Mr. Choi was irritated by Yi, even though he was gasping and sweating. Mr. Choi thought that they shouldn't go back now.

"Look up there. Isn't that the slope where you said you were going to bury me? Right? Now I know. Let's go back down."

Yi was gazing at the slope as if he were to be buried on it right then and there. Near the spot where Yi was looking, there were many graves among dense bushes.

"No, you have to go up there. Go around to the southeastern side. There is the most auspicious site," Mr. Choi said, holding a compass in his hand.

"Southeastern direction?" Yi craned his neck and followed Mr. Choi's eyes.

"Yes. Unless you have a diviner's eyes, you can't see it. I've seen hundreds of sites in my life and I know a good one when I see it. Now try to get up. If you are absolutely unable, I'll carry you on my back."

Mr. Choi pulled Yi's sleeve. Mr. Choi thought that his friend was scared now that he could really see his own burial site, and that his old desire for survival might flare up.

"All right. I can see it even without climbing up there. You may carry your daughter on your back, but not me. Let's go back, so we won't miss the bus." Yi was adamant.

"What is this? Do you think this is some sort of joke? Why did you nag and badger me all this time and now give up like this?"

Mr. Choi felt like giving up the whole thing because of his friend's obstinacy. The site Mr. Choi had in mind was a magnificent site on a dragon-like mountain. It was an unusually good site, with water to the south.

On the south side of Mt. Tal, the villagers had buried their dead for generations, so it looked like a cemetery. However, on the southeastern side, there were still some important sites left. Moreover, the mountain was not owned by an individual, so there was no fee to pay. Mr. Choi was really annoyed that Yi would not go up to see such an excellent site. Suddenly Yi pulled himself together and spoke seriously.

"Damn it, my friend, this is not a good site at all. It's not fit for me. Look over there. I don't like that contour because it will always be exposed unless my grave sits toward the northwest. In that case, even after death, I'll be under pressure to leave and roam again."

"You don't know what you are talking about. Good waterways and roads should be open at their entrances and closed at their exits. From here, the road is cut off in the front and back, it's true. The mouth of the river cannot be seen but its exit is visible. A mountain that may have auspicious dragon signs can be on the decline, at the same time. Such a mountain is called an unlucky mountain. But this mountain is on the rise, so to speak, and its soil is of excellent quality. It's a lucky mountain."

"That's what you say, but this mountain is scrawny and unsightly in appearance. There is something flippant about it like the bottom of a frivolous woman. That means she's to go through several men. Such women may be all right, but one's burial place ought to be serious. This mountain looks as if it might rise and sashay the minute it sees a pair of women's shoes beside the river. For some reason I just have such a feeling," Yi said. "Besides, I feel that today is not a favorable day. Those crows made me uneasy, too."

"Now, look here. Have you said everything you wanted to say?" Mr. Choi's pride was hurt. His beard was shaking as he began to retort.

"I'm sorry. Let's just go back down first. Then one of these days, we will go to see the other site on the Susŏk Mountain that you told me about."

Yi continued to cough without showing any intentions of rising. His deep eyes looked so sad that Mr. Choi couldn't press any further. Truthfully speaking, his eyes were like the very eyes of a mouse in front of a cat. They were pathetic. The burning fire-like glow was completely gone. When God created the universe, he made two sides to everything—night and day, summer and winter, the warm sun and the cold storm. Just like this cosmic dualism, Yi's temperament and expression followed the Yin and Yang principle.

"You are truly pathetic," Mr. Choi wanted to spit out, but he restrained himself. How could the Japanese torture him when they saw such eyes? How could anyone refuse table scraps to this man with his pitiful eyes? His protruded mouth like that of a rabbit, his misty, pitiful eyes, the myriad of wrinkles around his eyes, all of these reminded Mr. Choi of a remark Madam Wolp'o had made sometime ago. She said that he had a silly horse face and he was childish and small-minded in many ways.

"If that's how you feel, there is nothing I can do," Mr. Choi yielded. Immediately they began to descend toward Hap'yŏng. Neither of them spoke. Under the bus stop sign, a couple of people were waiting for the P'ohang bus. One was a middle-aged man in a cotton overcoat, and the other was a woman with a baby on her back.

Yi opened the dust-covered glass door to a small shop and went inside to rest his legs. His legs had been hurting for quite a long time. Mr. Choi stood beside a willow tree, waiting for the bus.

"Mr. Choi, why don't you come in here? You have good teeth, don't you? Won't you have some dried squid?" Mr. Choi, however, paid no attention.

"I've known for a long time that I'm not living really, just existing. I didn't know dying was so hard," Yi said to himself.

Around noon, the bus came and brought them back to Ibam. From that day on, Yi was very sick for a whole week. He could not urinate, so he lived on herb medicine day and night. His swelling was so severe that he could not put on socks. The worse his disease became, the more persistent he got about finding the right site. He repeated himself all day long that as soon as he got better, he was going to the Süsŏk Mountain with Mr. Choi.

As seasons change and day wanes to night, sickness and pain have cycles, too. After a period of agonizing pain, there comes a period of relative ease, to be followed by another period of searing pain. When periods of pain get much longer than pain-free periods, one knows the time of death is at hand. At such times, even great doctors like P'yŏn Chak and Hŏ Chun would not be able to do anything.

Yi, after a week of agony, gradually began to recover. At the insistence of Preacher Min, on Sundays, he waddled slowly to the day-time services at Ibam Church. People in the market place would say to one another, "Yi Tae-mal must be nearing death. He goes to church, you know."

"Why on earth have you become a Jesus chanter?" salt-seller Kim asked.

"I know nothing about the church. I'm going there simply to get a little share of the flour they hand out," Yi said.

As soon as the war ended, various U.N. organizations such as the F.A.O. sent an enormous amount of aid, most of which was channeled through churches and orphanages. Ibam Church was no exception. It handed out flour and used clothing to the believers and many people registered themselves as new church members for the sole purpose of getting the goods.

On Sundays, the church was packed. Yi sat among the crowd, listened to the sermon, and pretended to sing the hymns. But most of the time, he sat there and dozed. Wearing thick reading glasses, he read the Bible(The New Testament) diligently both at church and at home.

"I hated the sight of my daughter going to church, and now you've become a Jesus follower, too. Maybe we should build a special heavenly room," Madam Wolp'o said sarcastically.

"I'm not a true Christian. I just want to know what kind of places heaven and hell are and what kind of people go to heaven or hell," Yi answered. He was seriously studying the subject.

One day after Myŏng-ku went off to gather wood, Preacher Min came to Wolp'ook. He was wearing one of those free suits he got at the church, a shirt with a dirty collar, and a tie. He brought his usual leather briefcase. Once inside the inner chamber, he took out a bible and a hymnal and conducted a family service. He tried to convert Madam Wolp'o too. Preacher Min explained the stories in the Bible and told of his own experiences, but the Madam was adamant. She refused with absolute conviction.

"I don't believe in anything. I have no sons to remember me with ancestor worship rites. The only thing I believe in is money," she said. Her answer was the same no matter how many times Preacher Min tried to convert her. She didn't believe there existed a heaven and hell. Once a person died, his body would rot away and his spirit would vanish. There would be nothing left.

Many self-made people, who had had to fight tooth and nail to accumulate some wealth, wanted to live well with a vengeance. Madam Wolp'o was one such person. She firmly believed that money made it possible for her to enjoy life and be respected by others. Her belief was unshakable.

When Preacher Min pointed out in detail the reasons why worship of money was not right, Madam Wolp'o rushed out of the room as if she had been insulted. Preacher Min, like a good shepherd, knelt and prayed fervently that God would redeem this lost lamb.

His face was pockmarked with acne scars, his cheekbones were two unsightly protrusions and his lips were thick and ugly. In short, he was a homely man. He went on, "O, Lord, you loved children and widows. Lord, save us and save the lost lamb." In between words, he sobbed and moaned. He was so earnestly praying that he shook his unwashed hair till it shed a shower of dandruff. His bony hands were shaking.

Yi sat there with his hands clasped and his head bowed, but he looked at Preacher Min with the expression of a spectator at a show. He seemed to marvel at the eloquent wise words that tumbled out of the young man's mouth.

Suk-kyŏng opened her eyes often to look at Preacher Min.

Since his prayer was for her mother's sake, she seemed genuinely moved. She showed in more ways than one how deeply she admired him.

"Sir, in the Bible, it is written that the late comer is better than the early comer," said Preacher Min after finishing his prayer. His eyes were red.

"If you believe in God with a sincere heart and accept the resurrection of Jesus Christ, please pray often and earnestly and hang on to Jesus. Jesus will cure your disease and He has made lepers clean and raised the dead."

When he noticed that Yi watched him with unbelieving eyes, he quickly opened the Bible.

"Look here, Verses Five and Six, Chapter Eleven of Matthew. 'The blind receive their sight, and the lame walk, the lepers are cleaned, and the deaf hear, the dead are raised up, and the poor have the gospel preached to them. And blessed is he, whosoever shall not be offended in me.' These are the true words in the Bible. If there were in the Bible even one single line that wasn't true, the whole western civilization would collapse because the Christian Church is what has made today's western civilization." Preacher Min's voice was that of a sure and true believer.

"I am not saying that what is written in the Bible isn't true. But I have no intention of curing my disease, or prolonging my life by faith. I've lived long enough. No, I should have died long ago when I was young. The fact that I've lived until now is a kind of bonus I was given. The only reason why I bother going to church is to find out how the church goes about forgiving the sins one has committed," Yi said with an ironic smile that embarrassed the young preacher.

"If you believe in Jesus Christ and repent your sins, He will forgive you, regardless of the kind of sins you committed. All men live in sin, and I am no exception. That's why Jesus came to save us. Christianity is a religion of forgiving and love. Jesus died on the cross in order to save us sinners. He was a sacrificial lamb. Three days after he died, he was resurrected. Jesus...."

Yi stopped him by wildly waving his hand.

"Do you mean that whoever repents of his sins will be forgiven and led to heaven? No matter what heinous sins he might have committed?"

"First, believe in God. Second, let your repentance be sincere and true. Third, do not sin anymore. If these are done, then anyone can go to heaven."

"If that's true, it's not that hard to go to heaven, is it?" Yi grinned and looked at Suk-kyŏng. "Don't you think so? According to Preacher Min here, going to heaven isn't hard at all."

Suk-kyŏng looked down without a word. She bit hard on her lips. She wanted to say that her stepfather would never be allowed to go to heaven, but she controlled herself. She knew every detail of his sordid life and never considered him better than an animal. Whenever he looked at her, cold shivers went down her spine as if she were facing a coiled snake.

"The gates of heaven are always open to anyone who repents," Preacher Min said and opened the Bible again to Chapter 23 of Luke. "The part I'm going to read to you is the conversation between Jesus and the two criminals who were hanging beside him. I'll read from Verse 39. 'And one of the malefactors which were hanged railed on him, saying, If thou be Christ, save thyself and us. But the other answering rebuked him, saying, Dost not thou fear God, seeing thou art in the same condemnation? And we indeed justly; for we receive the due reward of our deeds: but this man hath done nothing amiss. And he said unto Jesus, Lord, remember me when thou comest into thy kingdom. And Jesus said unto him, Verily I say unto thee, Today shalt thou be with me in paradise.'

I've read from Verses 39 through 43. When Jesus saw that the malefactor on his left repented his sins and believed in him, He told him that he would be with Him in paradise. This is the proof that God forgives all sinners with His infinite love."

"Preacher Min, the part that says, 'Dost not thou fear God, seeing thou art in the same condemnation? And we indeed justly; for we receive the due reward of our deeds' is really true."

Yi's sarcastic smile disappeared suddenly from his face, and he became serious.

"In the Bible that you gave me, I found those words too. If one sows for one's body only, he will reap the decayed body. I think this means one always has to pay for his sins, in life and in death. I'm afraid of God's judgment. You say God will forgive any sin if the sinner only repents, but I don't believe that. If Jesus forgives us just because we say we repent and shed a few tears, then it's just too easy.

In that case, we may sin all our lives as much as we want, and then repent just before death. Who wouldn't do that?

I've also found in the Bible that if your hand or foot makes you sin, cut off that hand or foot. How horrible ! The Bible said it was better to go to everlasting heaven being a cripple than to go to hell as a whole person. What an awful thing to say ! When I read those parts, I was amazed. Then the next moment, I gave up, because there was no hope for me."

As Yi spoke these words from the Bible in a serious tone, Suk-kyŏng couldn't help turning away. She wasn't surprised at his memory of God's words, but considered it a blasphemy that he even so much as mouthed the holy words.

"Sir, you are truly afraid of God. That fear is the very beginning of true faith. Please continue to read the Bible. You'll find that God's words are everlasting truths."

Preacher Min smiled shyly. His face was shining with joy and he thought that he had saved a lost lamb.

"By the way, Judas sold Jesus for 30 silver pieces, didn't he?" Yi's expression was grave. He continued on.

"But Judas threw away the pieces and hanged himself. He could have lived well on those silver pieces, but he hanged himself. Didn't he repent? But why doesn't the Bible say anything about Judas going to heaven? At least I didn't find it."

"No, Judas didn't repent. Later, he regretted but it was too late. Furthermore, suicide is a sin in the Christian Church. Sir, think of Peter. He betrayed Jesus three times, but Jesus forgave him and appeared before him after his resurrection. So Peter repented deeply and kept on spreading Jesus' words. He was crucified upside down in Rome. So Judas' suicide and Peter's martyrdom are as different as hell and heaven."

"Regret led to suicide, but repentance brought martyrdom? Therefore, regret is hell and repentance heaven?" Yi slowly shook his head. "That's too deep for me. I'll read the Bible some more and ask more questions."

The day's discussion between Yi and Preacher Min ended. Preacher Min left hurriedly saying that he had two more families to visit.

In the meantime, Yi didn't miss his exercise—walking with a cane around the market place during warm sunny hours.

He went to the horse-lender Han, and negotiated to lease a donkey for one day. Han earned money by transporting goods from one market to another. He would put a cart behind a donkey and drive the cart himself.

Within Yŏngil County the five-day markets opened along the P'ohang-Ch'ŏngsong Road. There was the Top'yŏng Market, and the P'ohang Market. Among the markets, P'ohang Market was the biggest. Han would sometimes take that day off and lend out his cart instead. That was how Yi leased a donkey for one day.

The other burial site Mr. Choi had decided on was on the Susŏk Mountain. It was about 10 ris from Ibam over a high pass. The road there was so narrow that two people could hardly squeeze through, let alone a horse-cart. Yi wasn't sure he could walk the distance but he would rather be dead than be seen being carried on an A-frame like Kye-yŏn. Thus he had arrived at a solution, which was to ride a donkey up to the site.

People in Ibam, who had been surprised to see Yi going to church, were treated to another surprise—seeing him practice riding a donkey.

"When I was in the Independence Army, I used to ride horses and gallop at full speed to every corner of Manchuria. We were trained to ride and use swords at the same time. Of course, we were taught knowledge and self-discipline, so that we could eventually save our country and build a new nation."

Yi bragged about his old days, but few people could see the slightest resemblance to that young fighter in the present stooped figure in a loose Korean costume. The day when Mr. Choi and Yi had promised to meet, via a message from Myŏng-ku, turned out to be a fine day. Yi had consulted astrological signs and watched the stars and felt the wind. The day he had picked was indeed a good day.

It was the time just before autumn turned into winter. The sky was clear, the wind gentle, and the sun bright. Madam Wolp'o made Myŏng-ku go with them as the donkey handler. She made sumptuous lunch boxes for all three of them. Sitting on the borrowed donkey, wearing an overcoat and a hat, Yi looked like a dignified court official.

Around nine o'clock in the morning, Yi left on the donkey led by Myŏng-ku. In the fields, white-clad farmers were here and there, sowing wheat and barley. Others were busy getting mulberry bushes ready for the winter.

As the donkey trod on a quiet narrow path, the bells around its neck tinkled merrily. Neither Yi nor Myŏung-ku said anything until they came upon the Sŏwun Temple.

"This is an absolutely beautiful day. I've traveled through three countries in Asia, but I never saw finer autumn weather than the Korean autumn weather. Heaven put too many rugged mountains in our small peninsula, but heaven also gave us this kind of autumn."

Yi looked up appreciatively at the cloudless blue sky. There were dragonflies flitting around in the warm sun.

"Uncle, did you ever go up the Paektu Mountain?" asked Myŏng-ku, who had learned of this tall mountain in grade school.

"Of course, I did. That magnificent mountain is the mountain of all mountains."

Yi leaned his head back to see the top of Mt. Pohyŏn, but the Kyeyang Pass was blocking his view.

"Mt. Paektu, as you know, means White Top Mountain. And

it is indeed white. It's not white because it is covered with snow, but because it is covered with white volcanic rocks. Myŏng-ku, my boy, try to imagine a mountain two and a half times taller than Mt. Pohyŏn and a huge crystal clear lake on top. Just imagine how magnificent and awesome it must be! If you went up there and looked into that deep lake, you'd feel as if the whole universe were in the lake and the lake could see through you. Suddenly you'd feel breathless and tears would well up in your eyes. You'd feel so small in the face of this supreme cosmic mystery. You'd also feel a deep sorrow because Koreans, traditionally white-clad by preference, could not call this white mountain their own. When I climbed it, it was under the Japanese occupation. But I tasted the water of the lake and yelled at the top of my lungs, 'Long Live Korean Independence!' Now those old days are the mere memories of an old man."

Yi's reminiscence caused small ripples in the brilliant autumn air.

"I hope I might go up the Paektu Mountain someday."

"Unless the country is unified, it will be impossible. But then, by the time you get to be my age, perhaps...."

"Like you and Kim Sat-kat, I want to roam around, to Manchuria, Japan, and the whole wide world, roaming to my heart's content," Myŏng-ku said. At that time a popular song, "Kim Sat-kat," the name of the legendary romantic and wandering poet, was sung in every part of the country.

"Roam around? I haven't heard such words in a long time. A man should go out into the wide world, to see and learn as much as he can. In my case, I barely managed to survive. I merely wasted time, I'm afraid."

"Since you stayed for so long in Manchuria and China, you must have had much hardship. Uncle, if you don't have money or acquaintances in a strange country, what is the most important thing you need in order to survive?"

Myŏng-ku had made up his mind to leave Ibam as soon as the winter was over, so his question was not an idle hypothetical one. He meant it.

"In order to survive with empty hands in a strange place, you must have guts and quick perception. You need guts to endure hardship and sorrow, to overcome them and to proceed to your goal. At the same time, you need to be quick not to cause hostility in others and to get food."

Yi gave Myŏng-ku a mischievous grin. "My words are drawn from actual experiences, you know."

Yi's grin was an odd mixture of staring into the other's eyes, and sneering. It reminded Myŏng-ku of the bedroom scene he had witnessed through the peep hole. Madam Wolp'o used to say to him,"When you smile that provocative smile of yours, I feel hot and sexy down here." Myŏng-ku looked at his face more closely. His face muscles were smooth and bouncy like fish cakes, and his eyes were lewd and leering. His cheeks looked like two cheeks of a baby's bottom or two halves of a ripe peach.

"Uncle, I may be quick, but I am not gutsy. How can you become more gutsy? Is there a way?"

"Gutsiness and quickness are something you are born with. If you are not born with them, you need a lot of experience to acquire them. However, there is one thing you can do, and that is to learn to fight well."

"Fight?" Myŏng-ku looked at Yi with uncomprehending eyes.

"Even if you don't cause fights, you'll be forced to fight. Besides, a man must have a sense of adventure. Once you get involved in a fight, you must win. Otherwise you may lose your life."

"Were you a good fighter, Uncle?"

On every market day there were invariably at least a couple of fist fights, so Myŏng-ku had seen his share of fights in the past three years. But he had never seen Yi get involved in a fight.

"Yes, I was, if I may say so. I didn't really learn to fight except to pick up a few tricks. You have to be smart, first of all. My trick was to attack my opponent suddenly, before he was ready. If words could not solve a problem, I would butt him in the face with my head. Then no matter how strong the other guy might be, he was bound to cover his face. At that moment, I would kick him in the crotch." Yi sounded like a young street fighter.

"But how can you do that if there is more than one opponent?"

"In that case, you run away. As the old '36 Ways to Fight' tells you, running away is one of the basic strategies. When the enemy outnumbers you, you must run away for your life. Whatever danger you may be in, you must keep a cool head. If overpowered, you must act as meek as a lamb in order to get by the critical moments. If you happen to be superior, you bluff and swagger as if you had an army behind you."

"However," Yi suddenly changed the subject, "to survive in an alien country, you need at least one skill. It will make your life a lot easier."

"What skill?" Myŏng-ku asked, remembering the gossip about Yi's bedroom skills.

"A man must learn a skill to make a living, you know. For example, carpentery, automobile driving, salesmanship. You need a lot of knowledge. At least learn a beggar's chant that will help you get food. As for me, I had no skill. I was an aimless wanderer, but I knew a hand trick or two that I used at crucial moments."

Yi smiled at Myŏng-ku. It was the same weird smile.

"What kind of hand tricks?"

"Don't get me wrong. What I mean by hand tricks are such skills as cheating at card games, making two eggs out of one, and sticking a chopstick into a wine glass and lifting it, and...."

"You mean you can do magic tricks?" Myŏng-ku interrupted him, laughing like a child.

"Sure. I learned a few tricks while traveling around in Manchuria."

"But I've never seen you doing any of the tricks."

"Why should I? I am not starving or cold. Tricks are desperate measures."

"The egg trick is getting another egg that you hid in your sleeve, isn't it?"

"A magic trick is no longer magic if you know the secret."

"How do you do the chopstick and wine glass trick?"

"Well, we have nothing to do now, so I'll tell you a story. It was in Kilim, Manchuria. For days I survived on bad food I begged on the street. I was famished. I had no money, absolutely none. I went to a street of cafes and restaurants and finally entered a small shabby kaegwan."

"What is a kaegwan?"

"It is a restaurant. I thought I'd use some of my tricks. I also thought that eating to my heart's content and being sent to a jail were better than dying of starvation. I walked in and looked around to see if there was anyone I could fool. Then I spotted two middle-aged Chinese men at a table, drinking hard liquor and talking.

They looked like they were half drunk already. And the way they ordered side dishes showed that they had money. So I walked over to a table next to theirs and ordered a bottle of the same liquor and a bowl of Ch'wan-yang-rou."

"What on earth is that?"

"It is a Chinese stew of lamb meat. And just to attract the attention of as many people as I could, I began my chopstick trick, loudly bragging." Chinese chopsticks are much thicker and longer than ours. Chinese are people of a huge country, as you know, and things they use are bigger. I poured the liquor into a glass, stuck a chopstick into it, lifted the glass with the stick, and drank the liquor. It looked like I was drinking the liquor out of a ladle. The two men looked at me curiously and then tried to imitate me. Of course, they failed. So I told them that I would drink their liquor with my chopstick. They said okay. They said if I succeeded, they would pay for my liquor. Chinese are famous for betting. They bet on everything. So I put my chopstick into one of their glasses, lifted it and drank. Everyone in the restaurant watched me and applauded. One of the two men got suspicious and suggested that he try with my chopstick."

"So what did you do?" Myŏng-ku was so interested in the story that he almost tripped over a stone in the path.

"Mind you, such a moment was critical. Of course, he would succeed if he used my chopstick. So instead of handing over my chopstick to him, I used another chopstick. As I knew I would, I failed. Then I used the magic chopstick and succeeded."

"And people didn't find out right away that your chopstick was a special chopstick!" Myŏng-ku laughed. Myŏng-ku knew that Yi had carried around the special chopstick and replaced a restaurant chopstick with his own.

"So you see how it was. That chopstick was my very own. But my trick was to expose my trick on purpose. Such a strategy is a higher-level trick."

"Didn't they get mad at you? Didn't they call you a charlatan?"

"Of course, it was cheating. If you want to fool people, you must be very quick. When one of the Chinese men got suspicious, he demanded that I hand over my chopstick. At that moment, I said in a very dignified manner, 'Sir, it is a mere trick. I cannot let you pay for my liquor. If you use my chopstick, you'll be able to do it too. Therefore, I'll pay for your liquor.' Then I handed my chopstick to him. But the Chinese man must not have been very bright, because he dunked the chopstick only halfway down into the glass and tried to lift it. Of course, he failed. You see, there was a suction cup on the tip of my chopstick and you had to push it down firmly to the bottom of the glass. Anyway, the important thing was to get acquainted with these men by acting in a gentlemanly way. After that, I moved over to their table and began the real contest of who was to pay for the liquor and food."

"Oh, so your trick was a kind of sampler to attract their attention?"

Myŏng-ku had seen many shows, magic and otherwise, because troupes of drug peddlers, dancers, singers, and magicians often came to Ibam on market days. They always showed easy tricks in the beginning to arouse everyone's curiosity and interest, and then did everything to postpone the really hard ones.

"When you want to get acquainted with a stranger, the first and most important thing is to make him trust you. Remember this always. If you looked honest and sincere and you were, that's the best. Anyway, you cannot do anything unless people trust you. In a strange country, winning the trust of others is all the more important. You have to do everything you can to ease their suspicions of you. You must make them think that you are trustworthy and good at heart. Once you gain trust, you are in for a smooth path. For a liar like me, that first part of winning trust required all the mental concentration I could muster. The old saying that 'you should give your own liver' expresses what I'm trying to tell you. Once you win trust, you can say you've succeeded 90 percent."

"After the chopstick trick, what other tricks did you show them?" Myŏng-ku asked. He got bored with Yi's sermon.

"Shall I tell you what I showed them? The Chinese liquor bottle is a long-necked ceramic affair which we call here a goose-neck bottle. It is not big. Its body is not round but rather oblong and its mouth is the size of a small coin. I put this bottle on the edge of the table, in fact so close to the edge that it looked like it would topple over. Then I put a coin underneath the bottle. Next, I borrowed a big kitchen knife. The trick was to hit the coin off the table without toppling the bottle. The winner would be treated to free liquor."

"But that is not magic."

"As with all things in the world, a trick becomes a bore if it is repeated. You must always come up with new ones. The coin-hitting was a matter of mental concentration. You concentrate all of your energy for one second and use the knife as quickly as lightning flashes. Of course, make sure that your opponent tries first and fails. If you haven't practiced it, you will fail in ten out of ten tries. Remember to catch the falling bottle, too. Then you try your hand. The moment you succeed, you stick the knife hard into the table for dramatic effect and also for a threatening effect."

"When did you learn all that?"

"As I told you, I learned this while wandering around. They were useful for my survival."

"But those tricks were for older times. Nowadays people don't get fooled so easily."

"You are right. People were much more gullible then."

"If I go to a big city or a foreign country, I'll try to learn a solid and useful skill," Myŏng-ku said. He couldn't bring himself to say, "not like your tricks."

"That is a good idea. You have the right attitude," Yi said, but his boyishly enthusiastic expression was gone.

"By the way, did you succeed at the coin-hitting contest?" Myŏng-ku asked to encourage Yi, whose dark face was devoid of the enthusiasm he had had moments ago.

"Of course, I did. So I got a free meal, free liquor, and comfortable free lodging at the home of one of the Chinese men. His name was Song. Once you become acquainted with a group, you can stay around a few days at their expense. You teach them a card trick or two in return. Then as soon as you get some money, you go off, like a whiff of wind."

Myŏng-ku looked up and realized that they were near the Kyeyang Pass. The donkey was breathing hard, but he wasn't tired at all. He wanted to hear more stories.

Yi's stories, whether they were his own experiences or made-up tall tales, were endless. People would gather at Wolp'ook to listen to him. To the listener, whether a story was true or not didn't matter, because a story was a story listened to in order to kill time. They did not expect to experience or verify any of the incidents in it.

They thought, since their own lives were confined within a small village, that anything could happen in the open wide world, even weird things and unbelievable things. Besides, Yi was an excellent story teller. He had exaggerated gestures, an oratorical voice, and a special sing-song cadence that spellbound any listener even if the story itself happened to be ridiculously fantastic.

As Madam Wolp'o said once, if Yi drowned in a river, his

mouth would float up to the surface, his mouth being so special.

When Yi and Myŏng-ku arrived at the Odol Rocks, Mr. Choi was already smoking his pipe, sitting on a flat rock. The Odol Rocks were a group of rocks huddled together like soap bubbles. "Odol odol" was an onomatopaeic description of the bubbles.

"You look like some court official on parade," Mr. Choi said.

"Isn't it a beautiful day? Wouldn't it be wonderful to spend this day drinking fine wine and eating chrysanthemum cakes?" Yi looked around the scenery sitting atop the back of the donkey. Dry leaves and withered bushes made an exquisite picture under the brilliant sun.

Mr. Choi, in his cotton long-coat and hat, led the caravan. They followed a narrow trail south toward the Susŏk Mountain. The trail became narrower and deeper. After traversing the long winding path, they came upon an open valley across which they could see several round hills.

In the valley there was a village, sunken lower than Tuma-ri. Here nomadic farmers who burned land for cultivation had built a few cottages. During the war the village was deserted. When the war ended, a few villagers straggled back and lived there. Clean white clothes were on clothlines.

"How far is it from here?"

"About 5 ris. The last part has to be traversed on foot, so I want you to prepare yourself."

"The mountains here are more rugged than those in Hap'yŏng, but somehow they look snug and restful. Smaller mountains are huddled together like loving brothers and sisters, and the taller ones look like a screen to protect them," Yi continued to comment. The Susŏk Mountain, more than 800 meters tall, was gray with tall dense trees and rocks. In the distance, it loomed majestically.

"In the olden days when there were no airplanes, this kind of valley was an excellent refuge."

"It must have been. You can't see the inside from outside, but you can see the outside from inside."

"I don't know whether the guerrillas had a diviner with them, but they were very good at finding the right hiding places. That's why the Red guerrillas dug caves and built forts here."

"I've heard that Mt. Chiri is such a mountain. From afar it looks rugged and sad, the form of an old man with a heavy load on his back, but once you get in it, it is comfortable and generous like a mother's bosom. Besides, you can hide in it easily, I've been told."

"Whoever told you that was telling you the truth. In South Korea, Mt. Chiri and Mt. Kyeryong are such mountains. That's why those mountains have in their bosoms many sad and terrible secrets. If you get to know mountains, you'll find that certain mountains become mere sites for people's recreation or for vacation cottages of the rich, while other mountains become refuges for unjustly accused traitors who are pursued by authorities."

"If that's true, the Kŭmgang Mountains must be mountains for recreation and enjoyment because they are excessively decorative and beautiful."

"Mountains and rivers are the same as human beings. If a mountain is rarely visited by people, it is usually naive and timid. On the other hand, if a mountain is located conveniently for people to visit, it is usually decorative and smart-looking."

"So, the mountain you are going to must be naive and timid," said Yi, who laughed heartily into the clear air.

"Yes, it is a quiet, plain mountain. People can say whether a mountain is lucky or not by just looking at its shape. But they have a lot to learn. Even if a mountain is lucky, if it may not have good caves. Then so-called heavenly gifts such as a 'blue dragon on the left and a white tiger on the right' are of no use. On the other hand, even if a mountain has all these auspicious signs, if the mountain has exhausted its luck, they are useless."

"By the way, when and how did people begin to live in a deep mountain valley such as this one? My hometown Ttakpatkol has at least a road that is wide enough for a cart to navigate."

"Ibam and Tuma-ri were settled by people who took refuge here during the Japanese invasion of the Imjin Year. When the

Pyŏngja War broke out, more people came. There were those who got sick of the way the country was governed and took refuge here, with their families. Whenever there was a particularly bad administrator or a cruel landlord, people escaped into a deep, remote place where they could breathe freely, though their life might become harshier than before. They turned their backs on human affairs and went deep into the mountains."

"They sought a naive, timid mountain which would welcome them in its bosom?"

"Yes, you could say that. They worked on the rock-strewn barren fields, raising corn, potatoes, chickens and cotton. They lived in and with Nature."

"Then what made a person like me want so badly to leave and see the world? You yourself once had such a desire, you told me."

"It takes all kinds to make the world, I suppose. Almost everyone gets married and has children, but there are monks who sit and contemplate for years, facing a wall, without stepping out of a room even once in their lives. You know, life is a spider web. You happen to be on one thread. You traveled in the wide world but you came back to this remote mountain village. Who made you do that? As you say, human will has limitations. There are plants that become pet flowers in a wealthy man's garden and there are plants that live and die in this forsaken place."

"You are right. When I am buried in this deep mountain, who will remember that there lived a man named Yi In-t'ae? Even if someone happens to remember, what good would it do? I'll have rotted away in the soil. I'll be lying in a comfortable place and sleeping an eternal sleep." His high spirits gone, he said this as if reciting from a poem, and sighed deeply.

Mr. Choi became silent too. The only sound around came from the donkey's bells. On both sides of the trail, old gnarled pine trees spread their arms horizontally. From time to time, willow-warblers and yellow birds darted among tree branches and chirped their clear bell-like songs. Wild chrysanthemums, clustered together here and there, presented a refreshing autumn-al image.

"Master Choi," Yi called quietly after a long silence.

"What? You are not feeling well?"

"No, no. Look at those flowers there. Aren't they beautiful?"

"Yes, they are but they will soon wither away."

"That's what I wanted to say. Trees and plants become more majestic as they grow older, but why do men and animals become so ugly as they get older? I wonder. Compare a twisted old pine tree and a stooped old man. They are two extremes, two opposite poles, infinitely apart. It suddenly occurred to me."

"How true. Trees and plants gradually fulfil themselves and become more beautiful as they grow older, but humans and animals break down and decay. They become unsightly. While trees and plants know and keep their places, humans and animals fight and struggle. The former grow old gracefully whereas the latter fight and destroy themselves."

"That must be the reason why plants have pretty reproductive organs while human and animal reproductive organs are ugly. You know, a stamen and a pistil are so cute and pretty, but human and animal organs are really unsightly...."Yi looked down at Myŏng-ku and stopped his discourse.

"You don't sound like yourself today. Does this mean that you are going to live a beautiful life from now on, like trees and plants?"

"All my life I believed that when I died, everything else would disappear with me. But these days, I am beginning to think that one life can disappear like a puff of smoke and be gradually forgotten by everybody and everything."

"I've never believed in either the Christian or the Buddhist religion, but I never thought death was the end of living. Religion merely makes a man change his way of life."

"That means you believe in an after-life."

"Of course. If I didn't, why would I go around searching for a good burial site?"

"That's right. It just slipped my mind."

"I've learned a great deal from listening to your conversation," Myŏng-ku said, "but if I may speak my mind, as men are born to live with and among men, competing and fighting are unavoidable. They should not live like trees. They have to take action and win in the great struggle for survival."

"That is truly the idea of a young man. People in the world, especially the young, tend to take everything in a competitive spirit, which usually causes bloody conflicts and wars. But this attitude can also bring about scientific advances. But I do not think scientific advances are necessarily advances for the good of mankind. When you get old and sick, you realize that the best way to live is to live according to natural principles. Alas, it is usually too late when you realize this," Mr. Choi said.

"By the way, how is Kye-yŏn?" Myŏng-ku suddenly thought of her when Mr. Choi mentioned the decline of the human body.

"I've made up my mind not to worry too much. One's life span is decided by heaven up there," Mr. Choi said.

"Hey, you upstart of a young boy, you are no better than a nameless animal or a nameless plant! You are a mere errand boy at a tavern. Don't you know your place? How dare you speak the name of the daughter of a wise master?" Yi teased Myŏng-ku.

"The way you talk, you'll never get a good resting site," Mr. Choi joked along.

They passed two small houses with grass roofs and began to climb a 40-degree steep mountain trail. The donkey was tired. It blew out steamy breaths and brayed as it plodded with heavy steps. The trail was covered with coarse sand and eroded rock pieces, and the donkey slipped down the slope several times.

"It's just like the old saying that you follow a path hoping not to have to climb any mountains, but you end up going up one anyway," Yi said, holding tightly to the saddle.

"Now you have to get off the donkey. From here up, there is no trail," Mr. Choi said as he stopped under a huge oak tree.

Myŏng-ku halted the donkey. Yi carefully let himself down and untied his cane from the saddle. Mr. Choi walked in front, followed by Yi and Myŏng-ku with the donkey. They foraged through dense tangles of brush on uneven rough ground. It was an extremely strenuous walk for Yi, who nevertheless endured it with clenched teeth. He remembered his childish, shameful behavior the last time they went together, and he reminded himself that it might be the last outing for him before he died.

He fell into a reverie about his youthful days when he rode horses tirelessly over the rugged mountains of Manchuria. His dysfunctioning kidneys pulled him down like iron weights. He bit hard and said nothing.

As for Myŏng-ku, who had never handled a horse or donkey before, pulling the animal up the mountain was an impossible task. He wished he could tie the donkey to a tree and just carry the lunchboxes and the straw mat. But Yi said nothing.

"How much farther do we have to go?" Yi finally asked as he could not take it any longer. He was out of breath. His yellowish swollen face was drenched with sweat.

"Over this hill and to the south."

"Don't hurry so. I'm not going there to be buried today."

As Yi spoke they sat down in the shade of a tree. The two men smoked pipes. A light breeze coming through the bushes dried their sweat. It was very pleasant. After a few minutes of rest, they resumed their climb, this time turning around the hill to the south.

By the time they arrived at the site, it was almost 11 o'clock. The sun was straight over their heads. While climbing, Mr. Choi chanted and mumbled the funeral song "Talgujil Song," whose mournful tune must have been unsettling to his friend.

"It will be very hard for pallbearers to bring my coffin up here," Yi said in an obviously dispirited way. He was weak and he knew his body would be carried up here in the near future. His swollen yellow face was overcast with sadness. His gasping breath came out often with heavy sighs. Tears gathered in the corners of his eyes.

"It is too high up on this steep mountain, but it does look like a good site. There is hardly any wind," Yi said, staring down at the spot Mr. Choi pointed to with his cane. The soil there was dark red in color and looked rich.

"According to P'ungsu divining principles, the best site is a site that draws water and stops the wind. A dead person depends on 'Ki'(spirit or vitality), and this 'Ki' is scattered by the wind and comes alive with water. A truly good site is protected from the wind. In a famous book written by Kwak Pok of the Chin Dynasty, it was said that water leads to vital places, and a vital place is always with water. It also says that there should be no wind to scatter the vital spirit. Water is the antithesis of wind. In short, water gives vitality."

"How true. Especially for a man like me, wind should be kept away. I don't care about vitality, and I certainly won't want colorless, formless wind sweeping around," Yi nodded.

"The water down in the valley is from the Susŏk River. That river flows into the Chayang River. According to P'ungsu, a mountain is Yin, and water is Yang. Yin is static and Yang is movement. In other words, a mountain is static while water is mobile. The principle of Yin is form, and the principle of Yang is change. Water, being Yang, symbolizes the ups and downs of life. Therefore, when one decides on one's resting place, one should always look for water nearby."

Mr. Choi looked at his friend, expecting some sort of rebuttal, but there was no word from him. Closely observed, Yi's deep eyes were full of quiet resignation, the deep lines in his forehead resembling the thick bark of an old tree. For a moment Mr. Choi thought "Maybe this friend of mine is becoming like an old tree." Yet the stooped figure, the swollen yellow face with its gaping mouth exposing sickly yellow-green teeth, definitely were parts of an ugly old animal.

Yi gazed down at the valley without a word. The river flowing along the flat land was the Susŏk River, and over the river to the right stood a tall rocky mountain that was the Susŏk Mountain. On the west side of the mountain was a smooth slope that was like "the red peacock." "The white tiger and the blue dragon" of various peaks stretched like ocean waves, gradually sloping down the valley. In the background, there was a master peak, above which stood an even bigger master peak. This larger peak had a smooth, rounded top like the bald pate of its gazer.

"Look at that blue dragon on the left. It is beautifully rounded and sloped. If the blue dragon is too long, your posterity will move around much. If it is suddenly cut off or has a sharp hump, there will be someone in your posterity who will die abroad. But that blue dragon doesn't have either trait." Mr. Choi wanted to add a few more words to this, but didn't say anything because Yi was standing still, not paying attention to him.

In the meantime, Myŏng-ku took down the mat and lunchboxes. Under an enormous pine tree, he spread the mat and set the lunchboxes down in the middle. He knelt down on one corner of the mat.

"These silent mountains...," Yi whispered to himself.

"Now why don't you come and sit down? Are you going to be lonely here in this silent, deep mountain?" The two men sat on the mat facing each other.

"Well...," Yi took out a cigarette box from an inside pocket of his long coat. No one would be happy looking at his own burial site, but Yi's face was touched with profound pathos. He wore an expression of quiet sorrow.

"In another book called Sŏlshimbu, there are these words," Mr. Choi began, "there are two conditions required for a good burial site. The first is 'chŏk-tŏk', which means that one must have done much good for one's fellow men. In short, an accumulation of good deeds is an essential condition. It is said that good land is in the hands of heaven, and a good man can read the will of heaven. If a person has the insight to find his own resting place, that is good. Heaven knows that he is a man who has done much good. In principle then, a man who has not accumulated good deeds cannot have a good burial place."

"What are you talking about? You never said that before. In that case, a bad man can never be allowed to go down a good man's path. That's what Jesus said."

Yi's face took on an ugly expression. He looked like a man

suddenly hit by a devastating blow. He was desperate.

"What's wrong? Haven't you ever done anything good for others? All you did was sin?" Mr. Choi looked straight into his friend's eyes.

"You know my whole life story. I've never done any good for anyone."

Yi's hands were shaking like those of a stroke victim.

"Wasn't it a good deed to volunteer for the Independence Army and help save our country?"

"I was in it only for two short years."

"The length of time doesn't matter. Your intentions and dedication are what was important."

"I was a lowly soldier in the Army and I didn't do much, very little, as a matter of fact."

"According to P'ungsu, there is another condition that applies to men who have not done much good in life."

"Good. Unless you are a wise man, accumulating good deeds isn't easy. As you explained to me, P'ungsu started when men buried their dead instead of eating them, and there is a long history of burial. In this long history someone must have come up with certain secret methods of good burials. Men cannot find their own resting places, which is why they need diviners," Yi said and smiled, relieved at the new revelation.

"But you are not entirely right. Of the two conditions, the second necessitates the wise selection of a P'ungsu master. In other words, if you find a wise master, he will find you a good site. It was also written that Nature exposes her love for all to see."

"That last part is hard to understand."

"It means that Nature gives her love without hiding anything, but it is up to men to find a right place. A P'ungsu master is a human being like everyone else, so he might not have done much good in his life. And a man seeking his resting place may not have been a good man either. But the selected master is affected by him and may not find a good site," Mr. Choi said very seriously.

Every time members of a grieving family asked him to find a site, Mr. Choi told them the same thing. He also added that because he himself had done little good for others he might not be able to find a good site. In such cases, he would beg for understanding and forgiveness.

In truth, he firmly believed that a man who lived a good, honest and upright life, would be given, by heaven, a fine resting place. Furthermore, for such a man, heaven would guide the P'ungsu master to the right place. All the master would have to do would be to perceive heaven's will and follow it humbly.

But how could a man do only good deeds in this hard world? He himself had lived years of conflict, struggling between self-interest and altruism.

After listening to Mr. Choi, Yi hung his head and didn't move. Whether it was his illness or some psychological conflict, his nostrils flared and his face became full of pain. Looking at the pathetic man Mr. Choi regretted for a moment what he had told him, but changed his mind. It was something he would have had to tell him sooner or later.

"Sirs, why don't we have lunch now?" Myŏng-ku opened the wooden boxes, but neither of them paid any attention to him. Ants began to crawl on the boxes, so Myŏng-ku had to close them.

"There is definitely no way out for me," Yi mumbled to himself.

"What do you mean by 'no way out'?"

"Your words are the very words of wise men like Confucius. The problem is that I see absolutely no way out for me." Yi raised his teary eyes and looked imploringly at Mr. Choi.

"Master Choi, no matter what happens, please find me a genuinely good site. Since you have known all those excellent things, you must have accumulated several good deeds. Though you may not have made spectacular contributions to this world as some men have, you must have lived in accordance with the cosmic principles. Ever since I met you, I've believed that you must have."

"Maybe that is how I came upon this spot. This site lacks what we call the Master Peak, but Korea's Master Peak is the Paektu Mountain. Unless you are buried on Paektu, this is as good a site as any. Besides, there are very few special people worthy of a burial on Mt. Paektu."

"By the way, where is your family burial plot?" Yi changed the subject suddenly.

"In Tuma-ri. Why do you ask?"

"What is your estimation of your own family plot?"

"It has been there for six generations. It is what we call a Medium Master Peak. Though I may not be completely satisfied with it, I have no intentions of moving it to another site," Mr. Choi answered. In a flash, he was caught by the feeling that Yi was about to criticize his new site.

"Maybe I shouldn't say this, but if something happened to your daughter, would you bury her there?" Yi's eyes were intently observing Mr. Choi's reaction.

"What? Say it again!" Mr. Choi shouted angrily. Actually, when he had come upon this site while hunting for snakes for his daughter, he had thought of her. The site was precious. Why in hell did he ask that? Mr. Choi was furious.

"Come, come. I just wondered if you had a special site for her in mind." Yi was taken aback by his friend's vehement reaction.

"Frankly speaking, when I discovered this site, I thought it was too good for you," Mr. Choi said, and stood up glaring at Yi. His eyes reflected contempt for the sick man.

"Please, please, that is not what I meant. Come on, that's enough. I've made up my mind. This is it. Now, will you have lunch?" Yi apologized and pulled Mr. Choi's pants leg.

"Listen, there are just certain things you must never say. How could you be so irresponsible, huh?" Mr. Choi sat down, his anger subsiding.

"I'm sorry. I'm truly sorry. Even in this condition, I can't let go of this obsession. I'm really sorry."

Yi was secretly satisfied with Mr. Choi's reaction because it was what he had expected when he had asked the terrible question.

"Well, when I heard people say that there were snakes near the Susŏk River, I came here to gather some firewood and...," Mr. Choi stopped himself. He couldn't bring himself to say that he had thought of recommending the site to his future in-laws if Kye-yŏn got married.

"Myŏng-ku, bring the lunchboxes here. Master Choi must be very hungry. Please forgive me and forget what I asked. I know this mouth of mine has caused a lot of trouble," Yi said again, yet that mysterious smile hovered around his lips.

After lunch they looked around the surrounding area of the site, and descended down the hill. The sun was setting behind the Pohyŏn Mountain when they finally arrived near Ibam. Mr. Choi had gone off toward Tuma-ri after they had parted at the Odol Rocks.

"Thank you for everything you have done today. Please come to Ibam next market day, I'll treat you to a day of drinking," Yi called out to Mr. Choi.

"I don't know about coming next market day. I'll drop by one of these days, as I am planning to go away on a rather long trip very soon," Mr. Choi answered and tipped his hat at his friend.

Once Yi and Myŏng-ku began their descent, Myŏng-ku realized that coming down was much harder than going up. The donkey slipped and slid, and each time it slid Myŏng-ku had to hang tightly on and pull it back up. His palms were skinned and his legs ached. He thought however that this kind of struggle was good exercise for his planned flight to a big city, where he knew he would face greater hardships.

Pulling back the donkey with all his might, he said to himself that this was an experience he might find handy someday. In the meantime, Yi was sitting on the donkey's back without a thought in his head. He was swaying every which way, like a drunken official on his way home after a party. He yawned loudly and began to doze. He nearly toppled down when Myŏng-ku finally warned him.

"Please, be careful, you're going to fall."

"Ummm, all right. Go down slowly," Yi mumbled and swayed and nodded again. He had been suffering from insomnia, and the night before he had not slept a wink having been so excited for today's trip.

By the time they arrived at a forked road, with one path leading to the Sŏwun Temple, the sun had gone down and the evening breeze was quite chilly. Myŏng-ku was hot from his unfamiliar struggle with the donkey, but Yi looked cold, his shoulders hunched. Yi looked up and saw the sign for the Sŏwun Temple.

"It's still a long time before dinner, isn't it?" he asked.

"Yes, Uncle. But we are almost back in Ibam. Over there is the Chayang River."

"Why don't we drop by the Sŏwun Temple?"

"Why should we?"

"I want to see the chief priest."

"You are not going to church any more?" Myŏng-ku asked trying to stop the donkey.

"I know I won't be admitted to Nirvana, but I'd like to find out whether there are ways to prevent being thrown into an eternal sulphuric fire. I want to ask the master monk."

"But it is such a steep climb up to the temple that I'm not sure this donkey can make it."

"I know, but this is a rare outing that I am enjoying."

Myŏng-ku turned the donkey onto the path going north toward the temple. The Sŏwun Temple was located halfway up the Tal Mountain, facing south. It was about a ten minute walk from where they were.

In 1950 and 1951 when the war was at its climax in this area, the temple had been deserted. Now there was a Master Priest in his mid-40's, an old monk who did the kitchen work, and an errand boy of thirteen or so who lived there.

As a small temple, it had had five or six monks at the most, even before the war. As Myŏng-ku and Yi stepped onto a heavily wooded trail, it was quite dark. Between the trees, they noticed stone steps.

"I'm not sure this donkey can climb those steps," Yi said and leaned over to ask Myŏng-ku.

"I'm not either."

Myŏng-ku stepped in front of the donkey and pulled its rein. The donkey tried to go up but its hind legs kept slipping down. Yi was afraid of sliding off its back, so he leaned forward and hung tightly to its back.

"This is too dangerous. I'm afraid I may fall backward. I'll get down and walk." Yi got down, shaking visibly.

"Uncle, it's getting late. Can't we go there some other time?"

"No, I can't. I've got to see the Master."

He took down his cane from the saddle. He felt as if he were going to collapse at any moment, but he was determined to go to the temple. He walked in front. The stone steps were not even, and fallen leaves covered them.

Yi was barely managing to put one foot above the other, when his foot fell into a crack under the leaves. He fell over. When Myŏng-ku helped him up, he was gasping.

"Can't you just invite the Reverend to your home?" Myŏng-ku asked. Yi's eyes held a cold determined look.

"I always do what I set out to do! Let's go," Yi said in a surprisingly strong voice.

"All right, Uncle."

Myŏng-ku wanted to escape Yi's flashing eyes, so he held the donkey's rein in one hand and supported Yi with the other. Myŏng-ku was exhausted.

There were 50 steps. Another path opened up to a dirt road. Yi and Myŏng-ku, who had visited the temple on the last Buddha's birthday, knew that there was another flight of stairs before the temple.

"There's somebody coming down," Myŏng-ku said. They both looked up and saw two women in white mourning clothes, and a small boy.

"Good heavens, what are you doing here, Mr. Yi?" the older woman exclaimed in a husky voice. The young woman holding the child's hand hung her head down.

"Oh, Mrs. Han. Did you offer prayers today?"

"Yes, today is the anniversary of my son's death."

The old woman put her handkerchief to her mouth and began to sob. She was the wife of a tenant farmer of the Kwon family. Her son was drafted in the first year of the war and was killed about this time the year before. The young woman and the child were his widow and son.

"Is the Reverend in?" Yi asked.

"No. He left around noon. He said he had some business at the main temple," Mrs. Han answered, her eyes still full of tears.

"Then it's no use going up there."

Yi had to turn back. Myŏng-ku let out a sigh of relief.

CHAPTER VI

A week after he showed the burial site to Yi, Mr. Choi left Tuma-ri to visit his son at the Army Hospital in Taegu. He had been planning this trip for a long time ever since his last visit in the summer. A few days earlier he had sold some of the fall harvest for a good price and had made enough money for the trip. He left Tuma-ri late one afternoon and spent the night at Wolp'ook.

That night, before he went to bed, Myŏng-ku took 800 hwan out of his savings and gave it to Mr. Choi, who refused to accept it. Myŏng-ku finally persuaded him and put it in Mr. Choi's vest pocket.

The railway ticket prices had jumped three times, and a ticket from Pusan to Seoul, third class, cost 739 hwan. And 800 hwan was the entire sum of Myŏng-ku's two months' salary.

Myŏng-ku, handing over the money to Mr. Choi, asked him to look around the Pongdŏk-dong area near the American army base, and the Ch'imsan-dong factory district. Two years ago he had heard a rumour that his mother was living in one of the two areas. Myŏng-ku's request was so sincere and heartfelt that Mr. Choi reluctantly accepted the money.

"Sir, in a big city like Taegu, there must be pharmacies that

might have miracle drugs for people like Kye-yŏn," Myŏng-ku
said, blushing in spite of himself. Mr. Choi realized then that
Myŏng-ku was giving him money to use at least a portion of it
for Kye-yŏn's medicine. Mr. Choi felt all the more hesitant to
take the money.

"Even if I have to stay an extra day in Taegu, I'll look around
those places to get some information about your mother. Now,
take this money back," Mr. Choi said and took it out of his vest
pocket.

"No, no, please. If you find my mother, give it to her."

Myŏng-ku knew that trying to find his mother in Taegu was
like hunting for a pearl in a river, but he had to say this to make
Mr. Choi accept his money.

"All right, then. I'll try my best." Mr. Choi put the bills back
in his pocket, eyeing Myŏng-ku's height and body size. He knew
he couldn't spend the money on any personal use.

The next morning, Suk-kyŏng got up early and made him
breakfast—a hot bowl of soup and rice.

"Master Choi, this isn't much but I'd appreciate it if you'd
take it," said Yi, following his friend to the gate, putting two 100
hwan bills in Mr. Choi's hand. Wearing a cotton coat and a hat,
Mr. Choi had a cane in one hand and a bundle of rice cakes and
cookies in the other. Myŏng-ku walked with him to the edge of
the village. "Sir, I've heard that there are many pickpockets in
the city. Please be careful." he said.

If Mr. Choi rode a bus to P'ohang to catch a train to Taegu,
it would be a long detour, so in order to save on expenses, he
had decided to walk to Yŏngch'ŏn. In the old days when there
were no buses, people in Ibam used to walk to the Yŏngch'ŏn
market to do special shopping for weddings, funerals, and
family rites. When they had to go to Taegu, they took the same
route.

The road from Ibam to Yŏngch'ŏn along the Chayang River
was about 70 ris. It was the same road that Yi had taken eight
years ago.

The 40-ri distance from Ibam to Chayang was an unpaved

road, only wide enough for horse carts but not for buses. But the road from Chayang to Yŏngch'ŏn was a wide busy road on which many trucks and buses traveled. If you held up your hand, a truck would invariably give you a ride. When you reached Yŏngch'ŏn, you usually gave some lunch money to the driver.

It took Mr. Choi three hours to get to Chayang, where he got a ride on the back of a truck. He arrived in Yŏngch'ŏn, covered with dust, but it was a good ride. From Yŏngch'ŏn he took a bus to Taegu and arrived there around 2:30. The bus terminal was crowded. As Myŏng-ku had warned, he was wary of pickpockets, and his attention was constantly on the money pouch he had tied around his waist.

Mr. Choi went to the Army Hospital located in an old medical school complex, and requested a visit with his son. After twenty minutes, his son appeared in a wheel-chair, pushed by a nurse. His leg had already been amputated. The left leg of his pants was empty.

As he had received a letter more than a month before, that his son's leg was going to be amputated, he wasn't shocked. Even so, a cold chill went down his spine. Hak-su said he would be fitted with an artificial leg and released in a month or so. Even if Hak-su had an artificial leg and crutches, he would still have to be carried across the river just like his sister. Thinking of this, Mr. Choi couldn't help silently lamenting over his hard luck. Perhaps their family burial plot was in the wrong place, he mused.

"My son, you're all right in that part, aren't you?" As soon as the nurse left, Mr. Choi asked the same question he had asked during his last visit. He was looking at his son's lower abdomen. Hak-su was puzzled at first and then shyly realized what his father meant.

"I know you haven't had a chance to use it, but you know, don't you?"

The last time he saw Hak-su, Hak-su had answered him that the rest of his body was fine, but he wanted to make sure.

"It seems to be all right, but..." Hak-su answered with a slight sad smile on his pale, gaunt face.

"Thank heavens. I was so worried about the ceasing of our family line that I haven't slept at night. There are your healthy cousins, but you are the eldest of the main line," Mr. Choi said and smiled at his son.

"How can I marry a girl when I am in this condition? I'd rather live alone with you and Mother. I may not be able to do field work, but I can weave straw sacks and do such things."

"Don't say such a thing. Everyone in the world has a mate. I promise I'll find a fine girl for you," Mr. Choi said.

"At first, I wanted to die, Father. But some of my buddies, who were in worse shape than I, fought hard to live. They gave me courage."

"You are right, my son. You must live. You must. You'll live a good life and have several healthy beautiful children. People want to live in big cities, but Tuma-ri isn't bad at all. It has fine mountains, clean water, and good people. The war was terrible but it won't happen again, I pray. Heaven and our ancestors will watch over our family, I'm sure."

Mr. Choi held his son's hand tightly and fought back tears. He was thankful that his son wanted to come back to live in Tuma-ri. He was ashamed that he had once hoped his children would leave the god-forsaken village and live in better places. Tears were welling up in his eyes which he fought back as best as he could.

The visitors' lounge was filled with sounds of sobbing and weeping. Families were letting out their pent-up sorrows over their wounded sons. There were blind ones wearing dark glasses, and armless ones with their torsos all bandaged. Compared with them, Hak-su was much better off, Mr. Choi thought.

He stayed with his son for half an hour. The nurse came back to tell him that visiting hours were over and that it was time for dinner. Mr. Choi gave Hak-su 2,000 hwan and the bundle of goodies to share with his roommates. Hak-su tried to give the money back to his father, but Mr. Choi said, "You'll need it when you are released from the hospital. Besides, beef-bone stew is good for healing bones. If you can order it from outside, please do. I'll come back tomorrow. On my way here, I thought I had so much to tell you, but I don't know what to say now."

"Why don't you go home today? Staying at an inn costs money."

"I have some things to do yet in Taegu. I'll see you tomorrow."

Mr. Choi left the lounge with an aching heart. When he looked around to see his son again, the nurse was wheeling him down the corridor. He caught a glimpse of his son's hands wiping tears from his eyes. He too, must have fought hard not to show tears to his father. Mr. Choi was glad that he hadn't told him about Kye-yŏn's illness.

It wasn't yet six o'clock, but it was already dark. Chilly winds were sweeping fallen leaves on the paved street. Mr. Choi stood at the hospital gate, not knowing which of the two places to go to first. He decided to go to Pongdŏk-dong near the American Army base. He asked a passerby for directions to Pongdŏk-dong.

Three days later, Mr. Choi returned to Ibam. He walked all day from Yŏngch'ŏn and arrived in Ibam around five o'clock in the afternoon. The best thing that had happened to him on this trip was that he had had the luck of finding and buying the hard-to-get streptomycin at a Taegu pharmacy.

Mr. Choi was buying a winter jacket and black-dyed Army pants for Myŏng-ku when he happened to see a pharmacy. A middle-aged druggist explained that a drug called streptomycin would cure any kind of tuberculosis and veneral disease. But it was extremely hard to get. The druggist continued, "The antibiotics were invented by an American scientist named Waxman during the Second World War. A tuberculosis patient vomitting blood by the bucket could be cured by it. But it is very hard to get and very, very expensive. From what you told me, your daughter seems to be too far gone." The druggist said it might be already too late for Kye-yŏn. He explained that the drug, in tablet form or a liquid injection form came out of

American Army hospitals by illegal means in very small amounts. Mr. Choi begged him. He finally agreed to get some for Mr. Choi and told him to come back the next day.

The next day, as promised, the druggist had twenty tablets of streptomycin for Mr. Choi, who had to muster every penny he had brought to buy them. He also bought 200 hwan worth of kidney medicine for Yi. After he bought Myŏng-ku's clothes, he had 120 hwan left of the money My ŏng-ku had given him. This portion went to buying Kye-yŏn's medicine.

"Did you find out anything about my mother?" Myŏng-ku asked. He was surprised by the new clothes and deeply touched by Mr. Choi's thoughtfulness. In fact, he was so touched that tears came to his eyes.

"The American Army base in Pongdŏk-dong was huge. I visited every laundry in front of and behind the base. Nobody had heard of a woman from Yŏngch'ŏn or P'ohang. So the next day I went to Ch'imsan-dong where I looked in on every factory and eating place. Then, in one small tavern, I got lucky. I was told that your mother had worked there up until two years ago."

"Really?" Myŏng-ku moved closer to Mr. Choi.

"The news is not good, I'm afraid...," Mr. Choi fell silent and took out his tobacco pouch.

"Well, we'll see. Please tell me."

"According to the owner of the tavern, your mother left with a man who had come down south during the war. This northern-er used to have his meals there. He was said to be a junk dealer. Then sometime later your mother dropped by the place once, but didn't say where she lived. I didn't know what else to do, so I left your address with the owner and asked him to let you know if she ever dropped by again."

"Thank you very much. That is good enough news for me. Once I get a job and live in Taegu, I'm sure I'll find her one way or another." Myŏng-ku wiped his tears. In his heart he was disappointed that his mother had remarried.

Mr. Choi gave the kidney medicine to Yi, who took a small bottle out of a wall cabinet and showed it to Mr. Choi. "I never told you about this, but I too, have had this medicine for some time." It was a steroid hormone.

"I got this from a man who used to travel to big cities. But I found that there are diseases that can be cured and those that cannot be. Even people who have had every imaginable medicine poured into them, die with many regrets. Even an 80-year-old man may not die with a thankful heart for his longevity," Yi said, smiling sadly.

Autumn was short and winter was long in this deep mountain village. When the temperatures plunged below zero, pigeons and other birds came nearer to the village, as if seeking human warmth, and the cries of swans high up in the air seemed lonelier than ever before.

Yi's illness worsened to such an extent that it was very hard for him to go to the outdoor lavatory. His whole body was swollen like a balloon. He stayed in bed day and night. Madam Wolp'o urged him to get up and take a few steps at least once a day, but his reply was, "I'm dying. I've given up."

"I have no energy to please you at night or any strength to upbraid you. For eight years you've fed me and clothed me, for which I am very grateful. My gratitude will continue over to the other side of my grave," Yi said to the Madam.

As winter deepened, Mr. Choi had no reason to come to Ibam, and often skipped market days. Once in a while, he came and visited his friend. On such rare occasions, Yi would merely hold his hands and silently cry.

"My burial spot must be frozen over in this weather. These days that's the only thing I think about. If I die before the winter is over, everyone will have an awful time carrying me up there and burying me. You are the last true friend I've got. Will you go and look at the place for me?" he pleaded.

"Listen, my friend. No one can take it away. What's the use of going there? Besides, you are going to be here for quite a while."

Despite Mr. Choi's consoling and occasional scolding, Yi kept worrying about his funeral, his burial, and his after-life. He wondered aloud whether he would be forgiven for his sins if he were buried in a favorable site.

"Since you repent so much, I'm sure you are already forgiven. Stop worrying and start trying to gain some strength," Mr. Choi said.

Frost-covered cabbages had been collected from the fields for *kimjang,* the annual winter kimch'i-making. One day Mr. Choi brought red peppers and garlic to sell at the Ibam market. As he crossed the river, he was met by a quick middleman who bought diretly from farmers and sold for a profit to the market. The prices the man offered for Mr. Choi's produce were 30 percent less than he had expected. However, Mr. Choi thought, if he were to stand at a corner of the market, he would have to pay for use of the market space, and there was the possibility that he might not be able to sell at all. So Mr. Choi decided to accept the middleman's offer. As soon as he had the money in his pouch, he went straight to Wolp'ook. It was near lunch time when he arrived.

He went into the living quarters and noticed a pair of unfamiliar black rubber shoes. He coughed a couple of times to let his presence be known.

"Is that you, Master Choi?" Yi's voice called.

In the room, facing Yi, sat a Buddhist monk in his monk's robe.

"I knew you'd come today. Let me introduce you." Yi introduced him to the monk. Mr. Choi noticed his friend's worried face and weak voice signaling that his condition had deteriorated.

"This humble monk's name is Pŏbŭn, from the Sŏwun Temple," the monk folded his hands in front and bowed. He had clean-cut strong features.

"Today I invited the Reverend and learned a few words from Buddha," Yi said, and let out a heavy sigh. "After listening to him, my heavy heart has became ten times heavier."

"Exaggeration! How can you say a thing like that before the Reverend? Have you ever seen a man escape death by exaggerating his suffering?"

"Mr. Yi asked me to tell him the basic rules of conduct to be observed by all men, so I told him. I told him what Buddha taught," the monk said in a clear, ringing voice.

"My friend, I have lived all this time and abided by not one of the four basic principles. No, I have not only not abided by them but also have broken each and every one of them. Therefore I can see as clearly as I see the day that I'll be thrown down to a bottomless pit of fire.

The first rule was 'do not fornicate.' I didn't know it was the first, though I knew it was there somewhere. Ascetic exercises without discarding sexual desires are like cooking sand, because the sand will never become rice no matter how long one cooks it. Second was 'do not kill living creatures,' third, 'do not steal,' and fourth, 'do not lie.' I've lived all my life doing all these 'don'ts!' So, even if I am to be buried in an excellent place, it will be of no use."

Yi wiped tears from the corners of his eyes. Mr. Choi could do nothing but look at his friend in slight embarrassment. He felt like a person dragged into a lawsuit between two friends. He regretted that he hadn't gone straight back home. But he couldn't just get up and leave either.

"Carnal desire is the very source of life and death. All living creatures are born by it, but with different tempers and temperaments.

Samsara, transmigration, comes from it too. Moreover, because of it, love and hatred are born. If the object of one's love denies or betrays, hatred and jealousy are born. Hatred and jealousy in turn cause sins.

Therefore, one should get rid of sexual desire first. If one is controlled by carnal desire, one loses one's reason first, and then one's possessions. Unless one controls the cause, one can never aspire to Bodhisattva, let alone attain Buddhahood."

The Reverend Pŏbŭn concentrated on the problems of carnal desire as if he had researched Yi's past life. On the other hand, he might have had insight into Yi by reading his face. Perhaps he saw the depth of Yi's heart.

"Reverend, as you said, my life has been controlled by sexual desire. That is why I've ended up like this, with no children around me and only with a terrible disease. There is no hope for me," Yi shook his head slowly and continued, "There certainly is no hope for me. I committed sins and will be reborn most probably in an animal form !"

He looked up at the monk. His eyes were bloodshot.

"Reverend, would you tell me again the three wrong ways ?"

"First, avarice, second, anger, and third, folly," said the monk with a beatific smile on his face. He went on to say, "Sir, instead of blaming yourself, try to cleanse yourself of all the desires and pains. It's not too late for you to really 'empty' yourself. Try to observe the ten Buddhist precepts, and then you will get an awakening. According to Buddha, all men are born with a Buddha inside them, but they are blinded. Awakening must be done by and for oneself. If awakening leads you to wisdom and wisdom leads you to 'emptiness,' that is Nirvana."

"Reverend, sir, words of wisdom are fine, but men are animals with emotions, and men cannot live on air. Because we cannot kill desires, we commit sins, and we end up suffering for the sins we commit. We live a life in which our body goes one way and our spirit the other. Life is like a muddy swamp. Therefore it is extremely difficult to cut out all our desires. Once I tried to do that by sitting with my face to a wall and counting to one thousand several times, but I did not succeed," Yi stopped and looked up at the monk with imploring eyes.

"That's why ascetic training is a training of suffering. Next time I come around, I'll bring you a book. Do read it and try to cleanse yourself."

Brother Pŏbŭn closed his eyes, folded his hands, and began to chant a prayer.

"I hope I did not teach you Buddha's words the wrong way. Since I pass by here often, I will drop in from time to time," the monk said and stood up.

"You are leaving so soon ?" Yi asked.

"Yes, sir, this humble monk must take leave of you."

"Then please drop by as often as you can. If I were able, I'd visit you at your temple, but,..." Yi tried to get up.

"I think I will go, too," said Mr. Choi.

"You sit down, my friend, how can you leave me like this? Please sit down and have lunch with me."

Yi sounded genuinely hurt by Mr. Choi's haste to leave him. Mr. Choi sat down and decided that he'd pay for today's lunch to Madam Wolp'o. Yi followed the monk to the gate in the strange duck-like walk he had and handed him a white envelope. It was Yi's contribution to the temple.

After the monk was gone, Yi and Mr. Choi each had a large bowl of soup with rice. They talked about Christian and Buddhist teachings until almost 2 o'clock in the afternoon. It was time for Mr. Choi to leave, but Yi begged him to stay one more hour. Yi went so far as to hang onto Mr. Choi's pants legs forcing him to back down.

"It's so cold these days and you don't come this way often. As for me, every morning I get up, I pray that you'll come around after visiting Mr. Chang. If a magpie happens to caw outside on that persimmon tree, my hope goes up higher. As you heard yourself, neither Christianity nor Buddhism can save me. So the only thing I count on is my burial site. Whenever I see you, my worries and anxieties melt away like snow flakes. The minute I see your face, I feel as if I might cleanse myself of all my sins. Don't you think that such friendship is made in heaven? Moreover, you have lived a blameless life, and are a P'ungsu master to boot. You will guide me to a good resting place, won't you?" Yi said as he held Mr. Choi's hands and patted them tenderly.

"Now wait a minute. What is this anyway? You are patting me with one hand and slapping me with the other. You say one thing to the monk and another to me. Your greed has no limits. You'll never ever empty yourself, I know," Mr. Choi said and laughed.

Yi began to repeat everything he had said before. Listening to his lamentations, Mr. Choi remembered Madam Wolp'o's complaining about the difficulty of being patient with him.

Every time Mr. Choi visited Wolp'ook and went back to Tuma-ri, his heart was heavy and his legs were unsteady. The first time he came to Ibam was when his grandfather brought him to the academy to meet the teacher. He was ten years old. Since then, for nearly forty years, he had trod on the same road, hundreds of times.

He knew by heart every stone, every blade of grass, and every curve of the road. Lately however, he didn't seem to see these familiar things. The road was merely long and boring. It wasn't because of the winter weather or his age; it was because of his friend Yi In-t'ae.

Whenever Mr. Choi got on the road toward Tuma-ri after hearing his friend's interminable lamentations, he felt a strange foreboding about Kye-yŏn.

A vision of Kye-yŏn dying in horrible pain loomed before his eyes. He would hurry his steps, and as soon as he got inside the gate, he would open his daughter's door. Each time, Kye-yŏn would be found lying still, as usual. Then his legs would give way as if he had just awakened from a nightmare.

Yi's remark that he hoped Choi would go to Mr. Chang might have been an innocent expression of longing, but it gave him a chill, because more frequent visits to Mr. Chang meant a worsening of Kye-yŏn's illness. Another ominous feeling was that Kye-yŏn's illness was progressing at the same speed of Yi's.

To speak the truth, Mr. Chang had given up on Kye-yŏn, and had told Mr. Choi that there was nothing more he could do for her. It had been some time since she stopped taking any medicine. Mr. Chang also said that her life was in the hands of gods, and all the family could do was to give her nourishing food. So they stewed a whole goat, and made a pumpkin and bean gruel, which they fed her at every meal.

The streptomycin tablets Mr. Choi had brought from Taegu were almost all gone, but there was no visible improvement. For a moment, he suspected that the druggist might have cheated him and given him phony tablets. However, Mr. Choi always thought it a sin to suspect a person without evidence and came to the conclusion that Kye-yŏn was far too gone even for the miracle medicine.

For these reasons, he could not shake off the ominous feeling that both Kye-yŏn and Yi were going to die before the winter was over. He could not predict which one would go first. The worst, most chilling feeling he got was that Yi might take a virgin with him when he died, as he had had so many women in his life. Mr. Choi found this thought absolutely overwhelming. Consequently, he stayed away from Ibam as much as possible.

It was one early morning in November. Mr. Choi was digging a drainage ditch in the frost-covered barley field behind the Choi family shrine. While looking down over the field, he had glimpsed Myŏng-ku coming up with an empty A-frame on his back. Since Myŏng-ku didn't come here often, he sensed immediately that something had happened. He had skipped two market days and there would be another in two days, which meant that he hadn't been to Ibam for more than ten days.

Remembering Yi's longing for his visits, he felt a little guilty, as he sauntered down to his house. Myŏng-ku was coming up after being told that he was behind the shrine. They ran into each other. Myŏng-ku bowed and greeted him.

"Did something happen at home?"

"Aunt would very much like to see you. Unless you have something urgent to do, you must come with me, sir."

Myŏng-ku looked like he hadn't slept for some time.

"Why? What's the matter?"

"Uncle... he hasn't exactly gone mad, but he's acting that way. He is a little strange."

"What do you mean by that?"

"From the day before yesterday on, he has been sleeping in the empty pigsty in the backyard."

"In this weather? Why? Did Madam Wolp'o kick him out?"

"No, sir. He rolled up his covers himself and went to the pigsty to sleep there. He says he will stay there until he dies.

Yesterday we tried to pull him out, but it was of no use. Neighbors crowded into our yard to see the weird sight. Last night, no one slept."

"That is peculiar, indeed."

"The way he talks, he seems normal. I don't know what's gotten into him. I wanted to come here yesterday, but we all thought he wouldn't spend more than one night in the sty..."

"Do you think he will come out if I come?"

"I don't know, sir. He would have asked for you at other times, but he didn't this time. Still, you are the only friend he has."

Mr. Choi thought for a moment. He did not understand the meaning of Yi's behavior. Was he mad? He found it unlikely. His nagging about his burial site meant he had hopes for a good lot which certainly was not a sign of insanity. He wanted to stay in the pigsty until he died. Did that mean that he considered himself a pig? Like a flash of lightning, a thought came to Mr. Choi. Yi had often said that he was no better than an animal or a blade of grass.

Last time when the monk was visiting him, he said he would be reborn as an animal. Now facing death, he must have decided to lower himself like an animal or to practice being an animal in advance. Yi's strange eyes and the eerie smirk around his lips flashed in Choi's mind. Mr. Choi shivered. His friend's final eccentricity and remorse were awful.

"He may listen to you. He turned a completely deaf ear to Aunt's pleading and crying. She says only you can do something. Please come at once. Aunt is waiting for you."

"I am not sure I can help, but I'll come."

"By the way, how is Kye-yŏn?" Myŏng-ku asked shyly.

"Well, she can't even sit up anymore. She's as sick as your master."

Mr. Choi realized how many times Myŏng-ku had asked the same question, and his answer had always been the same. He looked at Myŏng-ku with pity as he knew Myŏng-ku was expressing his first love for a girl.

"I don't know whether you'll like it or not, but I bought this at the market," Myŏng-ku said, taking out a bottle filled with brown liquid. The coat he was wearing was the one Mr. Choi had bought for him in Taegu.

"What is it?"

"It is pure, natural honey. I know you don't have hives in Tuma-ri."

"Thank you. I really appreciate your thoughtfulness," Mr. Choi said and accepted the bottle.

"I'll be on my way now to gather some wood." Myŏng-ku bowed to Mr. Choi and went off.

Mr. Choi went into his room and changed into more formal clothes. He went over to his daughter's room and opened the door.

Kye-yŏn lay in the dark room with the covers pulled up to her chin. Mr. Choi's old mother sat at her side, holding her hands and telling her an old story. Day and night, the old lady took care of the girl. She told stories that always began with, "Once upon a time."

"Mother, I have to go to Ibam today. There is some business I must attend to."

"I understand. Be careful and come back before it gets dark. Mountain gods told me that the Choi family would have to be very careful this year," Mr. Choi's mother repeated the same admonition every time he went on a trip.

"I may not come back today. Please don't wait up and don't worry."

Mr. Choi looked over at his daughter. The gaunt, pale girl gave him a faint smile. To him the smile looked like a cry. He quickly turned his eyes away and shut the door.

Mr. Choi left for Ibam, flourishing his stick. As the morning frost and fog cleared away, the day became calm and warm. The stream of water rippling down between rocks tinkled like a bell. Before he reached the Kyeyang Pass, he ran into the mailman coming toward Tuma-ri. "You got a letter from your son."

It was indeed from Hak-su. Mr. Choi sat on a flat rock and

opened the letter. Hak-su's leg was almost healed and he was learning to walk on his artificial leg, but it would take him some time before he got used to it. He would be released probably around the end of the month. The letter continued, "I'm truly sorry to have caused you so much worry. At times I am at a loss as to how I will manage to live, then I recall all my friends who died in battles and it renews my determination to go on. Since there is no news from my brother, I'll take his place and work hard to be a truly good son to you and Mother. When they tell me my release date, I'll write you again. Till then, Grandma, Father, Mother, and Kye-yŏn, be in good health."

With trembling hands, Mr. Choi folded the letter and put it in his vest pocket. Tears blinded him.

As soon as Mr. Choi appeared at the tip of the market place, Madam Wolp'o ran toward him. She had been in and out all day, waiting for him.

"Ay, ay, Master Choi, I don't know what's happening. Did Myŏng-ku tell you? My husband has come down to that now? He had breakfast in the sty this morning. He didn't touch any of the side dishes. He just slurped up a bit of soup like a pig. I was going to call Reverend Pŏbŭn, but he insisted he didn't want to see anyone from the church or the temple. He seems really scared of going to hell. How do you know there are a heaven and hell? No one has ever came back from either place," Madam Wolp'o carried on.

"People around here are talking behind my back that I treated him so badly that he had to move into the sty. But you know me! I haven't done anything wrong. He was a beggar and a bum. He had no money, nothing! But once we got married, I've supported him with love and loyalty. And after all these years, he does this to me! What have I done to him to deserve this awful behavior? What injustice! What a bolt of lightning out of the blue sky!"

"All right, that's enough. I'll see him."

Mr. Choi stepped ahead of Madam Wolp'o, who was holding up a side of her skirt and shrieking like a shrew.

As soon as he stepped into the yard, he saw a fire burning in front of the pigsty. Apparently, Madam Wolp'o made the fire so that her husband would not freeze to death during the night.

Mr. Choi looked into the sty. On top of the thick bed of straw there was a mat and two covers. No one was in between. There was a sound coming from under the covers. It was a phlegmy groaning or low chanting.

"Look here, T'angnip," Mr. Choi called. There was no answer. "What kind of foolery is this at your age?"

"See? He won't answer to anyone. Ay, ay, I don't know what kind of spell has been cast over him. He wants to die there," Madam Wolp'o whispered. Suk-kyŏng was looking out from behind the kitchen door.

"Madam Wolp'o, will you go to your room? I have something secret to tell him." Mr. Choi thus got rid of the excitable woman and squatted in front of the sty. For years, the sty had been empty, and it was more like a barn. There were cracks between planks in the ceiling, otherwise it was a good barn free from any animal smell.

"T'angnip, this is me, your friend. Let me see your face," Mr. Choi coaxed in a soothing voice.

After a few moments, Yi barely uncovered his face. Mr. Choi pulled the covers off.

"Oh my God, whatever has happened to you? You look awful."

Mr. Choi was astonished at the deterioration in his friend's appearance. His complexion had become ash-grey and his eyes were two small pools of murky water. "This must be the face under the spell of a death messenger," Mr. Choi thought.

"Oh, it's you. Did you by any chance go and check on my resting place?" Yi asked without any sign of welcome.

"No, I didn't. The earth may move round and round, but your place will always be where it has always been. Besides, the land doesn't belong to anyone, so you won't have to pay either."

"Yes, yes, I know. Land doesn't move around like human beings so it is there, I'm sure," Yi said and closed his eyes. Then he began to chant.

"I'm going to be an animal in this final stage of my life. If I become an animal now, will I be an animal in heaven too? They say that hell, purgatory, and the beasts'-den are three evil places. Will I really be in the beasts'-den? Do you know? When a body dies, hair, nails, flesh, and bones all go back to dust. Tears, mucus, and other discharge go back to water. Warmth goes back to fire, and anything mobile becomes wind. So how in the world can the body and the soul meet again after death? When the soul goes up to heaven, does the King of After-life blow the soul back into the dead body? Does he blow a beast's soul into a sinner and a Bodhisattva's soul into a good man so he will live in Nirvana? Is one really born again as an animal? Amitabha, Amitabha..." As the chant died down, Yi's face went back under the covers like a turtle's head.

"T'angnip, my friend, you are going to freeze to death if you stay here. Besides, killing yourself is the biggest sin of all. As you were born by heaven's will, so will you die by it. Trying to hasten your death is against Nature's laws. To wait patiently for heaven's command is to gain wisdom. You are doing this to yourself as a sign of remorse and self-flagellation, but heaven already knows your mind."

Mr. Choi pushed down the cover to reveal Yi's face, a face that looked like a death-mask. Out of the straw-like gray hair crawled a few lice that had been living near the roots of his hair. The little creatures must have sensed that the end was near. Mr. Choi gently put his hand on his friend's forehead. It was cold as a slab of stone.

"You may think that this kind of masochistic punishment is a way to rid yourself of worldly attachments, but this behavior of yours is really embarrassing to others. Real self-flagellation should not cause others pain and worry. You may also think that this is a simple way to die, but actually it is not. It is as foolish as a beetle that jumps into thick gruel."

"Do you think I'm doing this for others to see or to gawk at ? No, no. This is not for show. I have my own reasons!" Yi spat out the words.

"I think I know what's inside your heart. There aren't many people who want to repent so deeply for their sins as you do," Mr. Choi said soothingly, changing his tactics from reprimand to flattery, hoping to get him out of the pigsty.

"You've already achieved some salvation in choosing this way of suffering and humility. Each man has a certain degree of self-importance and vanity, and it is extremely hard to get rid. But you've done it!"

Mr. Choi went on, but he realized that he wasn't just flattering his friend. What he said had much truth in it. When he looked down at Yi's face, his lips were moving as if he wanted to say something. Yi opened his eyes halfway and gazed at Mr. Choi's face, then slowly closed them again.

"Life is changeable, vain, and empty. Now I can see life and my own past footsteps from afar. Since I have nothing to leave behind, I have no attachment to anything. I have gotten rid of the last trace of carnal desire too. I can only say that I'm sorry. I'm truly ashamed of my past." Tears gathered at the edges of his eyes. Suddenly he began to shiver and his tongue hung out.

"Listen, let me get you into your room. We will talk all night, if you like, about P'ungsu, after-life and what not, just as we did the first night we met. You're going to die if you spend another night here." Mr. Choi went in and picked up the top cover.

"Don't! Leave me alone!" Yi screeched. No one knew where he had such hidden strength. Mr. Choi stopped himself and looked down. His friend's murky eyes seemed aflame, and his ash-grey face and long scraggly hair made him look like the devil.

"Oh my God. What's gotten into you? Let me hear your reasons for this strange behavior."

"Don't bother me anymore. I feel comfortable here. When I was a young man in Manchuria, I slept in the open air and survived in minus 30-degree temperatures. I won't die, don't you worry. I want to live like an animal until I breathe my last breath. After I die, I want you to lay me in the right direction."

Yi then pulled up the covers and held them tightly in his fists.

He was like a child having a tantrum.

Mr. Choi believed his friend's intentions. On the other hand, he had a sneaking suspicion that Yi's action might be a last desperate act of rebellion against losing his manhood. While he was hesitating whether to force him out of the sty or not, Madam Wolp'o came and squatted in front of it.

"Listen dear, I was wrong. It was my fault. Your best friend is here trying to get you back into your room. I can't go out anymore because people talk as if I drove you out to freeze to death. If you die, they won't let me carry on my business either. Is that what you want, huh? I don't know how long you're going to live, but I'll do my best to make you comfortable. Will you come in now, please?" Madam Wolp'o begged and wiped her tears with her jacket sash.

Four days earlier, she had gotten in bed beside him and had played with his withered penis.

"Now you are no better than a piece of wood or stone. Why don't we have separate bedrooms? I'll sleep better if you are not beside me, reminding me of the past," she had said jokingly.

During the night something made her suddenly wake up. As expected, the place beside her was empty. She groped around and found a matchbox. Holding a lamp in one hand, she went over to the guest room and found him sleeping, curled up like a baby beside Myŏng-ku. She went back to bed without waking him. Around dawn, her husband quietly crawled back to their room.

"You look like an old dog that has just screwed a bitch," she kidded him.

Then two nights ago, in the deep of the night, Madam Wolp'o thought she heard a strange noise. She wasn't sure whether it was real, or if it was a dream. She looked at her husband beside her. It was he, sobbing away.

She asked him if he was in severe pain. He didn't answer. She knew he was suffering from insomnia and that he missed all his children when he was alone.

"Ay, ay, what a bother you are! There's no need for an enemy!

Are you doing this to call out the ghosts? If you want to cry and carry on, do it in the other room. I need my sleep."

When Madam Wolp'o woke at dawn, she found he hadn't moved to the other room, but to the pigsty.

Snapping out her momentary flashback, Madam Wolp'o looked up to see the salt-seller Kim stepping in with a covered tray.

"Mr. Yi, please have some of this bean porridge. It's so cold out here, you should go in. Please pick yourself up again. Teach us all the knowledge and skills you have learned before you leave this world. You're too young for this kind of senile act. Please don't be stubborn like a child," Kim said and turned the tray over to the Madam.

"Listen, this porridge is hot. Have some, please." Madam Wolp'o uncovered the tray. The green bean porridge was steaming. But Yi continued to lie there under the covers, not saying a word.

"Look at these kind neighbors. You must have done something right to have such neighbors. Your sins have been forgiven, I'm sure. There is no one in the world who doesn't sin. Even at the church I was told that when Jesus told those who thought they were sinless to throw rocks at a whore, no one dared," said Mr. Choi, who in the meantime, gestured to Kim to move into the sty.

"T'angnip, let's go into your room and have some of that porridge. Then we can discuss the details of your funeral. When a human being is born, he is born naturally with his share of luck, but when he dies it is a different matter. From the moment of death to laying in the coffin, from the funeral procession leaving home to the third-day post-burial rites, the procedure is very complicated. When you die, I'll assume the duty of master of ceremonies. You're lucky to have a P'ungsu master who will also be your master of ceremonies. It means that your travels to another world will be smooth and easy. You just might get on the road to Nirvana. I say these things for your sake, my friend."

Mr. Choi pulled the covers off his friend and held up his head and shoulders while Kim picked up his legs. Mr. Choi's words must have calmed him because Yi did not resist.

"Neither a preacher nor a monk is as good as Master Choi. He is the greatest," Madam Wolp'o said.

Yi's unwashed body and the odor of urine reeked when they laid him gently down in his room. Madam Wolp'o asked Mr. Choi to go to the restaurant room and smoke a pipe so that she might give her husband a bath. She heated up a huge panful of water and brought it to her room.

"Let me wash you, my dear. Oh, when was it, how many years ago was it? That summer night you and I bathed in the Chayang River, I washed your back and you washed me all over. In that clear cool water, we made love! Think of that time and try to pick yourself up!" Madam Wolp'o untied his jacket strings.

"Don't you touch me! I ruined myself by sex, and now on my death bed you won't let me be! You bitch, you devil!" Yi screamed at her.

"Ay, ay, you frighten me. Lower your voice, people may hear you. I said I was going to wash you. What's wrong with that? You stink. No one will come near you because you stink so badly. Besides, a dying person ought to be clean."

Yi calmed down with these last words. Madam Wolp'o locked the door and undressed him. Every nook and cranny of his body was familiar to her, but his bloated belly and the withered inert little thing in his crotch belied the body of the strong, virile man she used to know. She soaked a towel in some warm water and began to wash him. Yi lay still while tears streamed down his face.

When she reached the lower part of his body, his limp organ gave her a momentary pang of yearning and sorrow. It was never going to make her wild again as it had done so many times before. She washed it lovingly. She swallowed the sob that filled her throat. She washed, rubbed, and stroked the dear little thing, but it lay in her hands, small and lifeless.

When Madam Wolp'o finished bathing him, she combed his hair and dressed him in clean clothes. Lying on the mat, he began to discuss the details of his funeral with Mr. Choi and his wife. His voice was calm at first but as he talked on, it became increasingly agitated, and finally ended up in a cry.

"I moved to the pigsty because I wanted to live the rest of my life as an animal, not because I hated you. So don't get me wrong. From long ago, I knew that the day I could not function as a man would be the day I would die. Moreover, I felt I should not die comfortably in a room. If I decide to sleep in the sty again, don't misunderstand me," Yi said to his wife.

As for his funeral, Yi instructed that it be a three-day affair. He asked Myŏng-ku to carry a message to his brother, saying that an obituary not be printed and that his wife not wear mourning clothes.

"But I'll have to wear a mourner's cap, won't I?" Mr. Choi asked. Yi didn't give an answer to the question. Instead he asked that the coffin lid that Mortician Pang made be used. He felt the framed name of the deceased to be unnecessary but he wished the coffin be decorated properly. Finally, he asked Mr. Choi to be the lead chanter of the dirge.

"I don't want you to come to the burial site," he said to his wife, "and after the funeral procession leaves, burn everything I ever had, my clothes, my hat, and my shoes. I don't want to leave even one single trace of my existence. Burn my pillow and my ash-tray too. Send my picture in the hall to my burial site and burn it there."

To Mr. Choi he said, "If grave diggers ask you to lay out travel money for the other world, please don't. Also, do not bury my clothes and shoes with me."

For a while Yi lay still, staring at the ceiling while streams of tears slid down his wan cheeks. His words, mingled with tears and sobs, created a solemn and somber atmosphere in the room.

"I'll observe your wishes to the letter. You don't want to wander around even after death do you, which is why you do not want your clothes and shoes to be buried with you," Mr. Choi said.

"All right dear, if that's what you want, I'll do as you tell me.

I'll put your picture in your coffin," Madam Wolp'o said and wept.

The two days that Yi spent in the pigsty had had a great effect on Madam Wolp'o.

"No, no. Don't put it in the coffin. Burn it at the burial site," he corrected her.

"Yes, yes, I'll do as I've been told." Madam Wolp'o's eyes lingered on her husband's face. He used to be so strong and so virile, like a piece of well-starched hemp cloth, she thought. Now he was a piece of limp rag. The vibrant summer was fading into a cold winter. Life was certainly a series of ups and downs.

In her mind's eye was the vivid memory of the night eight years ago. This man with the face of a horse and long hair spent the night at her tavern. The next day he won big money at a card game, and treated everyone to drinks. He was generous and manly. He said he had something to say to her. Despite his ragged looks, he was big-hearted and gentlemanly in his manner. Madam Wolp'o, who rarely let a man into her inner chamber, thought he was different.

He had ordered a kettle of rice wine and had looked her over, positively undressing her with his eyes.

"I've read Madam's face and I've come to the conclusion that you have a precious treasure that hasn't had an opportunity to shine because it hasn't met the right master. In life, there is something more precious than money and children. I've traveled widely and I once met a famous Chinese fortune-teller who taught me how to read faces. Tomorrow morning, I'll leave here, but before I do, I'll teach you a secret," he had said, as if he were a learned sage.

Under the flickering lamp light, his strangely provocative grin and the flaring nostrils of his big fleshy nose had mesmerized her. She remembered how fast her heart had beat. They did not have a wedding ceremony, but every night they had had the something that he called "more precious than money and children." Of course, there were as many stormy days as fair days, but all in all, their marriage had been a good one.

Unlike her first husband and the few occasional men she had had affairs with, Yi had given her a second youth in her middle age. She would never meet another man like him. Almost fifty now, how could she dare hope for a man who would love her the way he had? Her sorrow was deep.

"Listen, every year when the anniversary of my death comes around, do not have any kind of rite. If you still remember our days together, and if you feel like it, come to my grave for a visit," Yi said to his wife.

"No worship rites? Why not? How can you stop me from having them?" Madam Wolp'o asked, wiping the eyes of her husband, but he said nothing more.

"Do you mean that you don't want a monument, either?" Mr. Choi asked.

"Such things are all meaningless. I just don't want to leave behind any trace of myself. I thought of cremation, but burning, even after death, seems too horrible. If you bury me, I'll rot away, but my grave will tell people that a poor man, no better than a dog, once lived and was laid to rest here. From dust to dust, isn't that it? The dust will be forgotten after a generation," Yi said.

"You are not the only one who will meet with death. All men are born to die, and once dead, they are forgotten," Mr. Choi said. Yi was quietly gazing at his wife.

"Wife, I haven't done much for you all these years, but will you do me one big favor before I go?"

"What is it? What is it?" Madam Wolp'o moved closer to him.

"Will you invite a troupe of singers and ask them to sing for me? I want to hear the farewell song of Yi Toryŏng and Ch'unhyang, and also the farewell song of Shim Ch'ŏng before she plunged into the sea. For some reason I want to hear these two songs so badly. I know I am asking a lot, but this is my last wish." Yi's eyes were full of sorrow and pleading.

"Singers? Where do we find them?" Madam Wolp'o asked Mr. Choi.

"It's been years since singing troupes visited here."

"You may find them in P'ohang since there are fancy restaurants there. Or you can inquire about singers at stores where they sell musical instruments," Mr. Choi suggested.

"Master Choi, will you help her find them?" Yi smiled gently at his wife. His eyes were filled with tears.

"Thank you, my wife. I'm truly thankful to you for having taken care of me, a penniless bum. You have been a loving, devoted wife. God will bless you with more luck. I'll pray for that too. Please forgive me for what I did three years ago. I ran away alone, and I'm truly remorseful. Please forgive me."

Yi put out his big swollen hand and covered his wife's hand with it. His ash-gray hand was shaking visibly.

The year the war broken out, the North Korean Red Army had poured down toward Ibam. People had to decide between taking refuge somewhere and staying on in Ibam, taking whatever might befall them. Yi, who had had too many war experiences, insisted on leaving to find a safer place.

Most of the people in Ibam knew that the only place further south was Pusan and the ocean, so they decided to stay. They said that starving to death in a strange place was worse than dying at home. Able-bodied men and grown girls were sent deeper into the mountain. Some hid themselves in mountain caves and others went to live with relatives in more remote mountain villages.

Remaining in Ibam were the old people, women and children. Madam Wolp'o decided to stay with her two daughters. Yi on the other hand, didn't want to stay and face another war. He wanted to leave with the families of the Republic Army soldiers, policemen, and the townhall office workers.

Madam Wolp'o was furious at Yi. She had called him a bum, worse than an animal and other unmentionable names. He was absolutely impervious to her swearing. He was calm and cold.

If he were to die somewhere, he thought, his relationship with Madam Wolp'o was over for all practical purposes. He was destined to wander around all his life, he lamented, and he had left Ibam with a sack of rice powder on his back.

But at the first checkpoint in Yŏngch'ŏn, he was stopped by the Military Police and sent to a workers' group that was being formed at the Such'ang Elementary School. Knowing what the workers had been forced to do during the war, he escaped during the night. His memories of the Hokkaido mines were too vivid. For two days he ran only in the dark of night, and he returned to Ibam, which was already under the Communist occupation at that point. Those who had run to the mountains were also back in town.

He lied to Madam Wolp'o when he had come back saying his conscience had been bothering him too much. Even in Ibam, he wasn't safe though. For his life of wandering without concrete work of any kind, he was arrested, and tried by the Communist Internal Security Forces.

Yi managed to escape this crisis by insisting that he had been an independence fighter under the leadership of Comrade Choi Won-t'aek, a famous communist. In fact he had never even met Comrade Choi, who had later become a high-ranking official in North Korea, but he knew the name would be useful. For evidence of his activities in the independence movement, he showed them his missing ears.

When the Republic Army recaptured Ibam, he was once again a target of suspicion for his escape from the work brigade, and his self-propaganda during the Communist occupation.

"Mr. Yi is nothing but a bum living off his wife. He is said to have served in the Korean Independence Army under General Chi Chŏng-ch'ŏn and Shin P'al-kyun. He was caught by the Japanese who tortured him and cut off his ears. When the Reds came, he said something else, but who believed him?" some people said of him.

Yet others defended him to the Republic of Korea Army investigators, saying that he hadn't really done anything for the Reds because of his bad health. He was summoned here and there for about two weeks, and finally nothing more was said of him.

Yi asked his wife to forgive him for running away alone, yet another more grave sin was deeply hidden in his heart. Even on his death bed, he could not bring himself to confess it. He had to be forever silent on this particular sin.

It was committed before the Madam's older daughter was married. He had seduced her several times and taught her a few bedroom techniques. When he asked his wife for forgiveness, this unspeakable sin was silently included. Only he and the girl shared the secret, he thought, but now he knew God saw everything he did. He was deeply repentant.

Mr. Choi wanted to leave as soon as dinner was over, but Madam Wolp'o pleaded with him to stay, as she was afraid that her husband might move into the sty during the night. Mr. Choi could not refuse her. The Madam took her pillow and covers to her daughter's room where she promptly fell asleep. She was exhausted after two nights of vigil at the side of the pigsty.

As soon as Yi fell into a deep slumber, Mr. Choi left him and went to the lodgers' room where neighbors were playing cards and gossiping about Yi's odd behavior.

One remarked that Madam Wolp'o must have kicked him out because his organ was shrivelled and not functioning. Another said that if one died as an animal, one would be reborn as a human being, therefore, Yi pretended to be an animal. Yet, another pointed out that since he had played freely and wildly with so many women, he was under the evil spell of vengeful female ghosts.

"What do you think, Master Choi?" asked Sohn, the owner of the bicycle shop.

"Mr. Yi is a man of deep thoughts. He must have had reasons that he could not divulge."

"Are you saying that lowly people like us can't fathom a deep man like him?" Salt-seller Kim asked, but Mr. Choi didn't answer.

There were endless talks about Yi, but Mr. Choi paid no attention. Myŏng-ku had come back with an A-frameful of twigs, and Kwak, whose family had finally sent him money to pay to the Madam, was leaving the next morning. Mr. Choi talked with Myŏng-ku and Kwak.

Around 10 o'clock, Mr. Choi went back to Yi's room. By then, he was groaning loudly.

"Are you hurting much?"

"You can't die without hurting, can you?" Yi turned to the wall as he didn't want to show his pathetic face to his friend.

During the night, Mr. Choi woke up three times. The first time, Yi's low moaning and sobbing woke him. The second time, he dreamed that his daughter was falling off a cliff, screaming. He wished he could go over to her room and make sure she was all right. The third time he woke up, it was still pitch dark. There was not a sound.

"You don't seem to be sleeping well either," Yi said from where the door was. His dark silhouette was faintly discernible.

"What are you doing there?"

"I was sitting on the chamber pot. I sat for quite some time, but nothing came out," Yi said. He pulled up his pants and crawled back to his bed.

"Why do you talk so in your sleep?" Yi asked.

"Soon my son will come home with an artificial leg and my daughter's illness is getting worse. At least you don't have such worries."

Crickets chirped under the stepping-stone, and the winter wind shook the paper door.

"Only an animal has no worries, don't you think? A man has a past and because of this past, he becomes remorseful. The Buddhist monk told me to try and end all my worldly worries, but it is impossible, no matter how hard I try. If I had a more noble past, I wouldn't be so remorseful, would I?" Yi asked meaningfully.

"If it were easy, the word 'to' (the way, the awakening) would not have been invented. Finding 'to' is indeed difficult, but a man with a dark past will find it much more meaningful if he rids himself of all ties to the past and present," Mr. Choi said.

"You sound like a wise man."

"Whether in the Christian church or the Buddhist temple,

there are far more don't's than do's. There are ten command-
ments in Christian teaching and forty-eight in Buddhism. Ordinary people can in no way observe them all. For example,
Buddha taught us not to covet what we see, not to listen to
vulgar words, not to cling to sweet tastes, not to hang on to
anything of this world, not to be afraid when condemned, and
not to be proud when praised. And also to stay away from
avarice, meanness, anger, swearing, vanity, alcohol, and meats.
That's not all. One should not criticize others, not associate with
worldly people, not use people for profit..."

"When did you memorize all these?" Yi asked his friend.

"While I studied P'ungsu, I memorized 'prajna–paramita–
sutra,' too. But as I grew older, I realized that to live according
to nature and my conscience was the best way. I know my place
in this world and I am satisfied with it, according to what nature
gave me, so to speak. When one gets old and sick, one may cling
to a supernatural being," answered Mr. Choi.

"To me, Buddha seems more loving than Jesus. I don't know
why though."

"What do you mean by that?"

"The sight of Jesus bleeding on the cross is too horrible and
scary."

"That may be because you were so horribly tortured that such
a sight gives you that feeling."

"You have a point there. Anyway, a plump smiling Buddha
sitting on a lotus flower is far more endearing to me than Jesus.
Between the two saints, Buddha might be more likely to forgive
me than Jesus. I don't know why, but I just feel that way."

"Jesus, nailed to the cross, is too western to my senses. To save
human beings, he died horribly and tragically. To Christians
Jesus might seem more aggressive and positive, but Buddha is
much more comforting to me. Though Buddha is not action-
oriented, he is like a huge oak tree under whose shade one can
rest and be comfortable."

"I agree with you. During His life, Jesus preached love and
forgiveness, using beautiful words and beautiful images like

birds and flowers in the field. But his final image showed us how painful His life was. On the other hand, Buddha said life was nothing more than birth, aging, ailing, and death, but his image at his moment of death was far more peaceful and tranquil," said Yi.

He continued, "after meeting Reverend Pŏbŭn, a couple of times, I gave up the idea of becoming a Buddhist. I've committed too many sins already to be saved from eternal punishment. Moreover, I don't like the idea of cremation. My conclusion is that neither Christianity nor Buddhism is of much help to me."

"Why did you do such a weird thing as crawling into the pigsty?"

"It was my last gesture of struggle, I guess," Yi said. After a moment, he whispered, "You know, my wife nagged me so much that I wanted to do something to shock her."

Mr. Choi picked up his pipe and tobacco and prepared to smoke. Recently it had become a habit of his to suddenly wake up and have a smoke.

"I wish I could smoke just once more. But I cannot inhale without getting really sick."

"You should stop drinking first. Drinking alone in secrecy is like poison to your illness, you know."

Mr. Choi began to inhale deeply.

"Oh drats, this incontinence drives me mad. When I sat on the chamber pot, nothing would come out, no matter how hard I tried, and now it has seeped out."

"You can't even control that?"

"No, I feel like urinating all the time, but I cannot... It simply seeps out at all hours. The same with the big one. So I've begun to wear a diaper."

"It must be very hard on your wife. You are very lucky with women, though."

"That's why I should go quickly. I never thought I would live long enough to die in this condition. I always hoped that I'd die quickly and cleanly," Yi said, coughing and sighing.

"Dying is something one can't control. It is a blessing to die painlessly and peacefully," Mr. Choi said and shook ashes from his pipe. When he lay down again, Yi spoke again in a quiet voice.

"On sleepless nights, I lie here and think of my past. Among all the women I knew, I loved only three, my present wife, that singer I met in Manchuria, and the Chinese woman I lived with in Pokchu in southern China. Her name was P'aeng. I think of her often these days. For a year and a half, I lived in a cave with her and her daughter. It was one of my happier times. She was short, had a small face and was blind in one eye, but she was infinitely good to me. We were destitute, but she did everything for me with genuine love. When I was sick, she stayed up every night nursing me... I think human beings are happiest when they love truly, with no calculation, nor thought of reward. It stays in your heart. In southern China, the climate was damp and hot. We slept on the dirt floor in the cave. I do not know the exact cause, but the dampness must have something to do with her paralysis (palsy). I didn't know this at the time. She bore me a son and got sicker every day. I had to resort to homosexual relations to earn money to feed and nurse her. The woman kept saying how sorry she was. She would bury her face and hold the baby tightly and cry and cry. I wondered what sex was and why sex was necessary to produce a human life... I did everything I could possibly do for her. At first, I thought it was some sort of postnatal thing, but soon she began to develop a strange skin disease. When scabs were formed, they got infected again. Soon her nose and hands were a bloody mess, her eyebrows and hair began to fall off. I couldn't bear looking at her and the baby. My initial determination to support them began to waver. I could not face the fact that the woman had leprosy. One day I drank myself into a stupor and ran away. I cried for days."

"When the Korean War broke out, you ran away alone. Did you think of the Chinese woman then?" Mr. Choi asked, barely concealing his drowsiness.

"Yes, I did. While running along the Chayang River, I could

hear the distant roar of artillery and I remembered that poor woman I had left years ago. This time I came back, but I never went back to her. I often wonder what happened to her, her daughter, and our son."

Yi began to sniffle and sob.

"It happened so many years ago. A man's life is not very long if you come to think of it, but it is so full of pain and sorrow. It is true that human life is no better than dust," Yi went on in his weepy tone. Mr. Choi fell asleep.

At early dawn as the paper window loomed bluishly white, Mr. Choi felt that his friend had slipped out of the room. He sat up and found, to his great relief, his friend fast asleep.

"Master Choi, Master Choi, did you have a good night's sleep?" Madam Wolp'o whispered from outside. Mr. Choi got dressed and came out. He slept later than he usually did because of the uncomfortable night he had spent.

At the Madam's insistence, he had breakfast at Wolp'ook while his sick friend still slept. He decided not to go to Mr. Chang who had said that there was nothing more he could do for his daughter. Instead he went to a butcher and bought a pound of beef.

Mr. Choi was about to cross the wooden bridge near his village when he saw a young couple coming towards him. The man wore a cotton long coat, the woman a white jacket and a dark blue long skirt. The man had a small boy in his arms and the woman carried a baby on her back, and a big bamboo basket on her head. As they came nearer, he recognized Ch'an-kyŏng, Madam Wolp'o's older daughter, and her husband.

"Good morning, Master Choi, are you coming from town hall?" The young man greeted him goodnaturedly.

"Where are you going so early?"

"We're going to visit my in-laws. My wife has been anxious to see them. It's been some time since we visited them."

"Didn't you see them at Ch'usŏk?"

"No, my mother was ill then."

"Yes, now I remember. Is her asthma better now?"

"Yes, sir, just a little."

Ch'an-kyŏng stood demurely looking down. She and her husband were brought together by Mr. Choi when the young man came home on furlough during the war. Young men were dying by the hundreds every day, so the young man's family wanted to secure a male heir as soon as possible.

Ch'an-kyŏng was in full bloom when she had married him. Now, two years and two babies later, she had lost much of her youthful plumpness.

Before she married, she had been a friendly, loving, talkative girl, who welcomed Mr. Choi's visits. Now she seemed to have lost her laughter and chattiness. Except for running small errands, she had never done heavy farm work. But at her husband's house, she worked all day like an experienced farm woman. People in Tuma-ri stopped talking behind her back as they had done before. In the beginning they had been reluctant to accept the daughter of a tavern owner among them.

"I stayed at your mother-in-law's last night."

"You did? Did something happen?"

"No, nothing special except that your father-in-law was very sick." Ch'an-kyŏng finally looked up at Mr. Choi. Her eyes flickered like fire for an instant, and then the fire was gone.

"Ah, that kidney disease, you mean?"

"Yes, I don't think he will live out this year."

Mr. Choi didn't mention anything about his friend's stay in the pigsty. He didn't think it necessary, as they would hear of it soon enough.

"Then I'm glad we are going to see him today. We've been meaning to visit him for a long time."

"Your mother-in-law will be very glad to see her grandson. She will cook you the best hen she has, I'm sure," Mr. Choi said.

He pulled the young husband aside and whispered, "Living with your parents as you do, you won't find it easy to be especially good to your wife, I know, but you should pay more attention to her. I can see that she has gotten much thinner than before. Besides, she works so hard to help you and your family.

Be it as it may, she is an excellent wife and I am proud to have been her matchmaker. You know, young man, a woman makes such a difference in the rise and fall of a family."

"Yes, sir. I am always thankful to you," said the young man and he loudly kissed his baby son's cheek.

"Goodbye, have a good time."

"Goodbye, sir." Ch'an-kyŏng could not bow as she had the basket on her head, but her words were as friendly as ever.

Mr. Choi looked at them for a long time. The young father in front and the wife behind, crossing the bridge. The young man had been drafted two months after his own son, Hak-su, but he had returned in one piece. Now look at them! He had a good wife and two healthy children to boot. Mr. Choi felt tears welling up in his eyes.

CHAPTER VII

There are moments when one feels an utter futility of life, one such moment being when a healthy young man dies. On the other hand, there are moments when one is awed by the perseverance of a very sick man on the verge of death, yet who goes on for a long time. Yi's life was testimony to the latter.

In the week since Mr. Choi's visit, there was no news from Ibam. Yi once said if a magpie happened to caw in the morning, he would think of his friend and feel happy. This time it was the other way around. Every morning Mr. Choi listened for the footsteps of Myŏng-ku, who didn't come for a week.

Occasionally there was a Tuma-ri man who would go to Ibam, but Mr. Choi didn't want to bother him with an errand. Kye-yŏn's condition was on-again, off-again and whenever her condition worsened, he hoped that his friend would go ahead of his daughter.

After a week, Mr. Choi decided to go to the Ibam market. His son was coming home soon and he needed wall paper to redo his room before he arrived. It was a sunny but very cold day. The edges of the Chayang River were frozen over and children were sledding on make-shift sleds made of pieces of wood and wire attached to the bottom.

Mr. Choi bought wall paper and waxed paper for the ondol heated floor. When he arrived at Wolp'ook, few people were there as it was a little after the peak lunch hour. Madam Wolp'o saw him first and gave him a welcoming wave. Mr. Choi entered the tavern. The Madam had her hair oiled and combed neatly, and she wore a light jade-blue jacket. She was peppy and happy.

"You must have had a wonderful time with your daughter's family, I can see," he said.

"Yes, I did. That sincere and good-hearted son-in-law of mine makes me so happy. I'm deeply thankful to you. By the way, did my in-laws do their kimjang yet?"

"How would I know? It's their business." Mr. Choi looked over the Madam. She looked much brighter than usual. She had put white powder on her face, pencilled her eye brows, and had even put a dab of rouge on each cheek. She looked fine except for a few gray strands in her hair that belied her age.

"I sent each of them winter clothes, but if they are to do kimjang, I'll send some salt and salted anchovies."

"Your husband must be doing much better from all the things I see here."

"His life seems to continue on the strength of all the medicine he takes."

"He didn't go back to the pigsty, did he?"

"He did once. But Myŏng-ku carried him out the next morning. He didn't resist. No one can stand the cold nights we have these days, not even he," Madam Wolp'o said with a smile on her thin lips.

"He gave all kinds of advice to my son-in-law and asked everyone who would listen to help and support me after he's gone. It wasn't bad to hear him say that."

From Madam Wolp'o's face, Mr. Choi sensed a last attempt at seduction. Spruced up as she was today, it surprised him that she still had sexual allure left in her. He had heard that it had been more than three months since Yi had stopped functioning as a male. Looking at Madam Wolp'o's female flaunting, Mr. Choi felt a kind of sad pity. He also remembered that a woman didn't care too much for her looks if she had a strong husband, but she would often look into the mirror if she didn't.

"Did you have lunch?" Madam Wolp'o asked.

"Yes, I brought some steamed sweet potatoes from home and ate them a while ago."

"Oh my goodness, something almost slipped my mind. I had news to tell you," Madam Wolp'o again smiled that provocative smile, and said, "we're going to have a singing troupe here in our yard. We got them in from P'ohang. The singers will be here a week from today. You will come, won't you?"

"That's good. Who did the work to get them?"

"You know Mr. Kwon who used to work in P'ohang when the Japs were here? He did."

"Yes. Hmmm. He is a pretty powerful man. I heard that he squandered all his wealth when he was younger and now lives with his son."

"Yes, that is the man. When he was young and sowing his wild oats, he used to be crazy about p'ansori. He said he didn't know what happened to all the people he used to know, because of the war and everything. He told me to go and see a wealthy man named Ku. Mr. Ku knew many singers. So when the bicycle shop owner Sohn went to P'ohang, I asked him to call on Mr. Ku. Well, the old man was an invalid, paralyzed by a stroke, but he introduced a drummer to Mr. Sohn. So he is going to bring the singers with him. They are coming by train on November 21."

"That's very good news, indeed. T'angnip will have his last wish."

"We agreed on a price, too. It's 3,000 hwan."

"T'angnip will like that, but you'll have to spend a lot of your hard-earned money."

"What can I do? It's his last wish. I know nothing about such things. According to Mr. Kwon, 3,000 hwan is very low. In older times, a rich man used to send servants and horses to bring the singers. Then he would put them up in guest quarters and treat them royally. When they left, he gave them money worth several sacks of rice, I heard. Compared to that, 3,000 hwan is nothing."

"Seven days from now? That is two days after the next market day. If I am home, I'll certainly come, but I may have to go to Taegu to bring my son home."

"That's good enough. Please go in. My husband is waiting for you. I'll send in some rice wine, but please make sure that he doesn't have any of it."

Madam Wolp'o ladled the wine from an earthen jar into a kettle.

"If you go in, you'll see something funny," Madam Wolp'o said while wiping some wine from the kettle and giggling. The two curly strands of hair she had let down beside her ears looked positively obscene to Mr. Choi. They reminded him of a female cat in heat. The Madam's ears were small, without lobes.

As Mr. Choi stepped into the yard, he ran into Myŏng-ku.

"How do you do, sir?"

"It's been more than a week since I last saw you. You must be very busy."

"Master Choi, several days ago when Mr. Sohn went to P'ohang, I went with him to see my sister."

"So did you see her?"

"Yes, I did. P'ohang is a small place. It was easy to find her. She is a grown girl. We were so happy that we cried our hearts out," Myŏng-ku said. His eyes were teary.

"Is she treated well?"

"She is, about the same as I am here."

"You said she is the same age as Kye-yŏn?"

"Yes, she is."

Mr. Choi suddenly thought of a girl for his son. But Myŏng-ku's sister was too young to be married. Besides, it was not certain whether she would accept a man with one leg. Even if his son were an amputee, he would "never pay a price" for a bride, Mr. Choi told himself. If Kye-yŏn died, he thought he would adopt Myŏng-ku's sister.

"Someday you will get together, won't you?"

"Yes, sir. I'm determined to work hard and bring her home. In the meantime we'll keep in touch," Myŏng-ku said and went out.

Mr. Choi was a little disappointed that Myŏng-ku didn't ask about Kye-yŏn as he usually did. Mr. Choi was surprised at this turn of his thoughts. He had no blood relationship with Myŏng-ku, but he found himself more and more attracted by the young man, as if he were a son.

"T'angnip, it's me," Mr. Choi called aloud and opened the door without waiting for an answer.

Yi was fast asleep with his covers pulled up to his chin. His head was cleanly shaven! With a bald head and no ears, he looked so grotesque that Mr. Choi stood at the door, utterly astounded. His head looked like a rectangular lump of mashed beans, brown and fermented. His complexion was dark brown with a tinge of green, not the complexion of a living man.

Mr. Choi put the rolled wall paper against the wall, hung his hat on a nail, and sat down near his friend's head. Yi continued to sleep. He even snored. In contrast to the cold outside, the room was quite warm.

"Listen. It's me, your friend," Mr. Choi shook the covers.

Yi half opened his eyes and stared at Mr. Choi. Then he smiled that gentle smile of his when he wanted to be taken as a serious man. The bald head and the smile made him look like a boy. He stretched one hand from under the covers and held Mr. Choi's hand.

"Your hand is cold. It must be quite cold outside. Walking back and forth for a distance of 40 ris is not easy, I know. My wife said you were Buddha's disciple descended from the mountain village, but I say you look like the suffering Buddha himself."

Yi's voice was calm and clear. He had diapers on for his incontinence, but he kept his dignity, making friendly compliments. Mr. Choi thought maybe he was disciplining himself to be a Bodhisattva. Anyway, he showed a side of himself that deserved respect.

"You had your head shaved, I see. Now, you no longer feel ashamed of your missing ears?" Mr. Choi asked, smiling at his friend.

"Getting rid of all that hair on my head made my heart light too. What should I be ashamed on my death bed? I want to show my naked self before I die. And yet I cannot show all, can I?"

"You always say you're going to die, but look, you are still here. I feel cheated. Your life is certainly tough."

"Come down here on the winter solstice day and have a bowl of red bean porridge. You know the singers are coming on that day. Look over there, there are dried persimmons. They are particularly sweet this year. I've heard that some man in the village was eating a dried persimmon when he suddenly thought of his dead son. The persimmon got stuck in his throat and nearly killed him."

Mr. Choi picked up a persimmon among the pile on a wooden tray. It was soft and sweet, much sweeter than usual. He remembered a time long ago when he and his son were making straw ropes in the night. Under the flickering oil lamp, they used to take a break to have those sweet dried persimmons. Dried persimmons, like glutinous rice cakes, often got stuck in people's throats if they didn't drink water with them. Now one was blocking Mr. Choi's throat, not for lack of water but for a lump of sorrow he felt for his son.

"I feel really comfortable and relaxed now that all the preparations for my death have been made. Each day I feel light, as if I might fly off at any moment," Yi said.

That day, Mr. Choi found his friend's constant smile rather disconcerting. He figured that the cunning leer that hovered on his face might be an indication that his male organ was functioning. Flowing water might look the same, but it changed its color according to the wind and temperature, Mr. Choi thought, as did Yi and his wife. He, who lost the power of erection, acted one way, while she, who missed it openly, acted another. It was a truth he pondered over.

Mr. Choi repapered the walls and the floor of his son's room and waited every day for his son's letter. The mailman who came

twice a week apologized as if it were his own fault that the old
man didn't get a letter. He came to the conclusion that his son
wasn't coming home until after the New Year's Day.

The day the singing troupe was to arrive in Ibam, Mr. Choi
left home to get there around lunch time. It was an overcast,
windy day. By the time he reached the Kyeyang Pass, it began to
hail. The wind was so piercing that he regretted leaving his
rabbit fur earmuffs at home.

Holding down his hat with one hand, he barely made progress
against the wind. Hail stones stung his hand like tiny pieces of
glass. The singers, who had to sing outdoors, certainly deserved
3,000 hwan, he thought.

About the time he arrived at the Ibam marketplace, the wind
had subsided somewhat, and the hail stopped. In the inner yard
of Wolp'ook, straw mats were already in place. Myŏng-ku was
making an open fire beside the mats. It wasn't time for the act to
start yet, so there were few people around.

"It's so cold out here. Can they really sing on a day like this?"
Myŏng-ku asked Mr. Choi.

"Well, I don't know. You know, people chase away evil
spirits on the winter solstice day by sprinkling red bean porridge,
and that is why they chose today, I presume."

"They can't do the act in the house though. That's what I have
been told."

"I don't know about that. I guess they can sing in the house,
but they certainly can't do a dancing act there. This house doesn't
have a spacious hall."

Mr. Choi leaned his stick against a hall column and stepped
on to the stepping-stone when Suk-kyŏng came out of the
kitchen.

"How do you do, sir? Is my sister well?"

"Yes. She is raising two kids and does all the work too, very
well, I must say. Is the porridge ready?"

"Yes, it is. Please go in. I'll bring you a bowl of piping hot
porridge."

The door to the room opened and his friend welcomed him.

"Welcome, my friend. Hasn't your beard turned into icicles, eh?"

The picture of Yi taken eight years ago showed a completely different man from the brownish, swollen man with the shaved head sitting underneath it.

Yi was in a newly-made wine-colored jacket. He looked fine except for his shaved head, which startled Mr. Choi every time he saw it. As usual, it was warm in the room, thanks to Myŏng-ku's diligent gathering of firewood.

"Where is your wife?"

"She went to meet the troupe."

"I came just in time, didn't I?"

"The weather is wreaking its usual mischief for the solstice day, but I think it is just the right weather," Yi said happily, like a child on a holiday. But his face seemed more swollen and yellow than before.

"I'll never understand you. You threw a temper tantrum on the day we went to see your site on the Tal Mountain. It was a day like today. How can the audience stand the cold, let alone the singers who have to raise their voices?"

"You may be right. When they come, they will have to thaw themselves out first. But as far as I know, singers' throats never freeze no matter how cold they may be. I heard a story long ago that one famous singer sang on a cold winter solstice day for eight hours. He sang through the night until the sun rose, but his voice never faltered. Moreover, the audience sat through the whole thing without budging once. By the way, do you know why I want to hear the singers before I die ?"

"Because you used to roam around Manchuria with a singing troupe. You were in love with the female lead singer. You have the gall, though, to bring them here to recall your old romance when you have an adoring wife here with you. You are not an ordinary man. What gall! You are truly extraordinary!" Mr. Choi laughed.

"I don't care what you think. For recalling a cold Manchurian winter day, this kind of weather is just right, don't you agree? Even in March, it snowed and the rivers were frozen. Plum blossoms didn't bloom until nearly April. I guess there are still many Koreans living there. They must be longing for their homes in the south. The Japanese killed countless Koreans there, but some Koreans must have survived. I wonder...."

The door slid open and Suk-kyŏng carried in an octagonal wooden tray with a bowl of steaming porridge, another bowl of winter radish kimch'i, and a small dish of salt. A number of village people had gathered around the mats in the yard. They were squatting around a fire.

"Oh, it hasn't started yet. I'll come later," a woman said and disappeared.

"Have the porridge, please, and be in good health all year next year, sir, " Suk-kyŏng said to Mr. Choi. She smiled a charming smile.

"You, too, enjoy the porridge, and next year you'll be married to a fine young man. As I did for your sister, maybe I'll be a matchmaker for you too," Mr. Choi answered.

As he looked at the peach-ripe cheeks of Suk-kyŏng, the image of his son on crutches loomed in his mind's eye. If his son were whole, he would never take a tavern owner's daughter as his daughter-in-law. However, the situation was reversed now. He wasn't sure Madam Wolp'o would agree to give her daughter to a one-legged cripple. Human destiny was like that, he thought. Ups and downs could come and go within an instant.

Suk-kyŏng's ripe woman's figure foretold her fertility, Mr. Choi mused, and she would produce many sons. He glanced at her backside. He shouldn't ask for too much. It was beyond present circumstances to covet a girl like that for his son. It wasn't written in his son's fate. Greed results in sorrow. Mr. Choi quickly changed his mind.

"I'm sorry I have to lie down. Excuse me," Yi said and collapsed on his bottom cover.

"You're not going to have the porridge?"

"No, I don't have any appetite."

While Mr. Choi was eating, Yi lay still, staring at the ceiling. He had both his hands folded on his chest, quietly chanting

Buddhist prayers. A long time passed after Mr. Choi finished his bowl of porridge. He finally heard murmuring noises coming from the gate.

"Please step into the room and get warm," Madam Wolp'o's voice was heard.

Mr. Choi opened the door. The troupe was composed of four men. One young man had an old man on his back. The old man had on a long coat, a knit scarf, and a knit hat pushed down to his eyes. His face was pockmarked. The third man, in his late 30s, had a drum on his back, and the fourth man had thick wrist warmers on his hands.

The usual composition of a troupe was a female singer, accompanied by a male drummer and other troupe members.

Mr. Choi, who knew little about singers, was greatly disappointed by the absence of a woman, and the poor ragged look of the four men. The young man and the old man were pitiful, and the third one in an old Army jacket was not much taller than a dwarf. The drum on his back hung down to his ankles. The last one, wearing the wrist warmers, was a middle-aged cripple. His one leg was shorter than the other.

People in the yard began to snicker at these four grotesque men. Among the four, the young man was the only normal-looking person. But Mr. Choi did not dare laugh at the cripple. His own son was one.

Madam Wolp'o led them all into the inner room. The young man threw the old man down roughly on the floor and came out. He joined the people around the fire in the yard. Even before the show began, people were obviously disappointed.

"Did they come to do a cripples' fool act? The only normal one is the young man."

"The hunchback dance and the lepers' begging chant would have been better. These people are a cripple, a dwarf, and a pockmarked guy. Is this some sort of deformed men's variety act?"

"Well at least we will have a big laugh." Despite these snide remarks, the young man said nothing. He looked like a moron.

He merely headed toward the fire, poking his sockless feet in torn black rubber shoes near the fire, pushing between the knees and legs of others.

"Hey, are you going to broil your feet? Take them away. Can't you smell the rubber burning?" The bicycle shop owner Sohn scolded him.

The young man withdrew his feet and said, "God was it an ice box! The bus was an ice box." He pushed his head forward to get nearer to the fire.

Madam Wolp'o helped her husband around. The old man put his knit cap under his head and stretched out on the floor. He was paralyzed on one side. Mr. Choi gave his friend a pillow to make him more comfortable.

Mr. Choi, Yi, and the troupe members exchanged introductions. The old man was Mr. Ku, whom Mr. Kwon had recommended to the Madam. The dwarf turned out to be the singer and the middle-aged cripple was the drummer. He had on wrist warmers to keep his wrists supple to do the drumming. Usually it was the drummer who was one step lower in rank than the singer and had to carry the instrument. In this case, it was the other way around. The singer carried the drum, which Yi did not understand.

According to what he had learned, if the singer rode a horse, the drummer walked. If the singer stayed in a guest's house, the drummer stayed in the servants' quarters. If the singer ate at a mother-of-pearl inlaid table, the drummer ate at a wooden tray.

"It's really strange that the singer is carrying the drum. I've heard that even a singing teacher doesn't let a singer carry his instrument," Yi said.

"I am sorry, but he is my father," said the dwarfish man who looked normal when he sat down. His voice was husky and low. His name was Shim Chun-pyŏng.

"Is that so? I'm sorry not to have recognized that," Yi nodded to the older man.

"Because I play the drum at farmers dances, my older brother sent me all the way down to the Chŏlla Province to learn from

Mr. Chang P'an-kae," said the middle-aged man, looking re-
spectfully at the old man lying on the floor.

He continued, "For two years I learned and practiced diligently, but I didn't have talent or dedication. So I gave up, came
home, and have farmed ever since. But the attachment has
remained with me, and now my son is traveling with me."

The old man, Mr. Ku, interrupted.

"Why dig up all that old story? I may be wrong, but look
around at these people here. There isn't even one person who
knows a refrain. Does any of them know the scale? A beat? They
hear because they have ears, that's all."

Mr. Ku had a Kyŏngsang Province aceent, but his words were
standard language. Though paralyzed and pockmarked, he
sounded like a man of integrity and intelligence.

"Did you ever say that we should sing according to the level
of an audience?" the middle-aged man retorted.

"No. I was merely pointing out facts," said Mr. Ku. Yi was
rubbing the spots where his ears had been, because he was
embarrassed by the old man's remark that "they hear because
they have ears."

"I taught my son to play the drum. I was a stern teacher and
often whipped him on the legs. He doesn't carry the drum stick,
but he always carries the drum," the drummer Shim said
shamefacedly. He looked to be in his sixties. His manner was
dignified and gentlemanly, even toward younger people.

"That is how it should be. A son has to carry the drum for his
father. If he doesn't, people will call him the worst names,"
Madam Wolp'o threw in her share of the conversation.

"The lady of the house is right, but it is no longer true. During
the reign of King Sun-jong, Song Hŭng-rok was a famous
drummer. He also had a rare ear for tone, and many great singers
like Yi Nal-ch'i, Kim Ch'ae-man, Chang P'an-kae, and Park
Chi-hong were trained by him. These men were not only drummers but singers as well. During the reign of King Ko-jong and
through the early years of Japanese occupation, people like Park
P'an-sŏk, O Su-kwan, O Sŏng-sam, Chu Pong-hyŏn, and Han Sŏng-

jun were such famous and distinguished drummers that singers never dared to stand with them," Mr. Ku explained in his phlegmy voice, looking at Yi.

"When I heard that there was someone who wanted to hear our P'ansori singing at a chaotic time like this, I decided to come along. One can listen to music, alone in a quiet room, of course, but listening to music by a troupe of singers evokes a different feeling. The master of the house should understand that, I hope."

"Sir, you seem well versed in the lore of music and singers," Yi said.

"Oh, I am neither a singer nor a drummer. When I was young, I gave up on reading scholarly works and followed my wanderlust. I also fell in love with P'ansori singing. There are four requirements to be a truly great singer and showman : the first is to have a presentable appearance. I was not born with this, but I was given a chance to study with Chang P'an-kae, Kong Ch'ang-shik, and Park Chung-kǔn, all famous singers."

"I studied with a single-minded dedication, but I found my voice was naturally unsuited to singing. I had to give up. However, I have very keen ears and a basic knowledge and training to discern what good singing and drumming should be."

"I am surprised there are times when even you are so modest. As for presentable appearances, this applies to women, not to men. The famous singer Park Yu-jŏn was one-eyed.

In volume and clarity Yi Nal-ch'i was incomparable, but he was a cripple, and so was Park Ki-hong, another great singer. Chang P'an-kae and Kim Ch'ae-man had pockmarked faces like you."

"You are right. They say unless you throw up a bucketful of blood while training, you'll never make a singer. I didn't go near that level. I avoided whipping by staying around drinking and entertaining places. I wasn't cut out for singing fame. I was too lazy. My grandfather built up a fortune of 5,000 sacks of rice a year, which my father doubled by adding a successful fish store. But I squandered it all. I was the one who spent as if there was no tomorrow. Everything went up like bubbles. For this unforgivable sin, I am paralyzed on one side. I accept my punishment gladly," Mr. Ku said in a voice full of forced animation.

"I am truly sympathetic to what you've just told us," Yi said meaningfully, as he found similarities between the old man and himself.

"Anyway, my teacher's ears were truly remarkable. They say that under his ears great singers were produced. But I am far from..." the singer sounded so lacking in confidence.

"Though old and paralyzed, he was once the only son of a wealthy man. He was sent to Kyŏngsŏng(Seoul) to get a modern education. While a student in Kyŏngsŏng, he lost his heart to p'ansori and used all his wealth for finding and educating gifted singers from this part of the country. But this area had no tradition or history of music. The dialect was not suitable for this particular style of music, as was the dialect of the Chŏlla Province. He really dedicated his wealth and even his health to music.... Then, in the year the Korean War broke out, he had a stroke," the drummer Shim spoke and gazed at the old man lovingly.

"It's been more than three years since I myself stopped singing, so I am not sure how well I can sing today. I wasn't a good singer to begin with," said the dwarf singer modestly.

"With the war and everything, who could have practiced singing anyway?" Mr. Choi threw in a few words.

Though he knew little about p'ansori, the singer's voice had no strength in it, he thought. Worse, his face was as delicate and soft as that of a woman. A strong masculine vitality, big heart, and open hand were supposed to be the qualities of a great singer, and he could not find any of these in the little man sitting in front of him.

The drum beside him looked like an authentic drum of high quality. It was made of Korean willow wood and cowhide. It was obviously burnished by loving hands over a long period of time. The drum was a historical antique piece.

"Hmmm, the straw mat is not spread yet, I see. Young boy,

your name is Chŏng, isn't it? Make a fire on this side, too. A proper setting must be prepared for the singers and drummers," an old man's low voice said. It belonged to Mr. Kwon.

Madam Wolp'o opened the door. Hail was coming down profusely. Spectators had filled the yard already. There were a few old men who had come from surrounding villages as well.

"My toes are turning into icicles."

"When are they going to start?"

"The winter's short day is going to wane soon," several spectators began to grumble.

"Mr. Ku, so you survived the war, huh?" Mr. Kwon called to the old man as he stepped down on the stepping-stone. He wore formal attire of a long coat and a horse-hair hat. He leaned on his cane.

"Here I am, flat on my back. You and I had a wonderful time together traveling around the country, didn't we? Ah, those times are gone forever. Well, life is a momentary dream anyway. I had a good time and I have no regrets," Mr. Ku said, chuckling good-naturedly, like a true playboy philosopher. Mr. Ku struggled to sit up.

Mr. Kwon and Mr. Ku hugged each other, patting each other's back. Their friendship was moving to watch. When they talked about the war, during which they had lost each other, they were overcome with sorrow and wept.

Madam Wolp'o and Suk-kyŏng brought in two small tables with a bowl of red bean porridge and a dish of rice cakes on each. Mr. Kwon said he had already had lunch, but the members of the troupe heartily finished their bowls, except for the small singer who had only a few spoonfuls.

"Would you like to have a raw egg?" Madam Wolp'o asked, as if he were a child about to sing a solo at a school show.

"No, thank you. I'm fine," the singer answered, and he began to unpack a small bundle he had brought. In it were a singer's costume, a horse-hair hat, and a paper fan.

"Mr. Yi, you are the host today. You should dress properly too," Mr. Kwon advised.

"Yes, sir. I'll do so," Yi answered, and put on his long coat. Ever since the troupe came, Yi had been quiet and ill at ease. He would stare at everyone with his dreamy eyes while his hands continuously trembled on his knees.

On top of the coarse straw mat, another finer mat was placed. On the hall floor, three cushions were placed in a row. Yi sat in the middle with Mr. Choi and Mr. Kwon on each side. Mr. Ku, the old man, half raised himself against the doorsill and looked out.

It was two o'clock in the afternoon when the show started. The short singer in his formal attire looked like a school boy. He faced the audience. The drummer, also facing the audience, faced the drum in front of him. In his right hand, he held the drum stick. On both sides of the mat, the fire shot up its flames as hail hit the burning wood. Around the troupe sat old men. Amid the whirling hail and snow flakes, nearly a hundred spectators held their breath.

"For starters, I shall sing Im Pang-wul's *Memories,*" the singer announced, and he slapped open his folded fan on his left palm.

"When did he learn the famous Im Pang-wul's eastern style of singing?" Mr. Kwon asked the old man.

"He lost his wife in the battle of P'ohang. That's why he always starts with that song," Mr. Ku told his friend.

The singer coughed a couple of times and started in Chin Yang six-beat rhythm:

Mountains in front
Mountains in back
Where does the soul go?
How could you go so easily
Knowing not where heaven may be.

The sad song went on plaintively. Though his voice was not high pitched, it had the right tremor in it.

My love, my cold-hearted love,

How could you leave me so,
Why can you not come back to me

At this part, the singer's song turned into real sobbing. He couldn't go on. He began again a few moments later :

How I miss you
How I yearn for you
To see your face, one more time!

He finished the song with an emotional climax that expressed exquisite pain.

When the drummer hit the drum to signify the end of the song, the audience burst into applause. The singer's voice was neither strong nor sonorous, but it had the characteristic pathos and lingering appeal of the western style of singing of Yi Nal-ch'i and Kim Ch'ang-hwan.

"The singer is far beyond my expectations," said Mr. Choi to Yi, who apparently hadn't heard him as he was staring intently at the singer and the drummer. He was completely absorbed by everyone around him. After a minute, Mr. Kwon tut-tutted and criticized the singer.

"That singer boy may have studied under Im Pang-wul, but he didn't really learn much. His tone is unsteady."

"Your throat is not quite open yet. Sing that song, *White Hair*, " Mr. Ku ordered.

"All right, sir, I'll sing *White Hair*," the singer responded, and shook the fan open in one deft movement.

From ancient times until now
To travel the difficult road of justice
One ends up with white hair and inevitable death.
The king of heaven, earth, and humans,
Kings Yo, Sun, Woo, and Tang
Did those venerable kings die
Because they didn't do just and right things?

The foolish Emperor Jinshi
Built the Great Wall of China
Gazing at it long and hard
And it gave him little pleasure.
How sad it was to build the wall
And it gave him little pleasure.

The singer's voice deepened as he reached the halfway mark of the song, but it lacked strength when it hit the higher pitches. Yet he brought out the pathos of the song's message in such a deeply moving, husky tone that many women and old men wiped away silent tears. Yi's eyes slowly filled with tears too.

When a man dies
He is tightly bound by hemp rope
His hands and feet by thin rope
He is bound again by thick rope
His coffin is put on a bier
To be carried a long way
Through the green fields a far
How very sad it is to see it go
Without shedding tears aplenty.

By the time the song ended, there were those who shouted "Good!" "All right!" during pauses, but they were soon drowned out by loud applause. The atmosphere in the yard began to heat up and melt the icy air and snow flakes.
"The singer is very good!"
"He is short but he is as sturdy as anyone."
"The drummer is excellent too."
"Mr. Singer, please sing us *Kwangdaega* (A Showman's Song)."
"Please, sing 'Hail to Joy.'"
"We will pay you, Mr. Singer, please sing as many songs as you can." Everyone joined in the general excitement.
Despite the raves, the dwarfish singer was indifferent to the

adulation of the audience. His eyes and attention were turned
only to the two men up on the floor and in the room, Mr. Kwon
and Mr. Ku. The singer did his best to please Mr. Ku with his
gifted ears, and he anxiously waited for Mr. Ku's reaction.
Neither man had any particular expression on his face.

Only Yi was wiping his eyes with the back of his trembling
hand. To a man who was mortally ill, waiting for impending
death, the song *White Hair* must have been especially moving.

"I hear this singer endured unspeakable suffering during the
war. Such suffering and inner pain are good for an artist's soul.
His singing ability seems to have a firm foundation," Mr. Kwon
finally commented.

"No, he has a long way to go yet. His voice lacks clarity and
the rolling sound in the throat is not well done. Yes, I admit, the
basic training is there, but he'll have to spend years yet to
achieve a virtuoso level. Besides, his natural voice is not good in
quality. But where in this war-torn country can one find a good
teacher?" Mr. Ku responded to Mr. Kwon's remarks.

"Those short songs don't show much of the singer's real
ability. P'ansori is the true test," Mr. Kwon added.

When the singer began to sing the farewell scene in 'Ch'un-
hyang's Song,' the temperature suddenly grew mild, and the hail
changed to cotton-soft snow flakes.

The excitement of the yard appeared to have worked magic on
the weather. The singer began again :

Ch'un-hyang, my love, what shall I do? I can't leave you
behind, but I can't take you with me, either. If I decide to take
her my parents will forbid it. If I leave her, with her pure
virgin soul, She will end her own life. If I don't see her, I shall
die. Alas, there is no way out of this. Without knowing how
he got there, he found himself in front of Ch'un-hyang's gate...

The singer paused here and looked up, but neither Mr. Kwon
nor Mr. Ku gave any word of encouragement. The drummer beat
hard the twelve-beat rhythm, and the singer resumed in a strong-

er voice.

"The lover will come back as he promised. Please everyone forgive me for my many sins," Yi called to the whirling snow flakes as if speaking his last words in this world.

At that instant, Yi's slowly leaned toward Mr. Choi. Mr. Choi looked down. Yi's eyes were closed, but his face was twisted as if he were writhing from a terrible nightmare. Sweat was oozing out of every pore on his brownish-blue face. His breath was irregular and malodorous.

"Are you feeling sick?" Mr. Choi whispered.

"I am all right. I am listening to the song. I just need somebody to lean against. Just give me support," Yi said. As he opened his eyes, two streams of tears fell down his face.

The singer's mournful voice went up and down, sliding over long rolling passages, all of which deeply touched the very heart strings of the spectators.

Some were sighing and others wiped tears away with their sleeves. The singer sang on :

"Alas, my prince! Are you saying you are to leave me? You are jesting, you certainly are jesting, sir. We gave our hearts, never to part with each other. Last year, in May, you came and sat over there and I sat here. You swore upon heaven and earth that you would not leave me till mountains turned to oceans and oceans to mountains. Hardly a year has passed since then, and you are talking of farewell? You held my hand and pulled me to the field where you vowed ten thousand times, with heaven as our witness, that you would never leave me. Look up at the clouds upon which you made your vows. Tell me, please, tell me. You chased me and wooed me. Now you are going to destroy me. Hyang-tan, go over to Mother and tell her that her son-in-law is leaving us. Tell her I would rather die than let him go."

"Very good!" Mr. Kwon finally complimented the singer and clapped his knee.

The drummer was no less masterly. He followed the singer's singing with exquisite accompaniment. High and low, fast and slow, he beat with the appropriate strength and speed.

As if nourished by Mr. Kwon's encouragement, the singer sang mightily, telling of the scene in which Ch'un-hyang's mother emerges.

The audience, awed and moved to sobbing, wondered how such singing, like the flow of a long river, came from the small body of this singer. Except for the singer's lamentation and the audience's sniffling, it was eerily quiet in the yard.

Soft, petal-like snowflakes descended silently in thick whirls.

Yi took his eyes off the singer and looked up at the sky. Into his mind came scenes of Manchuria. When it snowed there, it snowed for days. The woman singer with the red hair ribbons and narrow shoulders must have been over sixty now. She had left him after receiving a telegram from her home. Her mother was near death, it had said.

She was from the Chŏlla Province. Yi wondered whether she had survived the war. The old days when he had roamed around in Manchuria with a group of musicians came rushing back to him and fanned a flame in his heart. He listened to the singer's words :

Ch'un-hyang, my love, I am going.
Don't cry, and stay well with your mother.
Ch'un-hyang held onto the horse's rein
and her lover's leg. Ay, ay, my sweetheart,
my prince, please take me with you.
Please don't leave me, my love.

The drum roll was long and mournful. In Yi's visions loomed a thirtyish woman and an old drummer with a long white beard. One stood and the other sat. They came near and their music sounded louder, they receded and their music faded. For a minute, their music came closer in faster beats, and he could see both of them clearly. Then, slowly they faded away far up into the sky. Now only cottony snow flakes were dancing in front of his eyes.

Snow flakes, millions upon millions of them, surged toward him, screaming and yelling. "You are too low to be killed. you're no better than a dog. You're a pig," they seemed to shout. They were crowding upon him, swearing, condemning, and villifying him.

Long ago, when he was a soldier in the Independence Army, he was caught and tortured by the 74th Military Police Regiment. The head of the regiment was a Japanese man named Akiyama, who spoke fluent Korean. Yi still remembered the words of Akiyama. When he released Yi, Akiyama said, "We considered you something lower than a human being. We tortured you for the sake of our great Japanese Empire. Yes, it was an unavoidable task we had to do for our country and people. We simply followed our orders. But, you... you are lower than a dog because you sold your own people. Now you are no longer useful to us. You are trash, you are not worthy of being killed by us. Therefore, we release you in the name of our Emperor. Koreans will never trust you. You will never join the bandits, either. Now get out and live like a dog or a pig!"

Yi had succumbed to unbearable beatings. Half unconscious, he confessed every detail of the Korean Army's composition, movement, and hiding places.

"If you had confessed sooner, you could have avoided all the torture," Akiyama patted his shoulder and grinned. Upon reaching the gate, however, Akiyama had said, "You dirty fool, you are lower than a dog!"

"Good heavens, he must have fainted," Mr. Choi cried as Yi collapsed on his shoulder.

"For a seriously sick man, cold air is very bad. Please take him into the room," Mr. Kwon said, not paying any attention to the unconscious man.

At these words, Madam Wolp'o looked back from where she was sitting. She jumped into the hall and moved her husband with the help of Mr. Choi. Yi was lifeless. People in the yard began to whisper to one another.

Stretched out on a cotton futon, Yi perspired heavily and breathed in small gasps. He was insensible. His lips quivered convulsively as tried to say something.

"You, yes, you…. As you said, I've lived like a dog. Yes, all my life, I've lived like a dog…." Yi spat out the words in gasps. His lifeless hands began to convulse.

"T'angnip, what are you saying? To whom did you make such a promise?" Mr. Choi prodded.

Yi's open mouth quivered again, but no words came out. Mr. Choi held his friend's cold hand and watched his lips anxiously. Mr. Choi guessed that Yi had a secret hidden deep in his heart and he was remembering it. While listening to the singer, a certain passage in the song struck him in the heart and brought home the painful secret that made him faint, Mr. Choi thought.

"Today I am going to find out why the Japanese released him after cutting off his ears. I'll find out today, no matter what," Mr. Choi made up his mind.

Madam Wolp'o rushed out, brought a wet towel, and began to wipe her husband's face and neck. Yi opened his blank eyes and closed them again.

"Uh, uh, he has a long way to go before sixty and yet he seems ready to leave this world. Maybe because he heard the sad farewell song," Mr. Ku commented calmly. He sounded as if he were above any human concern for life and death.

What a cold, unfeeling man! Madam Wolp'o's eyes were full of resentment. She gave Mr. Ku a sharp sidelong glance and asked Mr. Choi, "Shall I send someone to Mr. Chang?"

"His pulse is regular. He'll be all right after a while," Mr. Choi said while talking Yi's pulse on his wrist.

Outside, ignoring the commotion, the singer went on. The last part of "Ch'un-hyang's Song" floated up into the whirling snow flakes :

The moon in the sky reminded me of my sweetheart. Blooming flowers in spring brought me thoughts of my sweetheart.

Pouring rain in the night made me ache for my sweetheart.
Autumn passes and so does winter. I yearn for my sweetheart
at the cry of the wild geese in the sky. I sit, I think of my love.
Who is going to put out this fire that is burning inside me?
Alas, my poor life! I spend day after day, crying for my love.

When the song ended, Mr. Kwon told the singer to sing
Kwangdaega since the master of the house was so sick.

After a brief rest, the singer began the song with the accompaniment of his father's drum beat. The snow became thicker and covered the singer's hat and clothes, and his voice became
stronger and clearer.

"I don't think you can go home tonight. The snow must be
knee-high on the Kyeyang Pass," Madam Wolp'o said to Mr.
Choi.

"I don't want to impose on you."

"What a thing to say. We are the ones who always ask you for
favors," said the Madam while watching her husband, now
sleeping peacefully.

"Master Choi, please stay with him tonight. If he dies suddenly during the night, there are no men except for Myŏng-ku to
take care of matters. As my husband says, what is a friend for?"

"Well, it'll be impossible to go over the Kyeyang Pass tonight.
But it will be worse tomorrow when the snow freezes."

Mr. Choi wanted to accept her offer but hesitated.

"If you bind your shoes with straw ropes, you will be all right.
Please stay tonight. You are the only friend I trust. Tonight I
shall make you a delicious beef soup even if I have to spend my
last penny," Madam Wolp'o said. She knew she had persuaded
him.

Madam Wolp'o opened the door and stepped out. Long after
the show ended, the snow continued on until the evening. When
it stopped, it was dark. Eerie silence reigned. The sky was a
misty gray. Wind blew, occasionally brushing snow from the
roof and the branches of the persimmon tree.

Snow in the yard reached up to people's ankles except in the rectangular center where the mat had been. A thin layer of snow covered it. In the place where the fire had been, there floated down some snow mixed with dust. A flock of sparrows sitting on the persimmon tree flew up to the sky as Madam Wolp'o moved toward.

"It looks like snow again, so I didn't sweep the yard," Myŏng-ku said, as he stepped out of the lodgers' room, where he had been listening to the neighbors' comments about the show. The singing troupe had to stay overnight as there was only one bus a day going to Pusan.

"It may snow again, but sweep the ground, so people can move around," Madam Wolp'o said and went over to the room where the troupe members, Mr. Kwon, Sohn, and Kim were having drinks.

"Do you want more side dishes?" she asked.

"I am glad you asked. Bring more wine and more side dishes. You ought to treat your guests more generously," Mr. Kwon reprimanded.

"Didn't Suk-kyŏng serve you as you wished?"

"Don't sass back so much. Just go to the kitchen and bring more drinks and food," Mr. Kwon ordered. The way he talk-ed to the Madam showed that people in the upper part of the village traditionally talked down to people in the lower part of the village. Besides, Mr. Kwon was near seventy.

Before the liberalizing trend had started, children of the upper village had been forbidden to play with the children of the lower part.

"Please enjoy a leisurely evening and have dinner here. I'll serve you a fine dinner," Madam Wolp'o said, smiling entic-ingly.

"No, you don't have to. I will take these friends of mine to my house for dinner and an overnight stay," Mr. Kwon answered, and turned to look at Mr. Ku who was lying down, a wooden pillow under his head.

"My friend, can you sing that song, 'Sowing Wild Oats'? You may be paralyzed, but your tongue seems fine, which means that heaven created you to sing until you die," Mr. Kwon joked.

Madam Wolp'o stepped in the kitchen, only to find the pine branch fire dying down underneath the big iron cauldron. In the cauldron there was nothing but steaming water. She called Myŏng-ku, who was sweeping the snow from the yard, and asked where Suk-kyŏng had gone.

"I don't know," Myŏng-ku answered curtly.

"Where has this girl gone?" the Madam looked around the backyard, but there was no sign of her. She ladled more rice wine into a kettle, arranged some seasoned wild vegetables, and steamed and seasoned fish on two separate plates. She put all these on a tray to take to the guests.

"Myŏng-ku, try and find Suk-kyŏng, I need her to wash and cook some rice," Madam said, and she went off with a basket to do the marketing for dinner.

Meanwhile, Mr. Choi, sitting in the inner chamber, quietly looked down on his sick friend's face.

As hazy light filtered through the window, Yi slept soundly. His breathing was regular and his mien was peaceful. Once in a while, his lips twitched or his eyelids trembled as if he were having a nightmare or feeling pain. But a generally peaceful expression had come back to his wrinkle-free face.

After having a smoke, Mr. Choi left the room in order to join the others in the tavern room. The snow in the yard had been cleanly swept off, but Myŏng-ku was nowhere to be seen. When he turned into the tavern, Mr. Kwon and the young man carrying Mr. Ku on his back were just stepping out.

"Where are you going?" Mr. Choi asked.

"The service and food here are quite unsatisfactory, so I am taking these friends to my home. I have already sent word to prepare wine and side dishes, which I assure you, will be much better than those here," Mr. Kwon said.

Mr. Kwon and the troupe members went off, and so did Kim and Sohn. After seeing them off in the market place, Mr. Choi stood alone in the nearly deserted plaza. Only a few dogs and children were playing in the snow.

"Nature is indeed mysterious. Within a few hours, she has completely changed the world," Mr. Choi whispered to himself while gazing at the Tal Mountain.

The snow-capped mountain had the pristine beauty of a virgin in diaphanous underclothes. The round curves of the mountains and hills looked particularly appealing today. The tall straight trees in their density reminded him of well-combed hair on a young girl.

While Mr. Choi was thus musing, the members of Wolp'ook came home one by one. First, Myŏng-ku appeared carrying two drums of water from the village well. Then, Suk-kyŏng, holding a covered empty tray, came out of the nextdoor neighbor's gate.

"Your mother was looking for you," Mr. Choi said to her.

"Was she? I took some bean soup to the lady next door." Suk-kyŏng blushed and went in.

The next door lady was a widow with three children. She made a living selling bean curd and bean sprouts in the market and by renting a room to Preacher Min.

It was quite some time before Madam Wolp'o came hurrying home with a basketful of radishes, scallions and beef.

"Mr. Kwon took all of them to his home," Mr. Choi told her.

"Really? I went shopping to make them some special side dishes," she said, visibly disappointed.

As she promised, the dinner table that Mr. Choi and Yi faced was sumptuous. There were freshly harvested steamed rice and a mouth-watering beef soup. There were green onion crepes, red bean soup, and rice cakes for dessert.

"Dear, will you wake up and have a little bit of these? You hardly touched your breakfast and skipped your lunch altogether. You may starve yourself to death," she urged her husband.

Yi opened his eyes, but there was no light of recognition in them. An oil lamp was lit.

"Will you get up and have a spoonful with me?" Mr. Choi said.

"Oh, you are still here."

"How could I leave an unconscious friend?"

"Is it already dinner time? Are the singers gone?"

"Yes, they went to Mr. Kwon's."

Madam Wolp'o helped him up, and said, "They came here because you invited them. When you, the host, fainted, the performance lost its meaning. I spent 3,000 hwan for nothing. See if you can even find one single penny, no matter how deep you dig into the earth. Money is no laughing matter, you know."

"Thanks. If I didn't have you and Master Choi, my last years would be truly miserable."

"I don't want to hear anymore such words of thanks. I'm up to my ears with them. Hurry and have some dinner. I'll reheat the medicine you skipped at lunch time."

The beef soup had been made for Yi, so it needed salt. Mr. Choi put in a bit of soy sauce and sprinkled in half a spoonful of red pepper powder. This year's fresh rice and beef soup were delicious, Mr. Choi thought, but Yi dawdled and picked at the food for a while, then gave up. He had no appetite. When his wife brought in his herb medicine in a bowl, he drank it all.

Madam Wolp'o left the room with the empty bowl. Entering the kitchen, she found Suk-kyŏng gone again. "Good heavens, this girl of mine must be in heat or something," she mumbled. Suddenly she remembered she had forgotten to do an important ritual.

She put hot red bean porridge in a large bowl, and stepped out into the yard with a spoon in hand. Evening mist was slowly enveloping the village.

First she sprinkled a spoonful of the porridge at the fence gate, then in front of the tavern and the outdoor privy. Sprinkling red bean porridge on the premises was to ward off evil spirits for the coming year.

"Go away evil spirits. Go away sick spirits. Don't let disease spirits near my home. Let there be success at my shop! Let me find a good man for Suk-kyŏng!" she exhorted as she went around.

She finally went to the pigsty to splash a large portion of the soup when she heard a man whispering behind the wall that separated her home and the house next door. Her ears pricked up.

"Suk-kyŏng, I cannot marry you unless your mother converts to Christianity. Also, if we were married, we'd have to move away because a tavern is not a suitable business. People of my church won't understand. I know I ought not accept advances from the opposite sex, but as God's servant I must be the bridge between God and believers. In order to save His flock, my faith alone is not enough. I must be a model in every way."

It was the voice of Preacher Min.

"But you said a true believer is able to do anything. If God hears your prayers and mine, God will make my mother a believer. Let's help her become one and move away from here," Suk-kyŏng's answer was firm.

Madam Wolp'o realized for the first time the intimate relationship between Preacher Min and her daughter. Indeed, it was a case of "the immediate vicinity under a lamp being the darkest."

In the inner chamber, Mr. Choi and Yi sat facing each other.

"All day today, I haven't been able to urinate. Now that I have taken my medicine, I hope I can." Yi leaned against the wall. He picked up a towel beside his pillow and wiped perspiration from his face and neck.

While watching his enervated friend, Mr. Choi recalled the day Yi had ridden a donkey up the Susŏk Mountain. He had more energy then. Mr. Choi smoked his pipe for a while before he cautiously broached the subject that he had pondered for a long time.

"T'angnip, when you fainted while listening to the 'Ch'un-hyang's Farewell Song', it occurred to me that you would not live out this year. I didn't think you'd die then and there, but I saw the death messenger's shadow on your face. As you said when we went to the Tal Mountain, your face was under the shadow of death."

"You saw right. My time is near."

Yi nodded and answered in a barely audible voice.

"What I want to know is why you fainted."

"What?"

"The reason for your losing consciousness was not your sickness. Until you came to sit on the hall floor, your eyes were bright and full of spirit. Though the breeze was cold, it could not have felled you like that. You keeled over like a log." Mr. Choi looked straight into his friend's eyes. No matter how piercing Yi's eyes might become, Mr. Choi was determined not to turn away.

"Really? So are you saying you know the reason?" Yi asked with a grin.

"I know during the Japanese invasion of the Imjin year they cut off the ears of thousands of Koreans, but they never did it during their last occupation, as far as I know. I never heard of their making another 'Ear Tomb' as they had done nearly four hundred years ago. I don't believe that your ears were cut off by the Japanese torturers. When I first heard your story eight years ago, I knew immediately that that part of your history was somehow unconvincing. It didn't fit in," Mr. Choi said and deeply inhaled from his pipe. He sounded like an interrogator.

"How in the world did you decide that?" Yi asked. His voice was tremulous.

"Why do you answer my question with another question?"

"Did I say something in my sleep?"

"Yes, you did. When your wife was not around."

Mr. Choi knew this was an excellent opportunity to draw out an answer, but he suppressed the urge to add that he hadn't quite caught every word Yi had said in his sleep. Yi's forehead twitched in small convulsions and his hands shook visibly.

"What... what did I say?"

"My dear friend, you have a secret deep in your heart that you've never told anyone, not even me. Hiding it maintained a vestige of self-respect. I think perhaps that this secret of yours which you've hidden all these years may be the very cause of your sickness." Mr. Choi paused, in spite of other things he had to say. He wanted his friend to confess.

"Please, go on."

"You may think you can carry this secret to your grave, but you know you can't. Unless you deny an after-life and heaven's mercy, you cannot do that. It's just like the legendary Son-o-kong(a magical monkey in a Chinese story) who, in the end, had to admit that he was still within the palm of Buddha. There is nothing in the world that you can hide forever. Besides, if you have a secret in your conscience, your soul will never be saved. Have you ever heard of sacremental confession?"

"What is this long introduction? Come right out and tell me."

"Are you really going to hide it from me? I am your friend. I can keep inside whatever shameful things you might have done," Mr. Choi said while staring intently at his friend. He knew this was the time when he might have the upper hand in order to draw out the truth. Instead of beating around the bush he knew he had to hang on and dig in.

"Yes, I know you are my last friend, who will guide me to another world," Yi said and wiped his eyes with a trembling hand.

"My friend, when you were tortured horribly by the Japanese and you became almost insane, didn't you become a traitor? Wasn't that why they let you go?" Mr. Choi, no longer patient, spat out the word traitor. However, he did not know how his friend had lost his ears. He was told that the Japanese had threatened to cut off his ears, nose, hands and feet, in that order, and by the time his ears were lopped off, perhaps Yi could no longer resist and broke down. This was Mr. Choi's guess, at best, as Yi never gave him a clue as to the real truth of the matter. Whenever his life story came near that particular part, Yi would get furious.

"No, no, no. When I was released I was not insane. I desperately wanted to die, but I was not without my senses," he used to scream.

"Listen, T'angnip, I am neither Yama, the Lord of Hades, nor a heavenly judge. I'm simply your closest friend. I'm ready to keep a secret of all your past sins," Mr. Choi gently consoled him.

"Why don't you let it all out and regain peace of mind? Then your suffering will go away and you will sleep better. You will not lose consciousness again. When you stayed in the pigsty and had your head shaved, you thought you were paying for your sins. You also said that you had nothing to be ashamed of as you neared your deathbed, but as long as you have that secret of yours in your heart, God will see right through you. God knew your suffering too. That is why heaven heaps a thick layer of suffering on everyone. Truth and conscience are one. It is not approximate, around, about, above, or below. It is exactly one small dot, the truth."

Yi let the towel he was holding fall on his face. His tear-filled eyes had no fire in them. Instead his eyes were soft and loving, almost pitiful.

"You are indeed a true friend. No, you're more than a friend. You're a judge that heaven has sent me. More than a preacher or a monk, you move me deeply because you've truly looked into me, a worthless human being. Now, let me tell you the whole story. I'll confess everything to you and become free. Free from my secret suffering."

Mr. Choi swallowed loudly. Yi leaned weakly against the wall. His quiet voice began to penetrate Mr. Choi's ears.

"When I was released by the Japanese Military Police, I had my ears. Because of the repeated severe beatings I got, I could hardly walk, but my head was clear. Blood came out in my urine and feces. I spat out blood whenever I coughed. But if I had been put in a warm room and given lots of good food, I would have died, I'm sure. Such comforts would have taken away my survival instincts. There was no place to go and no one to give me even a drink of warm water. So I limped across the River Tuman and went back to Kando."

It had been summer time. Yi was in worse agony for the confessions he had made at the Japanese Military Police Regiment. A kind of mental collapse and despair ate at him. He had limped around in Yongjŏng, leaning on a stick. He was in tatters, barefoot, with an unwashed face, begging only at Chinese houses.

In his head, Akiyama's last words, "You are worse than a dog. Now go and live like a dog," echoed and re-echoed in his head, no matter where he went. After about ten days, when he was wandering around Tudogu, he happened to hear that the two Korean villages, Yajigol and Saemmulgol, had been devastated by an all-out Japanese surprise attack.

Yajigol was a Korean village of approximately 20 houses where his Independence Army regiment had had its last three-day rest. He had gone back there like a criminal secretly revisiting the scene of his crime.

At the entrance of the village, he hid himself behind some hazel-nut bushes and viewed the scene in front of him. Except for half a dozen houses, the entire village lay in ashes. The rumors he had heard were true. The Japanese had done a thorough job of ruining the village. From the corner of his eye, he saw a few figures moving around and felt at the same time a severe pang of hunger, but he dared not show himself.

Though his appearance was unspeakable, a few adults would certainly recognize him. His confessions to the Japanese nagged at him, and he wanted to find the true reason for their indiscriminate attack. Ever since the humiliating defeat they had suffered at the Battle of Ch'ŏngsanri, they had threatened that anyone who provided food and lodging or other provisions to Korean Independence fighters would be considered an enemy to Japan. They kept their word. They indiscriminately killed hundreds of Koreans.

Yi wanted to find out whether their attack on Yajigol had occurred because of his confessions. For about half an hour, he stood behind the hazel-nut bushes. Then he spied a girl of about twelve walking toward the village with a bundle of kindling on her head. While he hesitated to call to her, she suddenly put down her bundle and went into the bushes. In Kando, very few Koreans had bathrooms, not even outdoor privies. People relieved themselves in any convenient spot in the field, then dogs would clean up their mess. He knew right away that the girl had gone to do just this. He limped slowly to the girl's bundle and sat beside it. He raked his hair down over his eyes.

When the girl came out and saw him, she was too stunned to move or speak. Of course, she didn't know who he was. She didn't know what to do with this beggar-like stranger.

"Little girl, let me ask you some questions. When and how was this village burnt down?"

"In the night. One night Japanese soldiers on horses suddenly came over the pass. They set houses on fire, they killed people. I was so scared, I just cried." The girl said haltingly, petrified with fear.

"Why? Why did they do it, did you hear? For no reason at all? What did the grownups say?"

"Because people here gave food and room to Korean Independence fighters. The Japanese shot people and cut them with long swords. They cut off people's heads," the girl was on the verge of tears. She quickly put the bundle on her head. She seemed deathly afraid of the stranger. Scared beyond endurance, the barefoot girl ran away.

A flash of recognition came to Yi. He turned his back to the village and hurried off toward the Orang village.

As he was about to turn a corner, he heard footsteps from several people in hot pursuit of him. He looked back and saw three strong young men running toward him. They were brandishing scythes and clubs. Obviously the girl had reported to the village her sighting of a strange Korean man.

"Stop right there. Who in hell are you?"

"You son of a bitch, you are a Japanese spy, aren't you?"

The young men began to shout. Yi ran as fast as his limping legs would carry him, but he was caught before he had gone more than a hundred meters. One of the men got hold of Yi's shaggy hair, lifted it, and peered into his face.

"This is the guy. This is the Yi guy."

"Yes, this is the son of a bitch we've been looking for."

They grabbed him by the collar of his torn jacket and dragged him to the village.

At the village thrashing ground, old people, women, and children waited. He was ordered to kneel in the center of it. He dared not look up at their faces. With his head lowered, he trembled uncontrollably.

"Yes, he is one of the three men who stayed at our house for three days," a woman with a baby on her back pointed at him.

"You dirty son of a bitch! You are the rat who informed the Japanese Military Police!" The young man who had dragged him there screamed. He could hear the man's teeth grinding in anger.

Clubs, rocks, and kicks showered upon him mercilessly. He slowly lost consciousness. Someone poured cold water over him and the beating started anew.

"We fed you and kept you in a warm room. And what did you do to thank us? You opened your filthy mouth to the Japs. Can you still call yourself a Korean fighter? You deserve to be killed. It would serve you right to be killed by Korean hands!"

"Because of your betrayal, Yajigol, Saemmulgol, and Saribat-kol lie in ashes. In the middle of the night, Jap guards burnt down our houses and murdered people indiscriminately!"

"In our village alone, eighteen men, women, and children were hacked and burnt to death!" These vengeful screams pierced through his pain-numbed head. He no longer felt pain.

Though he knew he was lower than an animal that deserved to be slaughtered, he suddenly felt a desperate urge to live. His survival instinct raised its stubborn ugly head.

"No, no, please. When I lost consciousness during electric torture.... I must have said something...," Yi pleaded. He was being honest. He had only given the names of places to which he had gone.

"You dirty animal! Shut your filthy mouth! We know that only you were released of the three who were caught. Several men left five days ago to Yongjŏng to hunt you down!"

Clubs and kicks assailed him again. He could hear his flesh being torn apart. His clothes were in shreds and he was no better than a bloody hunk of meat.

"Let's tear apart his mouth! Pull out his tongue, and gouge out his eyes! Cut off his ears and nose! He shall never speak, hear, see, or smell. Then we will throw him away!"

These invectives came to him only faintly, as if he were far away. He knew he would rather die. Then he blacked out.

Right then, an old man with a long white beard, who was apparently the village elder, came forward and stopped the beating.

"Bitterness must never be repaid by bitterness. If we torture our own fellow Koreans in this foresaken alien land, we cannot call ourselves human beings. The reason why the Japanese released him was that they knew it would divide us. It was their cunning scheme. Listen, Suk's mom, come here and give me that knife."

The old man held the kitchen knife in his hand and spoke sternly.

"If you have ears, listen to me! I'm going to cut off your ears now. If you live long enough, everyday feel the spots where your ears were and repent and repent again! We've lost many of our people here but it is a suffering that we must endure, because we are a people without a country. Since you were once an independence fighter and suffered much in this strange land, I'll let you live. I'll let you go only because you are one of us. Our blood is the same!"

The old man then lopped his ears off. He fainted. Despite all the horrible beating and excruciating pain, he survived. Until he came around the next day, he lay like a lump of torn meat, abandoned in a corner of the thrashing area. He was naked. The hot sun shined on him.

"Wa... water, please." He thought he had shouted but it was no more than a whisper. There was no one to hear him. He didn't know how long he had been lying there before he heard foot-steps.

"Water, water, please," he begged a woman who happened to pass by him with a jug of water on her head.

"What? You want water? You dirty dog! My little son was burnt to death. So, you still think you are a Korean. Shut your mouth and don't speak Korean. Be thankful your tongue wasn't cut off!" She spat out a gob of spit that landed on the thick coagulated blood that used to be his ear.

"Get away!   Crawl away like a dog!   Feed on feces like a dog, like a pig!" she screamed at him.

After the sun went down, it became chilly. His legs broken, he could not walk. Naked, blood-covered, and half-dead, he crawled out of the village, truly like a dog.

He shed tears as much as he lost blood. He rolled in the dirt to cover himself. He crawled, crept, and rolled liked a worm.

He had no other choice but to hang onto life and live as dogs and pigs did. "Since I came out of the village alive, my fate from now on should be that of a dog," Yi thought. Unless he was able to do away with himself, he decided he would live out his life like a dog or a pig. Three days later, he managed to arrive in Tudogu, 30 ris away. It was then that Yi first showed signs of insanity.

CHAPTER VIII

Two days after the troupe had performed at Wolp'ook, Mr. Choi at last received a letter from his son. It came with another printed official letter from the director of the Army Hospital. Both letters informed him that Hak-su would be released on December 30.

The director's letter stated that : "Army Private Second Class Choi Hak-su is to be honorably discharged as a wounded soldier and is therefore entitled to a government pension, for which the Choi family's birth certificates and Mr. Choi's provincial I.D. card and seal are required."

A brief moment of joy was replaced by a deep sadness over the loss of his son's leg and the uphill struggle he and his son would face to make a living. This sadness was as heavy as the Pohyŏn Mountain, now a silhouette in the distance.

The day before Hak-su was to be released, Mr. Choi left home early. It was a bitterly cold day. The Chayang River was frozen over and ice was everywhere. He went to the town hall where they issued him his family's birth certificates. Concerned about the condition of his friend, Mr. Choi dropped by Wolp'ook, which he found to be gloomy and funereal.

He was told later that Yi had been refusing food of any kind, ever since the day the troupe had come. He only accepted a broth made of boiled corn husks, that had been recommended by Mr. Chang as having a medicinal effect on kidney diseases.

Yi's swollen body reminded Mr. Choi of a balloon, and his stomach looked like that of a pregnant woman's. His shaven head, blue-brown complexion, and deeply sunken eyes were the very features of a dead man.

"I, Yi In-t'ae, am truly going to die. You've done so much for me. I owe you much. After I am gone, I pray that you'll have a good, trouble-free life. I will bless you from another world. I am afraid I have lived too long. For a man worse than a dog, I have lived much too long."

Yi's voice was so weak that Mr. Choi had to put his ear close to his lips. Yi's gentle voice reminded him of a Chinese philosopher's words that a dying bird has a sad voice but a dying man has a gentle voice.

"Now are you at peace with yourself?"

"No, not really. I'm not cut out for such spiritual refinement, I'm afraid. All I know is that I want to die. It seems that I won't have peace of mind unless my soul leaves this world. I wish my soul would free itself from my body."

"T'angnip, my friend, shall I dig your grave in advance?"

Yi shook his head at this question. He knew the old saying that digging a grave in advance prolonged one's life. But he knew he didn't want to live anymore. Mr. Choi nodded.

"I don't know why my life perseveres like this," Yi said and continued, "Out of stubbornness and rebellion, I've lived like a dog, and I wonder whether the Lord of Hades will forgive me."

"After I'm dead and gone, spring will come and flowers will bloom. Then I hope you will come around and leave before my grave a lighted pipe."

Mr. Choi understood why his friend wanted to die so much and felt profound sympathy for his inner suffering.

"Sir, you saw that there is no hope, right?" Madam Wolp'o whispered to Mr. Choi whom she had called out of her husband's sick room.

"If he is going to die, I wish he would do so soon."

"Why don't you force-feed him at least some rice gruel?"

"I tried, but he absolutely refused to eat anything. I couldn't push anything down his throat."

"Is he really going to kill himself this way?"

"I don't know, but I don't think he will last beyond December. In the New Year, I will have to marry Suk-kyŏng off. As you know, we cannot have a funeral and a wedding in the same year. It's most unseemly."

"Oh, you've found a man for Suk-kyŏng?"

"Sir, you may think it rather sudden, but I've decided to become a Jesus follower. My husband will die soon, and when Suk-kyŏng leaves with her husband, I'll be all alone. I'll need something to hang on to, won't I?"

"But... but, you, a Jesus follower?"

"I don't know whether this Jesus is a western devil or not, but there is reason for me to pretend to believe him, at least for a while. I've made up my mind to try. Preacher Min, Suk-kyŏng and I told my husband about something called a baptism so that he might go to heaven. But he refused. He was stubborn as a mule. A baptism was useless to him, he insisted."

"One should live long! I've lived long enough to see you turn to Jesus! You are not in need, are you, of the American aid clothes or flour?"

"No, but I'm confused. I don't know what is what. When I think of running a tavern until I get old and gray, I cannot help asking questions. What is life all about? That horse-faced man in my room I gave up on long ago. I've gotten him out of my mind. I had his shrouds and coffin made already," Madam Wolp'o said. Tears welled up in her eyes as she looked up at the persimmon tree in the corner of the yard.

Mr. Choi left early in order to get to Taegu before sundown. The wind was blowing hard along the Chayang River.

The next day when he arrived at the hospital early in the morning, the hospital administration office was packed and noisy as it was the day before December 31. It took him half a day to go through the paper work. In the late afternoon, he left the hospital with Hak-su, who was on crutches.

They went straight to a railway station and caught the last train to P'ohang, where they stayed overnight in a small inn. The next afternoon, they arrived at Ibam, but didn't see anyone. They hurried home to Tuma-ri.

Hak-su refused several times to be carried across the river on his father's back, but Mr. Choi insisted. Thinking of his missing eldest son, crippled second son, and his fatally ill daughter, Mr. Choi swallowed hard to stop his tears. Climbing the Kyeyang Pass, while helping his son along, he remembered how lightly and quickly they used to walk over the Pass, even with heavy loads on their A-frames.

"Father, someday when you are old and weak, I'll carry you on my back and take you to Ibam," Hak-su used to say when he was younger. It seemed so long ago.

It took them twice as long to get to the top of the Pass as it used to. The sun was going down behind Mt. Pohyŏn and an icy wind blew against the father and son. Dry, bare trees were noisily swishing and swaying in the wind.

On a flat rock at the top, they sat and rested. Mr. Choi, for the first time since his son had gone off to the war, told him of Kye-yŏn's hopeless condition. Mr. Choi burst into sobs, losing control in his long-suppressed sorrow. Consoling his father, Hak-su ended up crying with him.

"All right, my son, let's cry as much as we want right here. Then let's not ever show our tears to anyone. You and I will work hard to keep our farm going and to take care of our ancestral place. Yes, you and I," Mr. Choi said, affectionately patting his son's thin back.

The day Mr. Choi heard the news of Yi's death was three days after Hak-su's return home. It was January 2. Mr. Choi and Hak-su were about to have breakfast when Myŏng-ku rushed in and shouted the news at them.

"Master Choi!"

Mr. Choi knew the message Myŏng-ku had brought. According to the boy, Yi had died in his sleep early that morning.

"Aunt said that at dawn she suddenly felt strange, so she put her hand under his covers. She said he was already cold. She noticed streams of lice crawling out of his covers and clothes. She said she didn't know when he died, but his eyes were closed and there was a peaceful smile on his face."

"I see. Come on in and have some breakfast with us. Then we shall go together."

As soon as breakfast was over, Myŏng-ku left to carry the news to Ch'an-kyŏng, the Madam's eldest daughter. Her house was a tiny, thatched-roof cottage situated behind mulberry bushes on the edge of the village. Ch'an-kyŏng lived with her mother-in-law, husband, his two younger brothers, and her two small children. When Myŏng-ku arrived, there were two chickens pecking for food in the yard. Ch'an-kyŏng sat on the floor of the kitchen, nursing her baby.

"Big Sister!"

"My goodness, what brings you here so early in the morning?" Ch'an-kyŏng asked as she came out of the kitchen with the baby in her arms. Her once peachy cheeks were cracked and her hair, loosely tied in a bun, had lost its luster. She was gaunt and untidy.

"Uncle passed away."

"He did?"

"Yes, at dawn."

Myŏng-ku tried to erase the memory of his nocturnal encounter with her under Yi's window three years earlier.

"I am going back to Ibam with Master Choi. You'll come with us, won't you?"

"I am afraid I can't. I have to get permission from my mother-in-law," Ch'an-kyŏng said and sniffled. She turned a resentful eye to the inner chamber where her mother-in-law was.

"Has someone come?" asked Ch'an-kyŏng's husband as he opened the door. He was having breakfast with his mother. His mouth was full of rice.

"Oh, Myŏng-ku. What brings you here?"

"Uncle died."

"He did? Alas. It's so cold today. Why don't you come in?"

"I already ate at Master Choi's. I must hurry back. I have so many errands to run," Myŏng-ku answered, and he turned and left. When he looked back just before he went out the gate, he caught sight of Ch'an-kyŏng wiping her eyes with her jacket string.

Mr. Choi put on his long coat, a tall horse-hair hat, and picked up a compass and a cloth ruler. In case snowed, he would need a rain hat so he put one in his vest pocket.

He walked over to the room where his mother was spoon-feeding red bean soup to Kye-yŏn, who was propped up against a wall. Kye-yŏn's arms were too weak to hold up a spoon.

"Mother, I have to go to Ibam. The man at Wolp'ook died very early this morning."

"You mean Mr. Yi? He was sick for sometime, wasn't he? But everyone must go when he is called. He wasn't even sixty yet, too young to die."

The old woman sighed, watching Kye-yŏn.

"With the help of gods, I hope you will live a long, long time."

"Mother, I'll be the master at the funeral, so I won't be back till the day after tomorrow."

"I understand. Do your best and lead him comfortably to another world."

Mr. Choi bowed to his mother and turned when Kye-yŏn called out, "Father." Her teary eyes were shy.

"Please give this to Myŏng-ku," Kye-yŏn said and took something from under her covers and gave it to her father.

"To Myŏng-ku? What is it?"

"He will know."

"All right. I will give it to him."

Mr. Choi put in his vest pocket the small, flat thing wrapped in a handkerchief. He thought it odd but decided not to ask any questions. When he came out, Myŏng-ku was not back. Moments later, he ran in, breathless.

Mr. Choi and Myŏng-ku were about to leave Tuma-ri when Mr. Choi gave the package to Myŏng-ku.

"Kye-yŏn asked me to give this to you."

"What is it, sir?"

"I don't know."

Myŏng-ku unwrapped it and found the small mirror he had given her long ago.

"This is a mirror."

"A mirror?"

"Yes, I bought this mirror at the Ibam market in the year I came to Ibam and gave it to her."

"Umm. That means she is returning it to you after three years."

Mr. Choi felt Kye-yŏn's behavior to be ominous, as if she were giving up hope.

"It was a cheap little thing. She could have kept it. Why is she returning it to me?" Myŏng-ku asked, holding the mirror in his hand.

"I don't know, Myŏng-ku."

Myŏng-ku stopped and said, "Master Choi, now that Uncle is dead, I am going to leave Ibam as soon as the winter is over."

Mr. Choi said nothing.

"Uncle settled in Ibam instead of going back to Ttakpatkol. I have no intention of going there either. Like Uncle...."

"You want to wander all over the world, don't you?"

"No, sir! I'm not going to wander with no useful purpose. I'm going to work hard and make something of myself. That is why I want to leave Ibam. Someday when I miss home, may I come back to you in Tuma-ri?"

"Sure, you may. For some reason, you are like...."

"Master Choi, I'd be very happy if you considered me as your son. Even if something happens to Kye-yŏn, I'll always think of you as my father and will write to you often, wherever I may be."

"Yes, I'd like that. In this short, unpredictable life, let's give love to each other while we can."

Mr. Choi felt a poignant sorrow deep in his heart, but gave a warm smile to Myŏng-ku. When they stepped into Wolp'ook, the Madam welcomed them brightly.

"It was quite unbelievable. He died exactly the way he wanted to, in his sleep. Anyway, he told us everything he wanted to tell us, so he had no other parting words, I guess," Madam Wolp'o said and wept. She was already in her mourning clothes. Yi had instructed her not to wear widow's weeds, but she insisted she couldn't send her husband away without this proper courtesy.

"Did he starve himself?"

"Yes, he said he knew what he was doing. He acted as if he knew exactly at what hour, and on what day, he was going to die. He was calm and dignified. Yesterday, he didn't say a word all day. He just lay on his back, staring up at the ceiling, deep in his own thoughts."

"Has he been washed and dressed in shrouds?"

"No, sir. Mortician Pang said he had to be dried out first, so he put him on a wooden bench and went home."

"Send Myŏng-ku to Mr. Pang. We need him to prepare the final shrouding."

In the meantime, Myŏng-ku had had an early lunch in the kitchen eating a bowl of bean sauce and vegetable soup with rice in it. He then ran to the bicycle shop to rent a bicycle, which he needed to take the message to Yi's older brother in Ttakpatkol. It was almost 60 ris, round trip. If he were to walk, he would not be able to return before nightfall.

Mortician Pang lived next door to a dye shop on the border between the upper and the lower parts of the village. He took care of funerals for everyone who had died in Ibam, and Yi had ordered his coffin and bier well in advance. Myŏng-ku went into Pang's yard, pushing the bicycle along.

"Are you home, sir?"

"Who is it?" The old mortician opened the door of his room. He had lost most of his teeth, so his wrinkly cheeks were hollow. In one hand, he held paper flowers for the funeral.

"Master Choi has come. He wants you to come for the shrouding."

Myŏng-ku stared at the white rice-paper flowers. They were beautiful.

"Are the flowers for the bier, sir?"

"That's right. I'm making them now. As soon as I finish, I will bring the coffin down too."

"May I watch you?"

"Sure. Come on in."

Myŏng-ku stood the bicycle against the wall and went in. The room was littered with pieces of rice paper. On one side, there was a pile of flowers on bamboo sticks. The old mortician was dyeing the flowers in red, pink, and yellow ink.

"They are very pretty."

"They will lead the dead man to another world."

The old man picked up a flower on a bamboo stick and dipped it in red water in a bowl. The absorbent rice paper instantly turned red. He put the red flower on top of the colored pile, and picked and dyed another one in yellow ink.

"May I try one?"

It was an easy thing to do, but Myŏng-ku found it interesting.

"Yes, you may. We need about twenty more. Don't dunk the flower in the water. Just dip the tip of it, then the paper absorbs the color."

Myŏng-ku picked up a white flower and dipped it in pink dye. The pink color spread only half way.

"That's enough," said the old man. Myŏng-ku looked on the pink flower and thought of Uncle who had told him of his magic tricks. Turning the paper flowers to different colors was no magic, but it reminded Myŏng-ku of Uncle's stories.

"How do you make these flowers?"

"You fold the paper this way and that way and then cut them with scissors. Instantly you see flowers blooming in your hands." The mortician smiled a good-natured, toothless smile. Almost seventy, he was wrinkled and shrivelled.

"Will you teach me how to make them someday?"

"What for?"

"I want to learn everything I can. They say that a man should learn everything he can except stealing, because no one knows what skill may come in handy someday."

"But a mortician has always been despised. I became one because I was born into a family of morticians. But I am the last. All my children went off to big cities."

"You must have made millions of bier flowers and shrouded many dead people."

"Yes, I have. I've dressed hundreds of people for their final rest. During the war, I did more than twenty people a day."

"What kind of dead body is the most difficult?"

"Pregnant women, frozen bodies, and bodies cut in pieces."

They dyed more flowers while they talked. The mortician was glad to have someone to talk with, though the boy was young enough to be his grandson. His toothless mouth went happily chattering on.

"Why is it difficult to do a pregnant woman?"

"Because I have to put my hand in and draw out the baby."

"You put your hand into a dead woman?" Myŏng-ku was shocked.

"Because you cannot put two people in one coffin. And as for a frozen body, you have to cut the arms or legs. Otherwise, you cannot dress it and put it in a coffin."

"Why do you cut the arms or legs?"

"A normal person becomes rigid after death, but the body softens in two days. But a frozen body never does. That's why. It is quite difficult."

They finished dyeing. The room turned into a flower bed of white, pink, red, and yellow blossoms. The old man stood up and put on a long black coat without a collar.

"I heard that sometimes a body suddenly sits up when you put it in a coffin. Is that true?"

"Yes, it does happen once in a while."

"The body has come back to life?"

"No, a person never comes back to life once he dies. People who say that they have come back from death are lying."

"Then how does a dead person suddenly sit up?"

"When you prepare a body for burial, you hide livestock in their pens and cats in a barn, because people believe that if a cat crosses over the chimney of a room where a body lies, the body will sit up. They used to believe that. But, it isn't true. The cat has nothing to do with the body sitting up. It happens... well,... I don't know how to put it into words," the old man tried to find the right words while tying his hat strings under his chin.

"When joints suddenly break or bones push through the flesh? Is that what you're trying to say, sir?"

"That's right. Yes. Though breathing has stopped, nerves can still be alive. It's just like a frog that twitches its legs even after death."

"If a corpse sits up like that, the mortician must be stunned, I guess."

"Of course, he is. At such times, he says these soothing words: 'Look here, if a dead person like you does this, won't your children be shocked? Now, lie down and go to heaven peacefully.' " The old man smiled another toothless grin.

"Those words are perfect. If you console them with such words, the corpse would have to lie down."

"Such stories simply show that for every dead person, death was hard to accept. People put him in a coffin, bind it securely, and put mounds of dirt on top of it, so he will never get out. Death is so very final."

Myŏng-ku thought about the old man's words as he rode the bicycle to Ttakpatkol. The more he thought about them, the more unacceptable death seemed.

The next morning after breakfast, Mr. Choi picked five strong men and headed to the Susŏk Mountain. Among them was the salt-seller Kim. Each of them had a lunchbox, a spade, and a pick. Though it wasn't as cold as the previous day, the sky was heavily overcast as if it might rain or snow at any minute.

As soon as they arrived at the burial site, Mr. Choi measured the spot with a compass and a ruler inorder to decide where they should dig. He pointed his compass north and searched for the right direction for water and mountains in relation to the corpse's head. Then he made sure that everything was placed properly in the right place. After Mr. Choi drew the rectangle in which the body was to lie, the men began to dig. The top soil was so solidly frozen that it was hard as rock. As their picks rebounded without digging in, one of the men complained about Yi's timing.

"Young man, no one can pick the day he dies just as he wishes. Besides, one should never say things against a dead person. Make a fire first and thaw the top soil," Mr. Choi chided.

The men scattered immediately to find firewood. After the fire thawed out the frozen ground, they began to dig again. Underneath the top soil, they found soft dirt they could dig easily in.

The salt-seller Kim was digging the spot where the dead person's head was to be placed when his pick caused a metallic echo and bounced back up. He and another man found a rock as big as a go-game table. The two men tried to loosen it but backed off suddenly, shocked.

"What is it?" Mr. Choi asked from a flat rock upon which he sat, smoking his pipe and thinking of his friend's curious life.

"Master Choi, it's a huge snake," Kim said, shivering.

Mr. Choi went over and looked into the hole between the rocks where several snakes were curled up in hibernation.

"Wow, they are plump! Just right for boiling and drinking!" one of the men exclaimed.

"Snakes mean that this burial site cannot be used. Am I right?" another young man asked.

Looking down at the snakes, Mr. Choi remembered how widely and how hard he had searched every part of this mountain last summer to feed boiled snakes to Kye-yŏn. And they were here in the dead of winter, which to his mind, seemed a bad omen. It occurred to him that his daughter might not last this winter.

"What are we going to do about them?" Kim asked.

"Even a king's burial site isn't without some defects. I never read any book that said one should move a burial spot because of snakes. Maybe they are dragon-gods who will guard Yi's grave. Now go on digging."

"Look at that big one. It's as big as Yi's famed organ," one tall young man pointed.

"Why don't you make snake stew for your daughter?" Kim suggested to Mr. Choi.

"Don't say such a thing. There are snakes that are suitable for that, and there are snakes that aren't. Scoop them up with the soil underneath them and bury them in another hole, so they will sleep a long winter's sleep," Mr. Choi instructed.

He remembered what Yi had told him long ago. In Tongu, Manchuria, there were murals in the tombs of the Koguryŏ Dynasty members. In the murals were dragons, birds, giraffes, turtles, sea monsters, and snakes curled up around turtles. Such murals indicated that snakes were animals that guarded the departing soul of a deceased.

"May you be guarded by those snakes and go to Nirvana," Mr. Choi whispered to himself while looking up at the overcast sky.

That night, Mr. Choi kept vigil all night. Incense burned in front of the picture of his friend, who looked as if he might say something to him. But alas, he lay dead behind the screen. In the tavern room, bier bearers practiced the dirge.

Mortician Pang criticized their off-key notes, but the men's singing did not improve much.

Since Yi and Madam Wolp'o were from another part of the country, the bier bearers were not relatives but men randomly picked for the job, and they sang the dirge as they would a popular song, without a trace of sad feeling.

The next morning, under heavy clouds and a light drizzle, the bier left Wolp'ook. The bier had been decorated with paper flowers of different colors.

Sending the bier off, Madam Wolp'o wailed most heart-rendingly. With a baby on her back, Ch'an-kyŏng cried behind her mother. Suk-kyŏng hid herself in the kitchen and did not come out.

Master Choi stood in front, holding a funeral penant, followed by the bier bearers. Behind the bier should have been a male heir. Instead there were Yi's brother, Myŏng-ku, his son-in-law, old man Pang, and several neighbors.

When they were out of the market place and walking along the Chayang River, Mr. Choi began the lead passage of the dirge in a clear voice. The bier bearers responded and moved forward to the plaintive melody.

> Once you go, you can never come back,
> Ay, ay, ay, you can never come back.
> Once you die, you are bound manyfold,
> Ay, ay, ay, you are bound manyfold.
> Bound and carried over the valley of death,
> Ay, ay, ay, over the valley of death.
> Covered under the shrouds ever,
> Ay, ay, ay, under the shrouds ever
> Pine trees and bamboos are your walls,
> Ay, ay, ay, bamboos are your walls
> Cuckoos and birds are your friends
> Ay, ay, ay, birds are your friends
> Mountains, deep and many,
> Ay, ay, ay, deep and many
> Lonely and sad are human souls
> Ay, ay, ay, lonely and sad are human souls.

As the funeral procession entered the narrow path toward the mountain top, the drizzle turned into rain. The unseasonable rain came down heavier as the bier bearers' voices fell out of unison and died down, in scattered noises here and there.

Mr. Choi stopped the procession and let the men set down the bier. Some put up paper umbrellas while others put on rain covers. One or two grumbled that Yi caused problems even in death. Mr. Choi covered his hat with rain headgear.

As the rain poured down, the dyed flowers began to bleed in

colored rain drops. Over the picture of Yi, placed in front of the bier between two lanterns, rain streamed down. Red, pink, and yellow rivulets crisscrossed over his face.

"As I told you when we left, there will be no money to be paid to you. I want you all to know that. There is a long steep climb from here. Let's go," Mr. Choi said.

As he turned around, Mr. Choi's eyes rested on his friend's picture. Yi, his long hair down to his shoulders, gradually soaked in tears of rainbow colors.

About the Author

Kim Won-il was born in 1942 in the town of Jinyŏng in the southeastern part of Korea. He was a student at Sorabul Arts College and later graduated from Youngnam University.

His representative works are novels such as *A Festival of Darkness* (1975), *Sunset* (1978), *A Carnival of Fire* (1983), and *The Wind and the River* (1985); and collections of short stories, *The Soul of Darkness* (1973), *The Wind that Blows Today* (1976), *Meditations on a Snipe* (1978), and *In Search of Disillusionment* (1984). He is a recipient of several prestigious literary awards: The Modern Literature Award (1975), The Korean Fiction Award (1977), The Creative Literatue Award (1979), and The Dong-In Award (1983).

About the Translator

Choi Jin-young is a professor of English Literature at Chung Ang University in Seoul. A graduate of Seoul National University, she received MA in English Literature from the University of North Carolina and Ph.D. in English Literature from Seoul National University. She taught for three years at St. Augustine's College in North Carolina. She has published several books on English and American novels and translated into Korean many literary works of both English and American authors.